I SO

Born in Preston, Patricia Fawcett has lived in various parts of the North including the Lake District. She is married with three grown-up children and runs a creative writing group as well as writing full time. She now lives in Devon.

RETURN TO ROSEMOUNT

Together, Clementine and Anthony Scarr had co-founded the school known as Florey Park on the headland. Then, after Anthony's tragic death in a car accident, Clemmie's priorities changed to making sure his memory remained untarnished for their two daughters, Nina and Julia . . . Clemmie is delighted when her grown children return home — Nina due to a doomed love affair, whilst Julia's reason remains a secret — along with Julia's feisty daughter, Francesca. And then Nina meets Alex and the promise of a new relationship blossoms . . . But, outside the beautiful gardens of Rosemount, forces are shifting that will threaten their happiness.

Books by Patricia Fawcett
Published by The House of Ulverscroft:

SET TO MUSIC
THE ABSENT CHILD
EIGHT DAYS AT THE NEW GRAND
OLIVIA'S GARDEN
THE CUCKOO'S NEST

PATRICIA FAWCETT

RETURN TO ROSEMOUNT

Complete and Unabridged

ULVERSCROFT
Leicester

First published in Great Britain in 2005 by
Robert Hale Limited
London

First Large Print Edition
published 2006
by arrangement with
Robert Hale Limited
London

British Library CIP Data

Fawcett, Patricia
    Return to Rosemount.—Large print ed.—
Ulverscroft large print series: family saga
    1. Mothers and daughters—Fiction
    2. Large type books
    I. Title
    823.9'14 [F]

    ISBN 1–84617–403–1

Published by
F. A. Thorpe (Publishing)
Anstey, Leicestershire
Set by Words & Graphics Ltd.
Anstey, Leicestershire
Printed and bound in Great Britain by
T. J. International Ltd., Padstow, Cornwall

This book is printed on acid-free paper

Prologue

Julia felt guilty that, by living so far away from Rosemount, she was dumping everything on to Nina. And, as mother grew older, it was bound to get worse. But, what could she do? She loved it here, she and Tom had good jobs and the house was their dream home. She wasn't moving from this house for anybody or anything. Not ever.

She worried about the future, about mother getting old, although she was not yet sixty and very lively at that, so she wouldn't be going ga-ga for ages. If ever. But it did mean that eventually Nina would shoulder all the responsibility, which was not fair. Why she was worrying so, just now, when they had years and years to sort something out was a mystery.

But then, she was a born worrier and it seemed to be exaggerated these days, very likely hormonal.

Julia stared at the hazy view of the flat, low meadows with the distant sea just out of sight. How often had she looked at this view, but lately she was looking at it with different eyes. The eyes of a mother-to-be. The panic that had encircled her from the very beginning clung to her still and she knew she had to get a grip. Tom was, to her everlasting irritation, completely relaxed about it all, amused rather that their long term plans could be completely scuppered.

She was being a pig to him and she knew it. It was his fault that she was pregnant, telling her it would be OK to take a chance, when it clearly wasn't. It was so unlike her to be cavalier about something as important as that but, after a celebratory anniversary dinner she had been heady with champagne and, for once in a while, had needed little persuasion.

She had threatened to have an abortion, knowing even as she said it, as she saw his shocked face, that she would not. The misery had unhinged her temporarily and, to her everlasting shame, she'd lunged at him at one point with a knife. If he hadn't moved fast, she might have caught him, although, thank heavens, the knife was so blunt it would hardly cut butter. Horrified at what she might have done, she dropped it and howled like a baby herself, as he caught her in his arms, smoothed her hair, and whispered that it wasn't the end of the world.

It just felt like it.

Her feelings swung and leapt from outrage,

frustration, fear, disbelief, all edged with worry. She enjoyed forward planning, knowing what was what, everything neatly pencilled in and this coming baby was a threat to that. It would turn all her beautifully laid plans on their head.

All her life she had had everything planned, to the nth degree. The right university, the right course, the right choice of career, Mr Right too. Oh yes, everything planned, her life plotted out for the next twenty years. Unlike Nina, who lived life on the run, staggering from crisis to crisis, scattering boyfriends as carelessly as the rose-petal confetti she had flung into the air at Julia's wedding. She might have suffered huge disappointments in her life but she seemed to rise above them and remained infuriatingly cheerful. Nina had missed out on university, opted instead for some lowly interior design course. In fact, sewing was the only thing Nina was any good at and where would that get her, poor love? Julia did the worrying for her little sister, little in the sense that she was younger, a darling but ultimately a loser. Julia was the bright one, the pretty one too, which seemed unfair but there it was.

The news of her pregnancy had been greeted with delight from northern shores: at last Nina was to be an auntie, Clemmie a grandmother. Over the phone it was easy enough to pretend, to sound as breathlessly excited as they. But the truth, which only she and Tom knew, could not be avoided. This was outside their life plot, a twist they had not bargained for. Their joint incomes were essential to their lifestyle, a professional couple who enjoyed the good things in life, wine, holidays, a lovely home with impractical child-unfriendly off-white sofas, a pond in the garden, for heaven's sake . . . freedom.

Tom was a born teacher with a natural talent for communication, passionate about his subject, unconventional in some ways but luckily in ways that got the best out of the children. There had been a lot of feedback from grateful parents, whose little darlings had done far better than expected, purely because of Tom's influence.

She had known Tom since he was head boy at Florey Park and she was the headmaster's daughter. Tricky situation, that, but they had managed their budding relationship with the discretion that father, her dearest beloved father, had insisted upon. She was so glad that father had known Tom, had given his stamp of approval to him before his tragic death. That mattered to her.

Off then to their respective universities. Again, all planned. In fact, their choices had forced them to be apart a while, a good test, coming together again in the happy realization that they needed each other.

Teaching might not be the profession it used to be but Tom loved it, unconcerned that Julia was bringing in more cash per month, the golden girl of the financial company she worked for, her future rosy. She was on target, or rather she had been for a more senior post, commitment the buzz word. Her boss, a single woman in her fifties, offered congratulations through gritted teeth. Julia's attempts to assure her it would not make a difference met with a cold stare. She was aware that she couldn't have chosen a better way of cutting the throat of her career. If she could have the baby late Friday evening and be back at work Monday morning, with the minimum disruption, then it might just be OK.

Seven months on, with the initial shock subsided, she had told herself so often that it wouldn't be so bad that she almost believed it. She would take a couple of weeks off, engage a good nanny and that would be that. A mere hiccup that's all. At work, her pregnancy was never mentioned as if, by not talking about it, it might just go away.

It would not, of course, and she was resigned to it now and, in the strangest way, a little sliver of anticipation was settling in, starting from when the baby gave that first slow lazy tumble and she had seen the movement of the sharp kick. Suddenly, this was real.

She had even found herself going into the nursery the other day, taking out all the little garments that were ready and waiting and just handling them, putting them up to her face and sniffing them, the newness of them. What would the baby smell like? Would that be a new smell too?

She had wasted a whole hour just messing about, which was most unlike her. True to form, once it was past the point of no return she had set to with a vengeance on the organization. The nursery, pale primrose, with its white baby furniture, was finished and she was going to interview for nannies next week. She wanted a no-nonsense type, middle-aged preferably and certainly not some glamorous young girl, not with Tom around. Tom was not handsome, not in the film star sense, but he had a smile that caught at you and this uncanny ability to attract the ladies. As he was completely oblivious to it, it made him all the more desirable.

The early mist was lifting steamily over the water meadows, the sun trying to break through and it promised to be a glorious day.

Pity she was going to spend it stuck in the office, trying to pretend that her wits were still as sharp as ever, that this dreaminess, this mumsy preoccupation, this lack of concentration that grabbed her occasionally was purely temporary.

'Right, let's go,' she said, turning from the window and talking to nobody in particular, unless it was the baby. She checked her appearance. She was carrying the pregnancy well on account of her tall, strong frame, with no sign yet of that waddling way of walking that some of the women at her pre-natal classes had already developed. She simply wore a looser blouse with her business suit and her long dark hair, sleek and swinging from a side parting, drew the attention it deserved.

Setting off for work that morning Julia had no idea that, before the end of the day, Francesca was to make her entrance into the world.

Far too early and far too small.

It upset all the plans but then Frankie was good at that, starting off as she meant to continue. It meant hastily rearranged leave, kicking several projects into touch, straight into the hands of her assistant, who, with no babies on *her* horizon, was transparently desperate to step into her shoes.

7

But, somehow, when that would have once driven her mad with annoyance, frustrated her beyond belief, it no longer seemed so important. There was important and *important*. The baby's survival was important and Julia abandoned everything to be at the baby-care unit for the next anxious six weeks, watching over the tiny scrap fighting for life.

Such a tiny scrap, but when Julia put out her finger the baby grasped it with a grip so tight and strong that she was taken aback. Stroking the soft cheek, watching the little chest rise and fall with the effort of breathing, seeing the perfection there in the little face, fingers and toes, Julia finally understood what it all meant.

Motherhood.

She willed the baby to survive, and, after some frightening set-backs when she had *real* cause to worry, she did just that. Against spectacular odds, she pulled through.

Her beautiful daughter, Francesca Clementine Scarr Vasey — Frankie.

1

Clementine Angelina Scarr dusted the silver-framed photograph lovingly and placed it in its position between the Royal Doulton figure and the Grand Napoleon mantel clock, the huge mirror above the fireplace reflecting the charming drawing-room.

Her home. Rosemount.

The photograph was of her only grand-child, Francesca. A formal photograph and the smile was therefore a touch forced. Clemmie knew what young girls were like and she was probably uncomfortable in smart clothes, much more at ease in that teenage uniform of jeans and T-shirt. Frankie was a miniature version of her mother, slighter, but with the same blue eyes, dark brown hair, although she had recently had it cut off, according to Julia.

Julia had been in quite a state about it in a recent phone call but then, in Clemmie's maternal opinion, Julia lived life on a tightrope and she had been telling her for years to relax.

'You'll never guess what Frankie's done, Mother. I could have cried when I saw it,' she wailed. 'All her lovely hair — gone. She never gave me an inkling.'

'Quite right too. She knew you'd have tried to stop her. And what about you?' Clemmie asked hopefully. 'Have you had yours cut yet?'

'No. I like mine as it is.'

'Oh dear! Far be it from me to offer advice, but long hair, and I mean really long hair like yours, ages you terribly, darling. The only remedy is to wear it up and what's the point of all that fussing. Find yourself a good hairdresser, insist they cut into a gorgeous shape like mine and have done with it. Long hair is for young women. Only for virgins, in fact. Didn't they use to do that? Hair pinned up as soon as you were married.'

'Mother! I don't know why I bother to ring you sometimes, you never support me in these things. You always take Frankie's side or Tom's.'

'Do I? Good heavens, I'm so sorry if I've given you that impression,' Clemmie told her, quite unperturbed. She always took their side because, quite simply, Julia was usually wrong, getting on her high horse for the most ridiculous reasons. Such as this.

Clemmie rarely saw Julia, who had disappeared down to Norfolk soon after she married, and it was still a sadness after all

10

these years that she had not really been there to watch Frankie grow up. Julia had never intended to have a child, Clemmie knew that, but she had put on a brave face and accepted it. But, alas, that little grudge would always remain and, whenever Clemmie did see the two of them together, Julia and Frankie, she detected a distance between them, small but important.

But that was Julia.

She'd always kept one step back, even from her, as if afraid to let go of her feelings. Anthony had known how to deal with her and Clemmie knew that it was Anthony she had always run to when in trouble, never her. He was her father so that was admirable, of course, but also a little upsetting. She had no idea what Julia's relationship with Tom was like. Clearly the man adored her, which helped, but she couldn't help the feeling that he was a saint to put up with her and her moods.

She would have liked to help out more, to be there for Frankie, to be a proper grandmother, whom the child could have talked to but it was such a trial to get herself down to the Norfolk coast, two trains and a taxi. She wished when it was too late that she had learnt to drive but then there had always been men falling over themselves to drive her and even now there was her odd-job man, Mr Harrison, for short trips. Edward Grantham had offered to drive her anywhere she chose, of course, but she would not take up that offer, if her life depended on it.

For visits to Julia she had to rely on Nina, who was unreliable and whose driving left a lot to be desired, or take the bull by the horns and suffer the awful train journey. So, since Frankie was born, she had very much relied on the occasional visits that Julia made up here. Twice a year maybe if she was lucky. A summer visit and Christmas. They always tried to have a family Christmas. The ones she clung on to were the ones when Anthony was alive, long before Frankie was born. Such a pity he had never known his little granddaughter.

So, she had watched Frankie growing in spurts. She was indeed a bright little girl, each time bigger and chattier and altogether wiser. On these visits it took time for them to get to know each other again, the sometimes shy little girl suspicious of this lady who was her grandmother, and then, just as that was beginning to happen, just when they were sharing confidences, when she was spoiling her rotten away from Julia's critical eyes, she was whisked away once more. Each time the goodbye made Clemmie ever more desolate.

Francesca was a mystery. Slight in build, as if she had never quite recovered from her premature birth, but robust enough for all that, by-passing most of the childhood illnesses, her slim frame hiding a deceptively strong will. A fragile girl with big expressive eyes, whom men would swoon over in a few years' time, if not already.

Clemmie had no idea what girls of seventeen did nowadays. She'd dipped into a teenage magazine recently in the dentist's waiting-room and been quite astonished to read the explicit details of the problem page. When Clemmie was seventeen, she had not yet had sex as they called it; that came later. Clemmie preferred to think of it as being made love to and she was of the opinion that nothing changed, whatever the decade. People talked about it more now.

Clemmie was not party to what made her granddaughter tick, what she really thought, though on the last visit, a year ago, she thought she detected a little welcome trace of herself in the stubborn look, the glint in the eye, a modicum of rebellion, confirmed by her choosing to have her hair cut and not telling her mother until the dreaded deed was done.

Good for her! Julia's steadfast nature had always been a bit of a disappointment. Julia

13

never did anything to surprise you. She was regrettably rather dull, whereas Nina was excitable. Two daughters, one an accountant and the other an interior designer — that said it all.

Nina, for all her bright intelligence, was hopelessly romantic, unable to see the wrong in people, hence the episode with that no-good ex-fiancé of hers. A little plain common sense wouldn't come amiss in Nina. Far too trusting, poor darling. She always looked for the best in people too, made excuses for them, imagined that everybody else was as utterly straightforward and honest as she was herself. No wonder that man had taken her for what he could get, played with her feelings, milked her dry, and then just tossed her aside when things went wrong. Clemmie hoped there would not be a reconciliation, for she would be hard-pressed not to cause a scene if she met him again. How dare he do that to dearest Nina? It had taken a full year for her to get over it and even now, two years on, there were times when her eyes took on a dreamy sadness and you just knew where her thoughts were.

As for her granddaughter, Frankie had always been, according to Julia, very nearly perfect, which is why the hair-cutting episode had come as such a surprise.

Anthony would have been so proud of her. The family had always been so important to him, the Scarr reputation paramount. He had traced his ancestors back to the court of Queen Elizabeth I, minor nobility. According to Anthony, sources undisclosed, the Scarrs had always been paragons of virtue, the very essence of English gentlefolk, with never a scandal to soil the name. Not one that he could unearth, anyway.

That, coupled with her own excellent Forsyth pedigree, meant that the two of them were well-connected, their marriage a delight to both sets of parents. Yes, he was marrying into the money that the Scarr family no longer had — one of them had gambled it all away — but that was by the by.

She was heiress to a confectionery fortune, an obscene amount that her father had trebled by careful handling and, indeed, she was herself no stranger to the stock-market. She was delighted to share her good fortune with Anthony and insisted that they call the money theirs rather than hers. She had never thought for a moment that he minded that. But, of course, he had.

And, ultimately, it had caused him to do what he did.

'Mother . . . I wish you wouldn't fiddle around with the duster. You pay Mrs

Harrison to do that,' Nina said, exploding into the room, bosom at the fore, as was her way. 'Remember what happened to the crystal vase?'

'That was an accident.'

Clemmie carefully removed her duster, hardly hiding the sigh that always came her way when she looked afresh at her daughter. Nina was a throwback to some far off branch of the Scarr-Forsyth family tree. Must be the Scarr side because none of her family was prone to fatness — like rakes — but Nina, a weighty ten and a half pounds at birth, had never let up. She ate like a sparrow, bless her, but it made no difference. A size fourteen, Clemmie reckoned, although she was pretty for all that and never short of men friends. However, if she had a fault, she was far too picky and running out of time. It irritated Clemmie immensely. That fiancé had been a mistake, of course, anyone with an ounce of common sense could have seen that, but Nina was making a mistake, too, in her persistent search for the ideal man.

There was no such thing as an ideal man. That was the fault of the male species in general. One had to make the best of what you could get. Mould them into shape. Although, come to think of it, she had once thought Anthony the perfect man and so he had proved to be, or very nearly.

'Accident or not, put that duster away or there'll be nothing left for us to inherit.'

Nina smiled broadly, startlingly aglow in a low cut lime-green top and hideous printed pink-and-lime cropped pants, an unfortunate choice in Clemmie's opinion, for it merely emphasized Nina's problem and the hastily applied fuschia-pink lipstick was a sorry clash. Her face was shiny from the sun, cheeks full of colour as usual.

Clemmie's pale cheeks, on the other hand, were subtly toned with blusher. She took ages with her make-up, seated at the dressing-table in her pink bedroom. It was a morning ritual she much enjoyed. The older she got, the longer it took to do something with her face. Close up, without make-up, her face resembled scrunched-up palest peach tissue paper. But then, nobody ever saw her close up without make-up, and going under the surgeon's knife in the name of vanity had never been an option. Her friend Dilys had had a nip and tuck years ago for what good it had done her. She had caught up with Clemmie now and also had a face like a ravaged prune.

'Have you spoken to Julia since Friday?'

Clemmie shook her head.

'If you're thinking about the job, then I'm

not sure I shall mention it. She's never interested. I don't believe she ever mentions it to Tom. For some reason that utterly defeats me, she loves it down there.'

She stuffed the duster in her pocket, although Mrs Harrison's half-hearted attempts at cleaning infuriated her. A furtive flick and a squirt of spray polish did not constitute cleaning. And how many times must she tell her that proper polish had to be used in the dining-room. She had caught her *spraying* her Rosebery Chippendale side chair the other day with some ghastly own-brand supermarket product and given her what for, but it would make no difference.

'I know she's never interested but you should mention it anyway,' Nina said. 'Just in passing. I'll tell her if you won't.'

Clemmie sighed. 'You don't give up, do you, darling. You have to face the fact that Julia will never move, not now. She's been there twenty years and that's a good stretch. I agree it would be lovely to have her near us but it's not practical, is it. Her life is down there. She has friends down there.'

'Are you sure?' Nina sniffed. 'She never talks about them if she has.'

'Of course she has friends. After twenty years? We all have friends. Of a sort.'

18

Nina moved to the pale-green sofa by the open French windows, plonking down on it, fiddling around instantly with the cushions. A restless woman, Nina. At her wrist a cluster of gold bracelets jangled. Clemmie glanced at them irritably. They would drive her to distraction but then she — and Julia for that matter — knew how to wear jewellery. Nina had no idea. The bracelets were gold but they might as well have come from Woolworths for all the effect Nina managed to create.

'I wish we could persuade her to come home though,' Nina persisted. 'Wouldn't it be wonderful for us to be together again, like old times? I hated London, mother. All the time I was there, I just wanted to be back here.'

Clemmie smiled. That told her everything.

Nina had never loved that man, not completely loved him as she had loved Anthony. Her dearest Anthony had been such a romantic. In the early days, when he was trying to persuade her to desert Edward, he had sent her a single red rose every day for a month and then, in a *coup de théatre*, serenaded her with 'How deep is the ocean?' singing it at full pitch below her window at Rosemount on a midsummer evening, until she was forced to go over to her bedroom window, open it and shush him quiet with a giggle. He hadn't remembered all the words

19

of the song but had improvised with a relish that delighted her.

Poor Edward. Plodding Edward. He'd never stood a chance. Why she had ever agreed to marry him was a mystery when they were plainly so unsuited, but war was in the thirties' air and things took on an urgency.

Nina's cheerful voice cut through her thoughts.

'I feel like a sheepdog, trying to round us all up. Our little family. It doesn't feel right, separated like this. It never has felt right. We've never got to know little Frankie, not properly. I wanted to see her grow up and I never did. Such a damned shame.'

'She's not so little now. She's seventeen, remember. A young woman.'

Nina sighed, glancing at the photograph on the mantelpiece.

'Seventeen. My God, I wish I was seventeen again. It's such a wonderful age. All her life stretching before her and it's hers to do what she wants with. I do hope they don't stifle her.'

'What do you mean?' Clemmie asked sharply, feeling she was being got at. Good Lord, hadn't she bent over backwards to let the girls do what they wanted? Anthony would have been most annoyed to know that

20

she had not insisted on Nina going to university, giving in to her instead and allowing her to do the design course. 'Stifle her?' she repeated, looking at Nina, seeking an explanation. 'How, pray?'

'I just meant that they should let her do what she wants. Like you did, Mother. I know Daddy wasn't around but you never tried to push me into teaching. Follow my dream, I seem to remember you saying, even though I hadn't a bloody clue what I wanted to do.'

'Don't swear, sweetheart.' Clemmie rebuked her mildly. She wanted suddenly to put her arms round her big girl and give her a hug. Poor darling. Life was passing her by. She ought to be married and a mother herself. Lots of children. Homely women like Nina were wonderful mothers, much better than she was. She'd always felt rather a failure as a mother, although she had rallied around on *that* occasion, years ago, done what had to be done for the sake of the girls.

'Doesn't she look lovely?' Nina went on, looking at the photograph again. 'She was a lovely baby too, wasn't she. So tiny. So precious. The time's just flashed by. I can still remember her so clearly as a baby.'

'I can remember *you* as a baby,' Clemmie told her drily.

'Can you really?'

'Of course I can. And don't sound so surprised. It's a mother's thing. I can remember the horror of your birth, the physical effort it took. Of course in those far-off days your father was allowed nowhere near. Just as well. I thought I was going to split apart.'

Nina laughed. 'Sorry.'

'I should think so. You were twice the size of every other baby at the baby clinic,' Clemmie said, smiling gently. 'Into second-size baby garments at once.'

'Oh, don't say that. I hate my baby pictures.'

'You were a beautiful baby,' Clemmie went on firmly. 'Quite the most beautiful in the baby clinic. You were born with a mass of dark hair and that's how it stayed. You were much admired.'

'Hmmn.' Nina looked doubtful. 'I can't remember what it felt like to be seventeen. Was I *ever* seventeen?'

Clemmie shook her head at the daft question, twitching to get at the dusting again. Mrs Harrison never lifted things, just went round them. Slapdash. But then, the younger generation — and Mrs Harrison at fifty counted as such — were a lazy lot. Dishwashers. Automatic washing-machines. Mixers. Whatever. Not that she had herself been especially good at housekeeping, luckily able to afford to leave it to others, but it was the principle. Certain values were given short shrift these days and it was to be deplored.

'I remember you very well at seventeen,' she said, smiling at her daughter.

At seventeen Nina had been cheerfully optimistic, unfortunately unwilling to buckle down to exams, or, even worse, beginning to develop the dreadful clothes' sense she now possessed. At seventeen she was only just beginning to recover from the pain of losing her father, which had quite bowled her over when it happened. It was a disaster for a daughter at any age, but sixteen seemed particularly awkward: such a tender age.

'Julia was already at college when I was seventeen,' Nina went on thoughtfully. 'I really missed her. Missed not having anybody there to grumble at. Missed not having a sensible elder sister around.'

'She was always that . . . *sensible*,' Clemmie said with a little sniff.

'And I wasn't?' Nina asked cheekily.

'Hardly, darling. Thank goodness. Having two sensible daughters would be completely unacceptable.'

They laughed, knowing it was meant as a joke — well, sort of.

'So, when you were seventeen, Julia was

23

already at college and still seeing Tom Vasey in the holidays. Your father liked him more than I did and that's the reason why I went along with it, although I did hope it might fizzle out,' Clemmie said with a sigh. 'You must remember she brought him home from time to time. You had a fearful crush on him. You used to blush furiously whenever he talked to you. You became practically fluorescent. It was most unbecoming.'

'Don't bring that up,' Nina said quickly. 'Please don't say anything about that, Mother. It is just so embarrassing when I think back. I hope he never knew. You don't think he guessed, do you? Or Julia? Even when they got married, I was embarrassed, although I was over him by then. It was just a teenage thing. Julia's welcome to him.'

'Yes indeed. She could have done a lot better. He's attractive enough in his way but he has no go about him at all, but then neither has Julia. I don't know where she gets that from. No drive. No ambition. You can't accuse me of being like that and your father was such a hive of activity. He wasn't satisfied with just being a teacher, he wanted to run his own school. He said he wanted to put his own stamp on education, produce a school that would be so excellent that parents would flock to it.'

'It must have been a huge thing to take on in those days just after the war,' Nina said with a small smile.

'Yes, they were difficult times. It was an anticlimax for so many people after the euphoria of victory. All that rationing. Such a bore. I must admit I would have preferred to relax and get to know him again after being apart for so long, but no. He insisted on rattling on with his pet project. He was supremely confident. As far as he was concerned, he had survived the war when so many of his colleagues had not and he was convinced that that had happened for a purpose. He had to do something with his life or he would be letting them down.'

'You must have had faith in him, Mother, to spend so much money on such a thing. What if it had failed?'

'We knew it would not fail. It took some time to find the right place of course. I was reluctant to move from Rosemount and that narrowed the search. When Florey Park came on the market it seemed like a miracle and we simply snapped it up. I had long admired the house and there were no other buyers, so it became something of a bargain. Then there was money to be spent on the conversion and so on. I think you could say we both had a vision. Anthony had a lot of contacts in the profession and once the ball was rolling, there was no stopping it.'

Clemmie smiled and sat down opposite Nina on the chair that used to be Anthony's. The same old chair, a quality chair, although it had twice been recovered and this new fabric, rust with cream elephants, was Nina's choice. The heavy cotton curtains, cream with a rust border, were her choice too. As was the Chinese rug in shades of cream, rust and dark blue. Clemmie allowed her to experiment in this room but she was not allowing her access to her bedroom for fear of what she might do. Nina became over-zealous when she got hold of a paintbrush and fabric swatches, although she had toned herself down a little to accommodate the wishes of the majority in this very traditional neck of the woods.

'I had all sorts of plans once upon a time but they mainly concerned my getting married and having hordes of children,' Nina went on, inelegantly splaying her legs. She pulled her top away from her and blew cool air down the neck, her face flushed and her shoulder-length curly hair, dark brown with a reddish tinge, was damp at the edges. Her eyes were a lighter blue than her sister's, giving her an almost Irish look. 'God, I'm hot. I wish this weather would break. There's not a breath of air out there.'

'If I didn't love this house so much, if I didn't consider it my duty to pass it on to you and Julia, I would have moved down to Norfolk years ago,' Clemmie said thoughtfully. 'Not with them of course. A place of my own. But it's too late now. Frankie will be off soon enough and she would be the only real reason I would want to live near. I feel I've missed out, Nina. We've never established a rapport, Frankie and I. We've never seen each other for long enough to do that. Never mind that we share our name, I'm just distant granny, that's all I am. I would have liked to get to know her, really get to know her, before I die. After all, I'm the only grandparent she has left.'

'Hey, don't get morbid,' Nina said, fidgety as usual, straightening her legs, kicking off her sandals and wiggling red-tipped toes. 'You could live for another twenty years. Think of that.'

'Yes, think of that,' Clemmie said, wondering just how many more wrinkles she could fit on to her face. She supposed there came a time when you had all you would ever have.

'You're only in your mid-seventies and that's young these days,' Nina said, determined to be cheerful.

Clemmie raised her eyebrows, gave a little snort.

27

'*You* are young, darling. Well, youngish, a couple of years to go until you're forty.'

'Thanks for that,' Nina said drily, glancing up as the clock chimed the quarter. 'I must go. I've got to check some curtains Mary's made up. Matching covers and cushions as well. Overkill but you know the saying: the customer is always right.'

Standing on the terrace outside the room, Clemmie waved her off, watching the car zoom off, rather too fast, down the drive and out of the gates without a pause. True, hardly any traffic passed by in the lane but even so Nina ought to be more careful, would be more careful if she had children. It sobered you, having children. When you had children there was always somebody other than yourself to consider. You adored them, of course, but they were a heavy burden too. If it hadn't been for Julia and Nina she could have told Edward Grantham to go to hell after Anthony's death. She would have weathered the storm, put the little matter down to Anthony's delightful eccentricity and his eternal desire to give her some pleasure in life. As it was, in order to protect her daughters she had had no option but to go along with Edward's perverted wishes.

★　★　★

She returned indoors and completed her dusting. Only when she was satisfied did she make herself a pot of Earl Grey, carrying the tray back into the sitting-room, where she could enjoy it in peace.

'Well, Anthony . . . '

She sat this time on the softly sage-coloured chair opposite the elephant-print one, closing her eyes so that she could drum up his presence. After a moment he edged through and she could smell him, that faint whiff of his favourite cologne. Anthony had worn cologne at a time when men thought such things soft, but then he had been a man of confidence.

Twenty-two years ago now. Twenty-two years since he died and she was still talking to him, he was still the first thing she thought of when she woke in the morning and yes, she did sometimes reach out for him in those blissful moments before sleeping and waking. Of course, in her dreams he was often there, young and vigorous, as she seemed to be herself. Odd — you never saw yourself in dreams, just felt yourself to be there, as an observer. As in life.

She could almost see him sitting in his chair, except he was still fifty-seven, forever a handsome fifty-seven, whilst she was ploughing on towards her eightieth. Good Lord, if he could see her now. What would he make of her? She was always beautifully dressed, for elegance was something that never left you and her hair was still short and sharp as it had been for decades, defiantly dark too. She dyed it black, not liking this tendency of older women to go several shades lighter. She vehemently refused to go blonde and had a constant battle with her hairdresser down in town, who also tried to inflict permanent waves on her. She did not allow the woman to intimidate her. It amused her anyway that, from the back, with her wickedly modern haircut, she might be mistaken for a woman in her forties.

Her shoulders were aching, a dull but persistent throb, but she had no intention of taking a painkiller. She suspected rheumatism or something equally age-related but she had not consulted a doctor for she did not wish it to be confirmed.

In any case, she had found a way of dealing with it. She propped a cushion behind her and lay back, trying to relax, visualizing the ache as a hard lump that was slowly crumbling and dissolving as an invisible hand caressed it. Anthony's of course. It required concentration but it usually worked after a while. In a fashion. And it was certainly better than being drugged to the eyeballs.

'Well . . . ? Shall I bother telling Julia about the vacancy at school or will I be wasting my time as usual?'

She opened her eyes and looked again at her late husband's chair, seeing the smile — such a dashing smile — and the twinkling grey eyes.

'What do you think, my darling? Worth a try? I know Tom seems to be entrenched in that school of his but this *is* a senior master's job and the cottage to go with it is lovely. It will do them very well until they find something of their own. Frankly, I never liked that house in Norfolk. Good position, granted, but ugly and with no character. Not like this. Not like Rosemount.'

She sipped her tea, weighing up the problem, and by the time she had finished it, the decision was made.

From the empty chair, Anthony had spoken.

2

At forty-two, Julia still wore her hair straight and long, very nearly waist length, and she used a colour now to cover a few grey hairs. She generally wore it loose, parted at the centre with the sides pulled up and off her face, held in place with tortoiseshell slides, maybe a little young for her age but she liked it and it showed off her excellent cheekbones. Her mother was always going on about cheekbones and good bone structure.

Caring for her hair was a nuisance, washing and drying it a mountain of a job, but Tom liked it and, absurd or not, she liked to please him still. Every so often she ventured into town and allowed the hairdresser to trim a small amount off, watching him like a hawk in case his hand slipped and he cut off more than she intended.

She might have known that life was trundling along too well, that something was bound to happen to upset the solid rhythm. And yes, she had sensed for some time that all was not well with Frankie. She put it down to the usual teenage anxieties but when she tried to talk about it Frankie clammed up.

As she recalled doing precisely the same thing when *she* was seventeen, she did not worry too much. It would settle. After all, when she was seventeen, she had already met Tom, fallen in love, determined to hang on to him and all her future plans included him. But, when her mother had asked her about that, she had not wanted to talk about it, worried that Clemmie would find some means of putting a stop to it. Tom was a scholarship boy, background fairly ordinary, and mother could be a terrible snob sometimes.

Funnily enough, she *had* talked to father, always found it easier to talk to him and he had been surprisingly upbeat about it. He liked Tom, perhaps because Tom had already expressed a desire to teach, and saw no reason why the two of them shouldn't make a go of it. They had a matching look about them, he told her, of which he thoroughly approved. But they had, for the sake of sobriety, to keep it under their hats whilst Tom was still at school. To their amusement he had pulled Tom aside for a man-to-man chat, telling him he could do what he liked once he was finished with school, provided he showed Julia the respect she deserved.

Tom had teased her about that but she thought it rather sweet.

And they had been discreet, although when they married five years later in the school chapel, poor Daddy was long gone and Julia had to struggle with her feelings as she was led up the aisle by an uncle she scarcely knew instead of him. She had felt his presence, however, very strongly, putting it down to her highly charged emotional state.

'Do you suppose she's in love?' she asked Tom now, bringing up the subject as they sat quietly, listening to a favourite CD. They preferred it to watching television. Listening to music, you could close your eyes and effectively switch on and off as you pleased. 'I seem to recall I fell in love when I was her age,' she added mischievously.

Tom grinned. 'Did you really?'

'Of course I did, you fool. And look where it's got me,' she added.

'A lovely home. A beautiful daughter. And me, you lucky girl,' Tom said lightly, before returning his attention to Frankie's moods, seeing that it was puzzling her. 'Stop worrying about her. She's working hard, it's always a different sort of challenge in the lower sixth, and she needs an escape valve. It's no bad thing for her to be thinking about boyfriends. After all, as you've just said, you were.'

'I know. It's different though when it's your daughter and there's such pressure on young girls these days. I worry that she'll feel left out if she hasn't had a sexual experience by now, although again I wonder how much of it is just talk.'

'She's sensible,' Tom said, giving her a reassuring smile. 'I should think it's very likely she imagines herself to be in love. After all, she's a pretty girl, so it's hardly surprising if the boys buzz round her.'

'Yes, but somehow I don't think it is that,' Julia said, swiftly considering the boys in Frankie's class, none of whom would be likely to set a teenage heart racing. She knew some of the mothers were already discussing contraception with their daughters which, although laudable in a way, disappointed Julia greatly.

They were seventeen for heaven's sake . . . she had no need to talk to Frankie about that, not for ages yet. She had only her own experience to go by but a certain amount of the self discipline she had imposed on herself would not come amiss in today's youngsters. She had said as much to Tom who laughed, accused her of being middle-aged and stuffy, saying things were very different these days. A horror of being pregnant and of having to face her father with that had been enough to curb her own desires and Tom had understood that. It was not easy for him to forget that, whilst Anthony Scarr was Julia's father, he was also Tom's headmaster and a remarkably upright and sober figure at that. They had therefore been remarkably staid during the early stage of their relationship, now she thought about it, admirably self-controlled, although at times it had been difficult and they had eventually caved in halfway through their protracted engagement.

Whatever the problem was with Frankie, her work was suffering and that *was* a worry. She would come home, go up to her room, ostensibly to study, but Julia knew otherwise. She was letting things slide, which was annoying because she had always been in the top set, effortlessly zooming along. She wanted to go to university, knew the importance of exams, so it was a bit of a puzzle all round. Her form teacher had had a quick word with Julia about it. She was not too concerned either and felt sure, like Julia, that it would settle but she had thought it wise to issue a warning.

And perhaps the wisest course of action, as she and the form teacher had discussed, was to keep quiet and not push her too much. She was not going to bother Tom with all the details, for the last thing she wanted was for him to come the heavy-handed father. He didn't usually, was pretty relaxed about his daughter, much more so than she was, but when it came to her education, if he thought she was risking failing her exams that would be a different matter. Being a teacher himself, albeit at a different school from Frankie's, he was alert for the slightest blip in her progress. She was on target, or had been, for straight A grades and nothing less would do.

However, there was no need to panic. Not yet.

For the moment, a low profile was called for.

Julia couldn't help watching her closely though, not able to work out what it was that was different about her.

Afterwards, of course, she wondered how she could have been such a fool not to have realized.

She was her mother, for heaven's sake, and mothers were supposed to know these things.

★　★　★

After a hot spell the weather had broken. It was pouring down. Torrential. Rain bouncing off the path, the flower beds thirstily soaking up the water, sky off-white, the clouds heavy and low-slung, and the summer temperature had plummeted as a result. Headache-inducing weather so far as Julia was concerned. She had started off the day in a summery top, had slipped a lightweight cardigan over it and was pondering whether or not to light a fire in the sitting-room when the doorbell rang.

Damn. Who could that be? She had some work to do for a particularly awkward client and had been putting it off too long today already. When the doorbell rang a second time she called irritably that she was just coming and hurried through the hall, quickly checking she looked presentable. The front door was solid and so it was impossible to guess who the visitor was until you opened it. Unsatisfactory in this day and age: they needed a little spy-hole for safety's sake. Screaming blue murder if she was in trouble — and their nearest neighbours were outside scream-hearing distance — was useless.

She saw instantly that the visitor posed no threat, standing as she was beneath a scarlet umbrella that had not kept her entirely dry.

'Mrs Vasey?'

'Yes.' Julia looked at the woman and small boy in the hooded jacket who stood on the path outside the porch. Jehovah's Witness was her first thought but then they didn't usually call you by name.

'May we come in?'

'I'm sorry . . . ' She held firmly on to the

38

door, taking in the woman in a single glance. Pregnant beneath the grossly unflattering dungarees, khaki-coloured at that, only a few weeks to go by the look of it, face a little bloated, eyes swimmy as if she had just had a good cry.

'Of course you don't know me, do you?' the woman said, cheeks pink suddenly. 'How stupid. I just assumed because I know who you are that you would know me. My brother used to be a client of yours: Brian Watson.'

'Oh yes, I remember Brian.' She smiled, directing another smile towards the little fair-haired boy, who was clinging on to his mother's leg, trying to interrupt. 'How is Brian these days? I haven't seen him for ages.'

'He's all right.' She shuffled on the doorstep, dark eyes taking in what she could see beyond Julia. 'I'm sorry to disturb you like this but this is a private matter, Mrs Vasey, and it might be best if I came in.'

Julia nodded. It was inconvenient but the woman looked so agitated that she decided to ask her in anyway. With a bit of luck it might not take long and she would catch up later. She couldn't think what it could be, unless Brian, who had amicably taken his business elsewhere, was in trouble. If so, she did not see what she could do to help. She had not been entirely happy with some of the aspects of his business affairs even if, on the surface, it was all above board.

The woman unclipped her umbrella, shaking it and leaving it, as Julia directed, in the porch. They made a few very English remarks about the weather as she led them through the hall into the sitting-room, taking a quick satisfied glance around, seeing it as the woman might newly see it. She might not be a qualified interior designer, like Nina, but she did pride herself on her style, which was comfortably traditional. Easy on the eye in shades of pink and cream. Pity about the lack of a fire, which would have added a welcome touch.

Julia had just finished arranging some flowers in a large glass goblet, a country-garden assortment of mauve sweetpeas and grasses, which she had placed on the table beneath the tall narrow window. Good classical-styled furniture, family photographs on another side-table and a bold rug over the plain cream carpet completed the effect she had been at such pains to achieve. Tom was no help and she had resigned herself to constantly picking things up and tidying after him. Arguments were a waste of time. You could always tell when he had been in a room from the debris deposited.

'Do sit down,' she said, waving a hand

towards one of the three sofas that draped cosily round a large rectangular coffee table in front of the fireplace. The dried-flower arrangement that graced the hearth at present was no substitute on a day like today for a real fire. Outside, the rain pelted against the window in a fresh frenzy and the frame rattled. 'Would you like a cup of tea? And what about you?' She smiled at the little boy clutching his comfort blanket. 'Orange juice or milk?'

'We won't bother, thank you,' the woman said firmly, seeming to get a hold of herself. 'Not until I've told you what I have to tell you.'

She was a petite woman and, sitting far back on the sofa as she was, her legs dangled.

'Would you like a cushion?' Julia asked. 'That sofa's not particularly comfortable I'm afraid. It's a little too squashy.'

The woman shook her head. 'It makes no difference. I can't get comfortable whatever I do these days,' she said.

'I know just how it is,' Julia said sympathetically. She had never actually got to the huge size of a full term pregnancy but she had some inkling of what the other woman must be feeling.

She waited, calmly enough but, somewhere inside, fear lurked as she caught something of the woman's apprehension. What on earth was the matter?

'I'll come straight to the point, Mrs Vasey,' she said, swinging the child up and on to her knee. He settled there, sucking his thumb, and absent-mindedly she stroked his hair as she spoke. 'I'm Karen Muncaster . . . Mr Muncaster's wife.'

'Mr Muncaster from school?' Julia asked, recalling the teacher at once. They had had a long chat before Frankie started in the sixth form. Undecided between history and geography, Frankie had asked them, rather to their surprise, to help her out with the choice and it was Mr Muncaster's gentle persuasion that had swung it for Julia. If she hadn't known his subject she would have had him down for History anyway. He had that look, that vague look, of somebody whose interest was deeply rooted in the past. In his middle thirties, tall, dark-haired, comfortably casual in jeans and sweater — her father would have been horrified at that — but it was par for the course these days and meant no disrespect. He had impressed her and, although the final choice was ultimately Frankie's, she liked to think they had had some influence.

'That's right, Mr Muncaster from school,' Karen confirmed. 'I can tell you have no idea what's been going on. They have been

42

discreet, I will say that for them. And that makes it easier in a way.'

'Discreet?' Julia's heart pounded and she found herself looking at Karen's ankles, which were puffy. Water retention — she should take care. 'I'm sorry, I don't know what you are talking about.'

'Your daughter Francesca and my husband are having an affair,' Karen Muncaster said flatly, her voice perfectly steady, although Julia had the feeling she had been rehearsing this conversation in her head. 'It's been going on for a few months now. I've been so caught up with the pregnancy and this one here . . .' she looked down at the blond head of her son. 'I've been a fool. I've never noticed. I believed him, you see. He told me he was at the gym and I had no reason to believe otherwise. It didn't occur to me to check up on him. Now I realize that he's been very quiet lately, preoccupied, and now I know why.'

'Oh my goodness, you're quite wrong . . .' Julia was locked into her chair, her body suddenly very heavy, pushed back into her seat, as if some gravitational pull was being exerted. Her eyes were riveted on the table with the photographs, to a particularly good one of Francesca taken last year. Happy and smiling and it dawned, even as she tried to

43

deny this to herself, that she had not been quite so happy and smiling for some time. Withdrawn and secretive, rather, and suddenly, looking at Karen, she knew in her heart that it was true.

She hadn't queried Frankie's occasional absences of late either. On Tom's instructions they had allowed her a looser rein recently, only proper, Tom said, now that she was seventeen and, provided she was back home before a certain time, she didn't have to account for her movements completely. Julia had been reluctant in some ways — *shouldn't we always know exactly where she is* — but Tom had been adamant.

'We can trust her,' he had said. 'She doesn't have to clock in, for God's sake. Let's give her some freedom.'

'Yes, but there are funny people out there. Young girls her age are being kidnapped, raped, murdered . . . '

'Darling, do keep a sense of proportion. She'll be perfectly safe.'

Oh really . . . Julia looked at Karen, knew it was true and didn't know what to say.

'She's only seventeen,' she said stupidly. 'Far too young for an affair.'

'Don't you believe it. I was married at seventeen,' Karen said. 'That's been the problem. We were married too young. Just kids ourselves. We married because I was pregnant, then I lost the baby. And it started to go downhill afterwards, but we persevered. It took ages for me to get pregnant again. So she's not too young, Mrs Vasey.'

'But . . . ' She struggled to understand, although anger was beginning to surface. How dare he? How dare he seduce a young girl in his class? He could lose his job for this. She would see to it that he did. 'How do you know?' she asked coldly. 'Have you proof?'

'I don't need proof. He's confessed,' the woman said. 'He says he doesn't know how it happened. But happen it did. He's told her it's over but she's taking it badly. She imagines herself to be in love with him.'

The telephone chose that moment to ring but Julia, glued still to the chair, let it ring again and again.

'Aren't you going to answer it?'

'The machine will pick up a message.' Julia said, sighing as the ringing stopped at last, grateful in a way because it had given her a brief chance to collect her thoughts, which were spinning and whirling all over the place. The calm of the room was no longer calming, the chill grey outside was depressing, and even the flowers, fresh in their pretty container, failed to lift her.

'We've talked and talked, hours on end,

about what we should do and, although he's been an absolute bastard, I've decided to stay with him,' Karen continued after a moment. 'I have to for the sake of the children but one thing I'm clear about. I am not going to be miserable *and* penniless. Philip can't afford to lose his job. Philip must not lose his job.'

Julia laughed shortly. 'He should have thought of that before he got involved with her.'

'That's easy to say. She was very persuasive, he says.'

'Oh come off it,' Julia said, anger flaring. 'I'm not having that. You're not going to tell me that it was Frankie's fault. He's not going to get away with that, thank you very much.'

'What does it matter whose fault it was? It's done and we have to decide what to do about it. We can keep it quiet. Nobody knows,' Karen went on. 'Just us. You and me. Francesca and Philip.'

'Why are you telling me this?' Julia said. 'You needn't have. I would never have known. I don't suppose Frankie is going to shout it from the roof, is she? And she's never been the sort to confide in me,' she added bitterly, instantly annoyed to have said this to a stranger. If the woman dared to look at her with sympathy she might very well clock her one.

46

Thankfully there was no sympathy, but then it was difficult to see beyond the blotchy face, the sad but determined eyes.

'I'm telling you because, as her mother, you have a right to know,' Karen said. 'We can work this out together. I know he should never have got involved but, in his defence, it's been hard for him these last few months. When I'm pregnant . . .'

'I know, I know,' Julia said quickly, before she went into details. 'But that doesn't give him the right to seduce young girls, especially girls in his class at school.'

'Only one girl,' Karen reminded her, quiet and dignified now. 'He's putting an end to it but that's not going to be easy if he has to continue to teach her for the next year and she continues to think she's in love with him. You can see how impossible that situation would be. So, we want you to take her away from here. We're settled. We're not moving.'

'We're settled too,' Julia said. 'And I think you've a cheek asking us to move. Frankly, he deserves to lose his job. It's madness for a teacher to do this. The sort of thing the papers love. What was he thinking of?'

'I've told you, it was a mistake,' Karen said, surprisingly defensive of him.

'A mistake?' Julia echoed in amazement. 'Is that all he can say? He deserves everything he gets and if that includes losing his job, then he deserves that too.'

She glanced towards the cabinet where she kept the drinks. She did not often drink but she could do with a double brandy now. For a moment she was tempted to go across and pour herself one but she resisted. Best to remain stone-cold sober.

'We could go that route. You could kick up a fuss and he would lose his job.' Karen said. 'I knew it was risky coming to you like this. It can go public and, believe me, if we leave things as they are it may very well go public. Do you want that? Do you want people pointing their fingers at Francesca? Because that's what they will do, believe me. Do you really want your daughter's name dragged through the mud?'

Karen Muncaster had thought this through.

Instantly it conjured up scandal, the Scarr name, the family reputation, her father's obsession with it. Frankie might be a Vasey but it would amount to the same thing, the Scarr name would be tarnished and she would be to blame. She couldn't face her mother knowing about this.

'How can we hope to keep it quiet?' she said, aware that Karen was beginning to wear her down. 'I can't believe nobody knows.'

'You didn't know.'

That was true. And none of the other mothers did either or there would have been a few sly digs.

'Surely there have been rumours?' she asked, though she was doubtful now.

Karen shook her head. 'Absolutely not. I've told you, nobody knows. It's incredible but there it is. Philip says they've always behaved impeccably at school and they were careful about where they met . . . ' she blushed. 'It sounds very sordid. He's been looking after a house in Norwich for a family friend whilst she's abroad. Philip said he would deal with it, check it out from time to time, so I assume that the neighbours thought she was me, if you know what I mean. Francesca doesn't look like a schoolgirl when she's out of uniform, does she?'

True.

Out of uniform Frankie looked like the beautiful young girl she was.

'Take it from me, there was no chance of bumping into anyone from school,' Karen finished with a sigh. 'Not there. Hole-and-corner stuff. Awful, isn't it? It makes me cringe just to think about it. And I'm amazed he could have abused our friend's trust like that. Using her things, her bed . . . ' she looked directly at Julia, eyes bleak. 'But that's what happened.'

'I need a cup of tea,' Julia said, forcing herself out of her seat, struggling for normality. 'And so do you. And I have some cheese scones. Would you like one?'

'Thank you.' Karen Muncaster looked hard at her. 'I'm sorry. I know this has hit you hard.'

'Do you love him? Do you love your husband?'

There was an uncomfortable silence.

'I love my kids,' she said at last.

3

Despite rehearsing what she would say to Frankie she made a mess of it, finding herself issuing what sounded like an order, directly Frankie was through the door.

In my study. Now.

Frankie appeared, looking puzzled, frowning down at herself.

'I was going to change,' she said. 'I'm soaked.'

'Sit down. You can change in a minute,' Julia told her, trying to soften her voice. Frankie's jeans were damp-splashed from the rain, her hair was clinging to her head. Julia couldn't get used to the haircut. It had the funny effect of making her look older and younger at the same time. It certainly emphasized her eyes and the silver hooped earrings she was so fond of were more clearly visible. Julia did not know when Frankie had developed such style but it was there, even in the habitual uniform of blue jeans and tops. She wore her inexpensive jewellery well, several silver chains round her neck, made it look a million dollars. Funny that, Nina did the opposite.

'Well . . . ?' Frankie asked, sitting cross-legged on the rug by the fire. 'What's happened? You look terrible. Dad's all right, isn't he?'

'Your father's fine. Mrs Muncaster called to see me today,' Julia began, coming straight to the point because otherwise she might never get round to it. 'She's told me everything.'

There was a silence.

Feeling her heart thud, Julia sipped the large gin and tonic she had poured for herself, the second today, and waited.

'What do you want me to say? Do you want me to deny it?' Frankie said at last, the movement of her chin defiant.

'I want the truth.'

'The truth . . . ?' Frankie's breath caught. 'She's never meant anything to him. He only married her because she was having a baby and then she went and lost it and it was too late then. He's going to divorce her and marry me. But he's not going to spoil things for me. We'll wait until I've finished my A levels and got a place at university. By that time the divorce will be on its way and we can marry as soon as it's through.'

'I beg your pardon?'

'You heard.'

Julia's anger, directed previously towards

Muncaster himself, switched to her daughter.

'How dare you speak to me like that?' she heard herself saying, shocked rigid. 'And you can forget all thoughts of marriage, my lady. I wouldn't let you marry him if he was the last man on earth.'

'I'll be eighteen. You won't be able to stop me.'

'A man who cheats on his wife,' Julia carried on, ignoring the interruption. 'On his pregnant wife at that, with a girl very nearly young enough to be his daughter. What kind of man is that?'

'I knew you'd bring that up — the age thing,' Frankie said, face flushed, eyes still defiant. 'So, what if he is older than me? It makes no difference. We love each other.'

Julia heard herself laugh. 'You don't know what that means.'

'It's you who doesn't know what it means,' Frankie said, her expression suddenly sly, a look Julia remembered from when she was small, a look that suddenly and inexplicably reminded her of her mother. Wise beyond her years. 'Shall I tell you what it was like, mum? With Philip. Do you want all the details?'

'I most certainly do not,' she said, appalled that she should say that. 'And I have no idea what your father is going to say.'

'Daddy will support me,' Frankie said. 'He

will go along with whatever I want to do.'

'Oh no, he will not. We will discuss it as a family and decide what we are to do,' Julia said, trying to calm herself, even though great waves of emotion were thudding through her, making her heart beat ever faster.

Steady.

She looked across at Frankie, only a few yards distant but it might as well have been miles.

Distant.

Julia couldn't help it. It was just the distance she had always maintained from her own mother, from Clemmie, as if she was afraid to bridge that little important gap that always existed between them, the gap that was not present with Nina and mother. She so envied Nina that closeness she had with mother.

With Frankie she blamed the circumstances of the birth, the baby's being whipped away so there was no chance of immediate bonding, followed by the very real possibility that she might lose her, which had the effect of making her take one step back, so that if she *did* lose her, it would not be quite so terrible. At least, that was the theory.

And that feeling had persisted over the years.

Always that little step back.

Always that irrational fear of losing her, the beloved only child. After Frankie she had briefly, but only briefly, thought of having another baby. They were lucky to have Frankie and she somehow didn't feel like pushing that luck. All mothers worried but she thought she worried more than most. Frankie's best friend had just passed her driving test and she knew she could not put it off much longer, the dreaded driving lessons. She would have to learn to let go but she did not want to, not until that gap had been bridged. And now look . . . this was going to pull them ever further apart.

'I want you to think very carefully about this,' she said, wanting to go over to Frankie but resisting because she needed to look at her now, see her reaction. 'We could be ruining a lot of people's lives here if we're not careful. Most important, your own. If it gets out, mud will stick. I don't care that it's his fault, it will still stick. And it's already played havoc with your work and that would get worse. You would lose out on university and you would end up bitter.' She paused, watching her anxiously, wondering if any of this was getting through. 'He won't marry you,' she went on, seeing that clipped look appear on her daughter's face. 'Karen told me that this afternoon. He's told her that he's finished with you and they're trying again. We have to let them do it, darling, no matter what our feelings are.'

Frankie murmured something under her breath.

Julia gasped at the obscenity. 'What did you say?'

'I told you to . . . ' Frankie stopped, the anguish on her face unbearable.

'How dare you do this to me,' Julia said, shocked by her own anger. For two pins she could have hit her. 'We were going along so nicely. We love the house and everything here. I've got the business well established. Good clients.'

'Oh, right. Be selfish then,' Frankie said, cold-eyed now. 'Don't spare a thought for me, for how I might be feeling.'

'I am thinking about you,' Julia said helplessly.

'No, you're not.' Frankie's face tightened, eyes huge in her pale face.

'Frankie . . . ' Julia pleaded, making a move towards her but finding to her horror that her daughter moved further away, rejecting the advance with a look that spoke volumes.

There was only one way out of this. It was the only way to avoid a scandal.

It might well be Muncaster's fault.

It was his fault, no matter how he might try

to shift the blame.

But the old saying was never truer — no smoke without fire — and she had no intention of staying around to see Frankie's reputation shot to shreds.

Not a daughter of hers.

Not a granddaughter of Anthony Scarr.

★ ★ ★

It was no longer merely torrential rain. It had upped a gear, the traffic had slowed to a crawl, and with his windscreen wipers failing to give him any clear view of the road ahead, Tom pulled into a lay-by as soon as he could to sit it out.

He had promised he would get back early and now he would be late, which would go down a treat with Julia. She was a good cook, liked to plan her meals, everything timed to last-minute perfection and being late would throw it into confusion. She would be in a sulk all evening. He sighed, reached for the packet of cigarettes that he stowed at the back of the glove-box, opened the packet and stared down at the solitary cigarette, the same one that had been there for the last four months.

It was one hundred and twenty-four days since he last smoked a cigarette.

He took the cigarette out of the packet, held it between his fingers, dare not raise it to his nose to sniff it. No, no, a thousand times no.

He had stopped on National Give-Up-Smoking Day. As good a day as any and these National Days of this and that amused him anyway. Who the hell thought them up, what gleeful committee conjured them out of thin air, and why didn't they include a National Pick-Your-Nose Day or Retch-and-Spit Day? Something equally horrible.

It was long overdue anyway, the giving up smoking. Julia hated the smell of cigarettes in the house and on him and he hated his dependence on them and the effect on his health. Forty-six now and he was approaching what he considered a critical time for guys. Heart attacks out of the blue, last-ditch affairs with nubile young women before the body completely lost it, trips to the gym, a new image and so on.

It was something to do with trying to hang on to the last remnants of your youth and it was bloody hard going.

He felt the wind buffeting the car and stuffed the cigarette pack back into its safe place, reaching instead for the paper bag with the fruit gums, searching for one of the last few red ones.

It had been a bugger of a day from the word go. They were out of Weetabix, the only cereal he liked and his boiled egg had been runny. He should have known then that it was a waste of time keeping the appointment on the golf course with Wetherby. They had managed a few holes, bravely soldiering on, Wetherby winning every single one, but when the visibility closed in they had to throw in the towel and retire to the clubhouse. His colleague Wetherby — mathematics — could bore the pants off the most generous-hearted guy and Tom's eyes had glazed over long before the cheese and biscuits arrived. A good golfer though and that made up for it. Half-hearted competition was neither here nor there. Tom liked a good scrap. They were already booked in for a return match and he would knock him for six next time.

Golf was the love of his life. After Julia and Frankie, of course. Francesca was his darling little girl, who looked like a smaller version of her mother, any trace of him deeply hidden. He wished they'd had more kids, a boy would have been nice, but Julia had been horrified enough at having the one and made damned sure they were very careful from then on. It took the edge off the lovemaking, the constant worry she had of being pregnant. She refused to take the pill, scared witless by some claims of possible side-effects. The calculation in her face before they performed the supposedly spontaneous act was a real turn-off. She'd suggested a vasectomy and he had agreed to that — in theory — but hadn't actually got round to it yet. Julia was now talking about having her tubes tied, something like that, but again she was terrified of hospitals and operations and was putting it off, just like he was.

Couple of cowards, the both of them.

He usually enjoyed the summer break from school. Of course, it was not a complete break, as people outside the profession seemed to think. It was a chance to catch up on some paperwork, that was all, collect your thoughts together for the new school year and he took that seriously. With most of the profession, particularly those out there in the comprehensive world, being frankly pissed off and bogged down, he never admitted just how much teaching meant to him, how he really wanted to make a difference to a few lives, have them remember him when they were grown up. A noble aim, though, and it was what he believed in, so bugger what anybody else thought.

Early in the summer break this year they did manage a couple of weeks away in Portugal, although this time, for the first time, without Frankie. At seventeen, she reckoned she was too old to come on holiday with them and, remembering the last holiday, when she had grumbled incessantly as teenagers do — bless 'em — he was inclined to agree. She stayed with her friend Amy this year at Amy's house, so they felt reasonably happy about the arrangement. Amy's mum, raucous but well-meaning, would keep her eye on the pair of them. There had been rumours of Frankie and Amy going off somewhere on their own but Julia had vetoed that. He would have risked it. He trusted his daughter but try telling that to Julia.

He sometimes thought that Julia ought to have lived in another century. She hated to be called old-fashioned but she was, more so in some ways than her mother. He had always found Clemmie strangely refreshing with that glint in her eye, which was not suppressed even at seventy-five. He recalled the closeness of her relationship with Anthony and how his sudden death had momentarily rocked her, before her natural determination took hold again. Peas in a pod, she and Anthony, and, although he and Julia put on a good front, were reckoned by most people to have what is known as a *good marriage*, he knew deep down that their relationship was slipping and he had to do something about that pretty damned quick before it slipped over the abyss. He knew what Julia thought about divorce and had never ever mentioned it but sometimes he wondered how long they could survive as their love loosened.

From his point of view the Portuguese holiday had not been a success. This time the moonlit strolls, the afternoon siesta, dinner and wine, failed to do the trick, failed to make Julia relax. Her mind was back home with Frankie and he found it a bit of an insult that she was incapable of switching off. Her incessant worrying about what might be was beginning to get on his nerves. He had tried to talk to her but she seemed incapable of acknowledging that their marriage was at a cross-roads, remaining infuriatingly complacent and shutting her mind somehow to the problems that were firing up.

His main problems were, one: that he was in the market for an affair before it was too damned late, and, two: that he might be falling out of love with her. They had been more acute since the last visit up north to Greysands at Christmas. He and Nina had been the only ones to brave the minus-two degrees weather and go out for a walk after Boxing Day lunch. They had left the others, zonked out in the sitting-room, watching *The Great Escape*, telling each other as they kitted themselves out in Scott-of-the-Antarctic gear, that the fresh air — and how! — would do them good, brush away the Christmas cobwebs anyway. Nina had enjoyed a hearty lunch and was desperate, she told him, to exercise the bloody calories away. He liked Nina. A bit dizzy, yes, but he'd felt sorry when she'd broken up with that guy of hers. He didn't know who had broken with whom — it wasn't the sort of thing you asked — but she did not deserve to be shabbily treated. She deserved somebody who would be seriously, madly in love with her.

At first, as they walked, they chatted about Christmas, one or two things they had seen on television, Clemmie's health and so on. Inconsequential stuff and he couldn't remember at what point it became more serious, verging on the confessional.

She was getting a bit broody, she said, now that time was marching on and she really wanted a child before she was forty. With no man on the horizon and the deadline a couple of years away she was not yet getting into panic mode but she was just the teeniest bit anxious, that was all. She and Harry had started talking about a family, or rather she had, and she wondered aloud if that had been the cause of his leaving. True, the state of their finances had been dire, but if only he had told her the perilous truth they could have buckled down and done something about it.

'We had a joint account,' she said. 'And it never occurred to me to look at the statements. I can't believe I did that now. It's stupid to trust somebody as much as that. He hid them, you know. Just in case I peeped at them. How can I have been so naïve?'

He had laughed it off — what else could he do? — told her not to worry that there was bound to be somebody lurking around, jollied her along in other words and, true to form, she had perked up and thankfully returned to her old determinedly cheerful self.

When she wasn't moping she was delightful company as ever, bundled up in a heavy duty green anorak, wearing a Christmas gift of scarlet beret, scarf and gloves, and they had taken the short cut over the top of the headland to Florey Park, a little nostalgic ramble for old times' sake.

When they reached the school, they stood quietly a moment looking it over and it brought it all back with a bang.

'Memories?' Nina asked quietly.

'You bet. I was scared stiff when I first came. Ten years old and the new boy on the block. I know it was great to be offered the scholarship and mum was pleased as punch and so proud of me but my God, I felt the pressure. I had to do well for her sake. I missed her that first term and it was a culture shock, boarding amongst boys whom I . . . well, I felt inferior to them at first. To their credit, they were a good bunch, put me at ease and after that I just sailed through. Your father was my inspiration, incidentally, and I'm not just saying that. I mean it.'

'He was proud that he knew every boy, their backgrounds, their problems, whatever. He used to go through the profiles at home, make damned sure he was never caught out wondering who somebody was.'

'He was an exceptional man. Tough luck, that accident.'

'Yes.' Her face clouded over and he wished he had not said that. 'You know, Tom, I always thought of it as my school even though I never came here, being a girl. I wanted to come here and I loved being here in the holidays. I used to come with Dad when he had work to do, and he let me wander round the classrooms and I used to sit at a desk and imagine I was doing lessons. It seemed so much more glamorous than my own school. Of course, that all stopped when . . . when Daddy died.'

Tom nodded, feeling a little awkward, surprised too, because the words conveyed a

65

sensitivity he had not thought she possessed. He didn't often see Nina in reflective mood. He tended to think of her as one-dimensional. If ever there was an image printed on his mind, it was of Nina smiling.

'You fancied me once upon a time, didn't you,' he said with a grin, feeling so comfortable with her that he could say anything.

'Maybe I did,' she said, mischief in her face. 'You had a lucky escape, Tom. Julia was a far better bet than me. You know where you are with her. I would just lead you a merry dance.' She tugged at her jacket, lifting up the collar and snuggling further into it. 'God, it's cold. My ears are going to drop off. Let's get back and have a hot toddy.'

The thought hit him hard as he snatched a glance at her. She looked gorgeous, face a bit shiny from the cold, her breath puffing out into the chilled air. She did not have the drawn look of Julia. Despite her mild grumbles about being overweight — and she didn't look that bad to him — she looked healthier than Julia.

Nina was all the things her sister was not.

Julia was as tense as a tightrope. She worried too damned much. About everything. And what had once attracted him so much now unsettled him, as he fought to regain his old feelings for her. His marriage was important and he wasn't giving up on it without a struggle. Male menopause probably, coupled with a vague dissatisfaction with his lot. He had no idea why. They had a nice house, he drove a decent car, Julia contributed significantly to the funds, even with the limited hours she put in and they had a beautiful daughter to boot. His sex life was not exactly a thrill a minute but then it never had been, had settled into being nice enough once in a while. He had imagined not so long ago that he would be happy with that for ever, so long as he had Julia.

He was bored, that was it. He needed a change. A change of scene. But, knowing how much Julia loved the house, its situation, he knew it would be an uphill battle to persuade her to move. They would have to wait a year anyway, until Frankie was at university, but in the meantime they needed to get their act together, to sort out locations, to look around. A year was nothing in house-moving terms.

He almost wished he had taken Clemmie up on one of those offers she was always making — a post at Florey Park — but that would be dangerous given the stupid crush he had on Nina. A crush at his age? What else could you call it? She was out of bounds and that was vaguely exciting. Good God, it would put the cat among the Scarr pigeons.

A pipe-dream. A middle-aged guy's fantasy, that was all it was. It would be laughable if it wasn't so pathetic. Nina was not beautiful as Julia was but she was exhilarating, vibrant and fun with a smile that truly lit up her face. He recalled that they had giggled their way back from that walk at Christmas, when she had slipped on the frozen path, lost her footing, done a sort of desperate ice-dance in an effort to regain her balance before ending up in a heap and, with his own feet sliding every which way, he'd had a helluva job to get her upright again. They had then clung precariously together for a moment, laughing uncontrollably before common sense took hold and he told her they would have to make a careful move.

'Easier said than done, Tom Vasey. Hang on to me, for God's sake,' she said, as they edged past the worst of the ice. 'A broken leg will bugger up my agenda no end.'

Julia would not have slipped. Julia would never have said 'bugger' either.

But then, Julia would have taken more care, not been so cavalier with her strides on the glassy surface.

In the lay-by he sighed as he rubbed at the steamed up window and peered out.

The rain was easing, just a straight downpour now, and it was time he got himself home.

A dread nudged at him as he started the engine, and he did not know why.

4

They were sitting in her study, she at her desk on the swivel-chair, Tom on the two-seater chintz sofa in the comfort corner by the bookshelves. Julia loved this room, was relaxed and happy in it and spent most mornings in here, concentrating fiercely on her work so that she could have the afternoon off if she wanted. She loved the flexibility of working from home, which she had done for years, and liked the freedom. Now she wouldn't dream of going back to the bustle of the workplace, the competition, the back-stabbing, for anything.

At home she could wear leisure clothes for work, only needing to dress up when she visited clients. She was quick, though, to notice when sloppiness was creeping in and guarded against it, making sure she had a good wardrobe of dressy clothes.

'Tom, I have to tell you something,' she began, wondering how best to say it. Frankie had not joined them for dinner, which was nothing new these days, and had now disappeared to Amy's. But Julia could not bring herself to tell him over dinner, as if

70

somehow, like the condemned man, she was allowing him his last meal before his life fragmented, as hers had done this afternoon. Frankie was his little girl, very much daddy's girl, and he probably still thought of her as that, his little girl.

'Sounds ominous,' he said. 'You've not been having it off with Mr Wallace, have you? He hasn't ravaged you in his rhubarb patch?'

She shook her head, unable to raise a smile. It was a running joke with them because the elderly man in the house down the lane clearly did admire her, courting her over his hedge as she walked by and she did sometimes pop round to enjoy a mint tea with him, sitting in the gazebo. Oddly, they were not on first-name terms. He called her 'my dearest Mrs Vasey' purring the words. He was eighty-nine and a half so he told her, and he would probably be delighted if he knew that Tom generally called him 'that randy old sod down the lane'.

'I'm afraid this is serious, darling,' she said, making sure she had his attention.

'What?' He stared at her. 'Good God, you're all right, aren't you? You're not ill?'

'Oh no, no. I'm all right. It's not that.' As a matter of fact, she was not quite fine, had been a little under the weather for a while but now was not the time to discuss that. She took a breath. Out with it. 'It's Frankie. You remember Mr Muncaster from school?'

'Yes. History.'

'That's right. Well . . . his wife came to see me this afternoon. It would seem that he and Frankie have been having . . . ' she could not bring herself to say sex, not in the context of Frankie. 'They've been having a sort of romance. A love affair.'

'Frankie? What do you mean, an affair?'

'They've been seeing each other,' she said in a rush. 'He's confessed to his wife. She's pregnant.'

'Frankie? Bloody hell, Julia, you're telling me she's pregnant?'

'No. Not Frankie. Mrs Muncaster. Karen she's called. It's she who's pregnant. Anyway . . . ' she swivelled her chair so that she could no longer see his face, to allow him a few private moments to compose himself, to get to grips with what she was telling him. 'The point is, they're going to try to save their marriage, the Muncasters. It's over, this fling with Frankie, although she thinks she loves him, poor sweet. She's very upset. He told her he was going to divorce his wife and marry her, you see.'

'Marry her. She's only a child. I'll kill him. The bastard.' The angry words slipped from him, edged with disbelief.

'Keep calm. Let's think this through. We don't want it to come out. We've got to keep it secret. They don't want it to come out either.'

'I should think not. He'd be out of the door before he could zip his pants. The education authority takes a dim view of this sort of thing. Any guy who teaches nubile young wenches has to keep a bloody tight grip on himself.'

'Quite.' She glanced at him. 'We have to get Frankie away from him. It's obviously going to be impossible for her to stay at school next year. I know it's a blow, darling. I know you love it here, I know you love your school, and we both love the house, but we're going to have to think about moving. Sooner rather than later.'

'Moving? Moving from here, you mean?'

'Yes. I'm sorry but we're going to have to put the house up for sale, move away.'

He managed a tired smile. Julia smiled too, imagining she looked pretty much as stressed as he did. He was still in his golf clothes, or his version of them. Try as she would, she couldn't change him, smarten him up a bit. He was just every inch a schoolmaster of the old school and very much the rugger player he had once been, the broken nose a reminder of that. Plenty of straight, fairish hair fading to grey, grey-blue intelligent eyes under his spectacles and a perpetual rather sweet worried frown.

She loved him.

She knew that their marriage was no longer in the first flush of youth, that it was going through a sticky patch. She was sure he was not being unfaithful, although she suspected he might be thinking about it. One of her well meaning acquaintances had recently commented that men of his age needed to be reminded that they were still virile and wanted and she supposed she was a bit short in that department. Sex had never been the be-all and end-all to her, but she trusted him. She could see no circumstances where he might stray. He might think about it but he would never get round to it. It was too much of a hassle for one thing, and he was much too nice a man to be devious.

They sat through a heavy silence, punctuated by sighs from both of them. Outside, the rain had sulkily run its course and the evening sky was prettier, patches of blue peeping through. The flowers were weighed down with raindrops, water was still dripping from the blocked gutter that Tom had promised to do something about. Fat chance. He was hopeless at do-it-yourself, the house was full of half-finished tasks that stayed unfinished, unless Julia did something about them. He was mean as mean though and objected strongly whenever she suggested they get somebody in to finish the job.

'I could do with a cigarette,' he said at last.

'Have one,' she said hastily. 'If it will help.'

'No. It won't help. I'll have to talk to her, won't I? Will she want to talk to me though? It's going to be bloody embarrassing. I didn't think she'd . . . well, you don't know what's going on with seventeen-year-olds, do you? An affair with an older man? God, that takes some swallowing. If it was one of the boys from school, from my school, I could understand that.'

'I know, darling. It's been a big shock. I'm very cross with myself for being so naïve. If only I'd talked to her before now.'

'Post mortems won't solve anything. It's done and we have to make the best of it.'

'At least she's not pregnant. He hasn't completely ruined things for her.'

They fell silent again, absorbing this.

'Suppose, to make things easier for Frankie, we do move,' Tom said. 'There is the small question of another job for me. They're not that easy to come by and I really don't want to get back into the public sector . . . '

'You might have to,' Julia said shortly. 'Beggars can't be choosers. Unless I ask mother . . . ' She looked at him, heard his sharp intake of breath. 'I know, I know. You'd rather hang up by your thumbs, but please don't dismiss it out of hand. She's forever telling me about vacancies coming up and we've always said no in the past. She has the headmaster in the palm of her hand and she's still got terrific influence there. She only has to say the word.'

'I don't like it,' he said. 'Pulling strings. It's no way to get a job. For a start, you always feel beholden to somebody. It means I would feel fettered somehow, always having to think before I spoke. Because there'd always be somebody there who might just say I wouldn't have the job were it not for my mother-in-law.'

'I don't like it either,' she said. 'But we might not have much option and better the devil you know . . . I can't think of anywhere else I really want to move to. Can you?'

'Abroad?'

'No,' she said firmly. 'Back home, if we can. Back to Greysands. At least it's familiar and it will be nice to be nearer mum and Nina. It's not fair that she should have to do everything.'

'You've never had any qualms about that before,' he said, raising his eyebrows.

'I have,' she told him, flashing an irritated

glance his way. 'I've just never talked about it, that's all. It's been a big worry for me if you must know.'

'OK.' He exhaled slowly. 'OK. Let's go for it. Ask Clemmie if there's a job going. Don't get your hopes up though. It's a long shot.'

★ ★ ★

Julia stayed at her desk a while, ostensibly catching up on some work but in fact staring out on to the side lawn and the roofs of the nearby hamlet. How could she consider leaving here? How could she? And worse, how could she consider going back to her other home? Going back home with her tail between her legs was not a welcome thought, although nobody would know that that was the reason. They could say they were coming back to be near to Mum as she got older, coming back to take some of the burden off Nina. Good reason, and Julia felt a moment's guilt that she might never have done anything about it were it not for all this.

They didn't need to say *anything*. They didn't need to explain. People did things for whatever reason. On the plus side, the move would be good for Frankie. Get her away from some dubious influences here. The school that Tom worked at was boys only and, whilst they had considered private schooling when Frankie was coming up for school age, they had in the end decided on the local state school because it had such a good reputation. And Frankie had thrived from the infant class onwards, doing so well until this last year. Julia had managed to keep all this, the recent downturn in Frankie's work, quiet from her mother and Nina, for there was no point in worrying them. A little rebellion, that was all, and she hoped Frankie would learn from it and make her proud of her again.

She was sitting and contemplating the rapidly improving evening sky when her mother rang.

'Julia darling, it's me,' she said.

'Hello, Mother. I was going to ring you,' Julia said.

'Really?' Her mother gave one of her little knowing sniffs. 'How are you, darling?' she asked, not waiting for an answer. 'I am very well as usual but it's hot up here. It's driving Nina mad. She's like an overdone lobster. She just sweats constantly.'

'Mother . . . that's not very nice of you.'

'Well, she does. If she lost a little weight, it might be easier for her to bear the heat but I dare not tell her that. You know how sensitive she is about her weight.'

'Is she? I thought she couldn't care less about it.'

'Well, yes. That's what she says. But she would, wouldn't she? I know her better than that. We mothers know everything about our children, don't we, darling? And if we don't, then we jolly well should.'

Julia sighed. Sometimes she could swear that Clemmie had installed 'bugs' in her house. It was quite unnerving how accurate she could be.

'It's been hot here too until today,' Julia said, returning to the safe topic. 'Clammy. Does the weather improve your arthritis?'

'Arthritis?' Clemmie bristled. 'What arthritis?'

'Oh. Nina said . . . '

'She doesn't know what she's talking about,' Clemmie said. 'I am perfectly well, darling. I am as supple today as I was thirty years ago. You have to work at it. It doesn't come naturally. I exercise by walking every day over the headland to the school. It takes me twenty minutes at a good pace. *I* don't need to go to a gym.'

A little dig. Julia thought of the member-ship card tucked into her purse. She had gone once, to show willing, but it had knocked her out for a couple of days afterwards. It just wasn't her scene, all those sweating, heaving, red-faced smug people, and it irritated her that Tom had imagined for a moment it was.

'You don't visit the school every day, surely?' she asked, more sharply than she intended.

'No, of course not. I merely walk as far as the gates and do an about-turn. But I do pay a formal visit once a week to see Jonty during term time,' Clemmie said. 'Do I detect disapproval? I'll have you know Jonty is delighted to see me. After all, I do still maintain an interest on the board of governors but I do not interfere with the running of the school if that's what you're thinking.'

'Did I say that?' Julia sighed. Mother jumped to the most ridiculous conclusions sometimes, although there was an element of truth in this one.

'This afternoon I was looking at the photograph of Frankie you sent me. It's in a silver frame now, sitting on top of the mantelpiece. She looks beautiful. I'm so proud of her.'

'Yes. It was a good photograph.' Julia twisted the phone cord, wondering how best to broach the delicate subject of a possible job for Tom. It was asking a lot and it would be just their luck if there was nothing doing, if everybody was happily settled for years to come.

'How is she doing at school?'

'Very well.' Julia hesitated, heard the doubt in her voice, decided to risk it. 'To be honest, she's going through a difficult time. She's slipped a bit this last term.'

'Oh dear. Seventeen is such a sweet age but it's also such a burden. I shall have a word. After all, strange as it may seem, I was seventeen once and I recall it vividly. It's all hormonal. Everything is when you get down to it. You spend your entire life going through hormonal crises. Does she have spots?'

'No. She has clear skin. Can't you tell from the photograph?'

'Photographs can be retouched,' Clemmie said sharply. 'I have mine enhanced now. It's wonderful. It just rubs out the wrinkles.'

'It's not that . . . ' For a moment, she was tempted to spell it all out. It might be easier over the phone.

'No spots? In that case, she's probably starting to worry about boys and it will be taking her mind off her studies. Have you talked to her about boys? Have you explained that boys of a certain age have the greatest difficulty in controlling themselves? She ought to be aware of it. The last thing we want is for her to end up pregnant. Maybe you should put her on the pill for when she's ready. Or perhaps not. I have no idea what we would have done when I was younger, if we

81

had had the pill. I just crossed my fingers and fortunately it worked.'

'Honestly, Mother . . . ' Shocked at the direction the conversation was taking, Julia felt herself flush, which was stupid when her mother was at the end of a telephone line. Why did Mother do this? Why was she acting as if she had talked freely to them, her and Nina, about sex?

'I know we never really talked, darling, you and I,' Clemmie said with a sigh, reading her mind. 'Put it down to a quite ridiculous embarrassment on my part. Skipping a generation, it's easier. Don't ask me why. I'll phone her. Have a long chat. When can I catch her in?'

'Please don't do that,' Julia said hastily. 'She's very uncooperative at the moment. Give her a little time.'

'As you wish,' her mother said in a voice that suggested the matter was not closed. 'Now, Julia, the reason I've rung is this. I've been in two minds whether or not to bother you but Nina insists I tell you. You know Nina, she's desperate for you to come back here so that she can pop round for coffee and have sisterly chats.'

'Tell me what, Mother?' Julia asked, feeling her heart thud.

'There's a vacancy at Florey Park in the

English department,' Clemmie said. 'There! I've told you and don't bite my head off . . . '

'I wasn't going to,' Julia said, taking it in slowly. 'Go on . . . '

'Senior English,' Clemmie said. 'He's gone off in a huff, the previous chap. I'm not at all surprised. He had one of those beards, unkempt variety, and eyes that never looked at you. Distinctly shifty. I would never have taken him on and he's proved utterly useless. He's gone before he could be fired. As I said to Jonty, he really ought to let me sit in on the interviews. I have a sixth sense and, after all, Florey Park is still my baby. There's a cottage with the job for as long as you need it, so you needn't worry about that.' Her sigh was slight. 'If Tom wants it, the job is his. I have absolute faith in his ability as a teacher.'

'Good.' Julia thought quickly. 'We might very well be interested. Can you arrange an interview? We could come up any time next week.'

There was a short silence.

'Of course,' Clemmie said, her voice giving nothing away. 'I'll have a word with Jonty and get back to you, darling. But if you do come up, do make sure that he wears a suit, will you? And get rid of that mustard tie, whatever you do. It offends my eye.'

83

5

Nina Scarr could not resist looking back at Rosemount as she swung the car through the gates. She'd seen it hundreds of times and yet it still had the power to impress. Men tended to be less impressed. She remembered Harry saying it was truly naff, a sugar-candy concoction. A pink thatched cottage maybe, if you must, but a pink house — never in a million years. It reminded Harry of those over-the-top mansions in Newport, New England, the stuff of Scott Fitzgerald's novels. It would have been all right in the thirties, suited all that, all those tennis parties, Cole Porter songs and endless cocktails, but nowadays it was the most ridiculous thing he'd ever heard of.

It was not ridiculous at all. Rosemount was beautiful. They could have changed the colour, of course, but it seemed wrong because the first lady owner had proudly called it her pink house and it was known locally as the pink house. In any case, father had maintained that it would be unlucky.

So it stayed pink.

An astonishing shell-pink confection of a

house with a white cast-iron tracery, almost like lace, around the gable and windows. Viewed from the bay, it stood out on its tip of land like a pastelled lighthouse. Totally out of character in this predominantly grey-stoned area, it was built in the early 1800s for a dowager countess and, when her family died off, it was sold into the wealthy Forsyth family, makers of confectionery, her mother's family.

Mother rattled around in it now and Nina had stayed with her at Rosemount for a while when she returned home after the couple of years spent in London with Harry. What a humiliation that had been, coming home like that, but the man had stripped her bare of funds after the failure of their business venture, making damned sure he had enough stashed away himself. She could have kicked up the most enormous fuss, made his name stink, but she didn't have the heart for it, even though it left her in a dilemma. It was a straight choice of taking a crummy job, opting for a crummy flat in an equally crummy area, or coming home and admitting she had made a mistake.

As soon as she could afford it she bought the flat and business with a little help — oh hell! — from her mother. She preferred to have her own place, even if it was incredibly cramped — 'charming' in estate agent's language. Her flat was over the shop, which was in the very heart of Greysands, nicely positioned for passing tourist trade but not, thank goodness, totally reliant on that. There were a lot of people with money in the surrounding area and they liked the idea of using an interior design service. She had slowly built up a reputation and she was now able to pick and choose the commissions.

The shop sold an upmarket range of sheets, towels and elegant lamps and ornaments with space set aside for local craftware. Her mother's friend Edward Grantham usually had one of his paintings in — variations on a bay theme — which did not go down well with mother for some reason. Nina could not understand that relationship. They had been friends for aeons but mother treated him with an icy politeness that was painful to watch. The man must adore her to put up with it. Funny that. Julia and Tom were a bit like that too. Julia was lovely but there was a coolness about her and sometimes she was unbearably short with Tom, who seemed to be happy to suffer in silence. Harry would have blown a gasket if she had ever treated him like that, but that was Harry. He might well have been roguish but she could read him emotionally like a book.

To Nina's relief there was a breeze as she drove along the coast road today, whipping in through the open window, ruffling her hair and sending long wispy strands across her face.

The road that skirted this hilly part of the headland was a demanding drive, up and down through the gears like a yo-yo, narrow and treacherous with a few scary bends and, at one turn in the road, a spectacular drop via ragged cliffs to the salt marsh and sands below. No safety barrier but then only half a dozen people used this road so why bother?

Why bother indeed?

The panic caught at her a moment as she eased the car round the worst hairpin and she wondered when, if ever, she would learn to relax about it. She couldn't stop a glance down over the cliffs, a sickening distance down, and she swallowed hard, clutching the wheel tightly until the road straightened out and the first of the town's road signs began to appear.

There was a better view of the bay now, glistening in the sunshine, the silvery water rippling its way across to the other shore. Nina bumped over some cobbles and drove into her little yard, thankful for the parking space because the town was heaving today with visitors, who had managed to clog everything up, bless their hearts. Tugging at her pants and top, feeling her knickers and bra sticking to her now, she pushed open the door to the workroom and stepped inside.

'If I could afford it, I'd have air conditioning in here,' she said to Mary, who was sitting at the workbench, almost submerged in a yellow floral fabric. 'But then, I suppose we can count the number of really hot days, can't we? And it would be an impossible extravagance. Tell me I'm right, Mary, and that you're not working in a sweatshop for buttons. I'll never forgive myself if that's what you think of me.'

'Don't be daft.' Mary told her, smiling. 'It is not a sweatshop and I wouldn't work anywhere else. Anyway, the weather is going to break by the weekend and then we should be back to normal. Grumbling about the rain.'

'Oh good.' Nina grinned at her. Mary was younger than she, married with two sullen and awkward children and a husband with a paunch, who ran a driving school. Why the hell she had to envy her, God only knew.

'Nearly finished,' Mary said, head bent over her work. 'Mrs Lawson has been on the phone. Can you take these over tonight and hang them for her? Bit of an emergency apparently.'

'Yes. I'll ring her back,' Nina said, taking a quick look at Mary's work, confident it would be perfect as usual. What a find! Mind you, she couldn't afford to pay her much but luckily Mary was happy enough with her miserable pittance and, commuting to work in Lancaster, not an easy trip on these unforgiving lanes, was not worth her while.

'I'll just pop up and have a shower,' she told Mary, checking in the shop first that there was nobody lurking. 'Can you hold the fort?'

Silly question. Mary was a treasure. Nina had no idea how she would cope without her.

The flat was so small that there was no room for sentiment and she had thrown much of her stuff away when she moved in. It reminded her of those old boarding-houses, the ones called Sea View, when you had to stand on a box and with a bit of luck might just snatch a glimpse. In her case, if she balanced on the sink in the kitchen and stuck her head out of the top of the window, she could just about see the bay.

Never mind. She knew it was there, so that was all that mattered. And she could smell it. The heavenly ozone flooded her head sometimes and when she was away from here she felt oddly bereft without it.

She had painted the flat, sitting-room, bedroom and minute study, in warm Mediterranean colours, and could not, at the last, bear to part with the Venetian glass, which turned out to be a mistake, for it served to remind her constantly of Harry and their holiday in Venice. Romantic creature that he was, he had chosen his moment, proposing in a gondola, just as they came out of a narrow water alley into the greeny-blue choppy waters of the Grand Canal, collided with another gondola and nearly tipped over. They had laughed about it, of course, and at the gondolier, who had been dour in the extreme, yelling at the fellow gondolier — Italian swear-words seemed so much prettier — apparently oblivious to the romantic event taking place under his nose.

The ring had nearly disappeared over the side, a beautiful antique ring she had worn so lovingly for a whole year. If it had, she told Harry, they'd have had to dredge the whole canal to find it.

'It's not worth that much,' he had said, his pragmatism taking over.

Nonsense. It was worth everything.

Tears pricked her eyes as she looked down at her now bare ring-finger.

Damn him to hell. She had wasted four

years of her life on him, four years she could ill afford to waste. And he still wasn't completely out of her system. She still hankered after him and for a long time she had harboured a secret notion that he might suddenly come to his senses and come to get her. Drag her off screaming.

The cool shower helped calm her down and she put on a bright-blue cotton frock, long and loose, and slipped some sandals on over her slightly puffy feet. She really was pathetic when the temperature soared. She used baby-powder and the smell of that always reminded her of little Frankie and that time she had looked after her when she was a baby. A whole week. How on earth Julia had trusted her to do it was beyond her comprehension but trust her she had and Nina had loved it, but it was over much too soon. Julia and Tom returned south and, thereafter, they saw each other maybe twice a year, sometimes only once.

And Frankie grew and grew.

And, somewhere along the way, they lost whatever it was they had had for each other. Now, when they met, they were almost strangers and that hurt a lot. They spoke on the phone sometimes but how could she expect scintillating conversations when the girl wanted to get back to her young friends.

Conversing with an aunt, whom she probably thought was incredibly old at nearly forty, was not the stuff of teenage dreams.

Damn. Thinking about Frankie and Julia only upset her.

Knickerless, but safe because the frock was down to her ankles, she went down the steep stairs into the shop.

* * *

They had driven the stupidly short distance to the beach but Amy, Frankie's best friend, had passed her driving test at her first attempt and borrowed her mother's car with dire warnings about bringing it back in one piece. It felt strange to be doing this after years of cycling across or simply walking. Amy parked proudly and neatly beside the shore and they slipped off their sandals and felt the hot soft sand of the dunes sifting beneath their toes. Frankie knew her mother would have a fit at the bare feet, mindful of the glass and sharp shells that might be embedded deep down. Frankie was more bothered at the sudden awful thought of hypodermic needles and it was enough for her to stop and awkwardly stuff her feet back into the linen sandals.

They took the harsh beauty of this coast,

the sand-dunes, tough grasses and sea for granted. This particular stretch of beach was awkward to get to and less populated by visitors, but today there was a fair sprinkling of people enjoying the warm afternoon.

They were both wearing shorts, cut-down jeans in Amy's case, and halter tops that showed off their sun-tanned midriffs. Three youths, one of whom they recognized from school, hollered at them from the shore, but although Amy giggled Frankie shooed her on, ignoring them. Boys of her own age were just boys.

'I'd tell them where to get lost,' Amy said, referring to the conversation they had had in the car. 'How can they think of moving when you're in the middle of the sixth form? You're going to get your schedule all mixed up and it's not going to help your grades, is it? Can't you stay here with me until you've finished? I'm sure my mum won't mind. One more will make no difference. You could bunk down in my room somewhere and we could come to some arrangement about your keep.' She flushed as Frankie glanced at her. 'We'd have to do that. Mum couldn't afford the extra food and things.'

'Thanks, but I don't think that's on,' Frankie said, wishing she'd not mentioned it now. 'It's not definite. Dad hasn't had the interview yet. But I think he'll get it,' she added, not wanting to explain about Granny and Florey Park and all the string-pulling. She'd heard them arguing about it. Dad was on about principles but she knew Mum would wear him down eventually. She always did.

'Where is it again?'

Frankie sighed. They had moved off the dunes and were now walking on the flat of the beach nearer the water's edge, where the sand, damp from the tide, had hardened and ridged. A few brave souls were venturing into the chilly water, water that took most of the summer to warm up. They stopped walking after a while and Amy threw down the car rug she had been carrying so that they could sit on it. Instantly, she began rummaging in her bag for her sun cream and began applying it to her bare arms. Amy was fair-skinned with reddish hair and had to be very careful.

'It's on Morecambe Bay,' Frankie said in answer to her question, lying now on the rug and digging her fingers into the fine sand, lifting her hand up and letting the grains sift through them. She and Amy had made sand-pies and castles when they were little, here on this very beach, but those days were over forever, until they had children of their own. Frankie wondered about that as it occurred to her that, if she did marry Philip, she would be stepmother to his kids. That was food for thought and not something she cared to dwell on too much. She did not want kids. They just got in the way, as she had got in the way of her mother's career. It came out occasionally, the what might have been, when mum was feeling particularly fed up with one of her clients.

'Morecambe Bay?' Amy echoed, looking completely blank.

'Look it up,' Frankie told her irritably. She loved geography and maps and prided herself on knowing what was what. It was pathetic how ignorant some of her friends were. Now, after all this, perhaps it might have been easier had she taken geography instead, because she would not have been in such close proximity to him.

'It takes ages to get there,' she continued with a sigh. 'Once you come off the motorway it's all twisty and turny lanes and you can only drive at twenty miles an hour or even less and you're always meeting tractors and things.'

'Don't go,' Amy said, stretching out, her legs already oily from a previous creamy application. The smell of the cream rose up, sweet and sickly. 'Put your foot down. Tell them no way.' Amy looked hard at her, close to tears.

'Oh, Amy . . . ' Frankie managed a smile, absent-mindedly putting a hand up to her hair and finding herself surprised at how short it was. She used to twist her hair before, a gesture she had been scarcely aware of and it was odd not to be able to do that any more.

'Parents . . . ' Amy went on with a big sigh. 'What can you do with them?'

Frankie nodded her agreement. The stilted conversations she had had since the news broke were very nearly funny. Her mother was having trouble taking it in and as for Daddy . . . oh dear, poor Daddy. He had been genuinely embarrassed, although obviously furious with Philip. She had warned Philip to stay well away, horrified that her father might cause a scene.

'I know what we can do.' Amy interrupted her thoughts, increasingly desperate now. 'We could get a place somewhere, just you and me. A flat would do.'

Frankie gave her an exasperated look. 'How?' she said. 'What would we do for money?'

'We could get jobs,' Amy said. 'I'm not really that bothered about going to college.'

'Well I am.' Frankie smiled a small smile.

She glanced at her friend. It would be a wrench to leave her. Amy was not so bad. Amy was not the bad influence her mother had her down for. Amy, for all her talk, for all her flirty ways, was innocent. Frankie envied her chaotic family life, the house always overflowing with her brothers and sisters and assorted friends. Her own home was much tidier and a lot quieter. Mum was not easy to talk to, wrapped up in her work or a book or something. Sometimes Frankie felt like a guest in her own home. She almost longed for the rows that Amy was forever having with her mother. She wondered if her mother cared enough about her to shout and yell like Amy's mum. When it all had come out, all this, her mother's prime concern had seemed to be how they might keep it quiet.

Being beautiful was a pain, Frankie decided. It led you into all sorts of trouble through no fault of your own. If she hadn't been beautiful — and this was not vain because she was only saying it to herself — if she hadn't been beautiful, then *he* would never have noticed her and none of this would have happened.

'If you do go, can I come and visit you?' Amy asked suddenly, in a small voice, as if it was only just dawning on her. 'During the holidays?'

'Yes. That would be good,' Frankie said, the pain of separation already beginning to gnaw at her. She would miss Amy a lot. Making new friends would be so hard and they would never be friends in the way Amy was. When you'd known somebody since you were three years old, it meant something. You could say *anything* to each other. You couldn't pretend with Amy, although, for Philip's sake, she had said not a word about all this, the real reason for the move north and, to her amazement, Amy had not twigged. Amy, terribly busy with her studying as well as the driving lessons, had believed the excuses. 'I'd love you to come and see me. Although there's nothing to do up there. It's dead.'

'There's not much to do here either,' Amy said. She was expected to do well in her exams, studying modern languages. She wanted to work as a translator eventually. And, contrary to what she had just said, she desperately wanted to go to college and get a good degree.

Frankie had no idea what she wanted to do. She knew with certainty that unless she got down to some work soon her results would be awful. She was already prepared for it: the post mortem of this year, her dad tight-lipped, her mother trying to console. She would soon knock the revision into shape and she would do well when it mattered because she had to, she needed to, not particularly because they wanted her to.

Other than missing Amy, she didn't actually feel too bad about leaving. She hadn't visited Greysands much over the years but she had enjoyed it whilst she was there and Auntie Nina was good fun. Shame she'd broken off her engagement and, at her age now, she might never meet another man. Maybe she didn't want to. Maybe she was getting on just fine with her interior design business. Maybe she had quite enough to do looking after Granny Scarr who was getting on now.

She told herself that Philip was doing the honourable thing in staying with Karen and the new baby, a little girl born two weeks ago. They had had a long talk and he had eventually convinced her that it was the only way forward, for the time being anyway. They were both being splendidly heroic, giving up on their love for the greater good, as it were. Something like that. He had made a promise to Karen but, after a while, when the reconciliation failed as it surely would, Frankie had promised that she would be waiting for him.

However long it took.

'You'll miss coming down to the beach any old time you like,' Amy said, turning a bit sulky now, probably thinking about whom she could latch on to when Frankie was gone.

'Bet it's not half so good a beach up there.'

'It's mudflats,' Frankie said, remembering. 'Miles and miles. It's just where the estuary widens out but it's not so bad. The town's got some shops, a department store of a sort, gift shops and all the usual stuff. And then there's the school where Dad might be teaching, Florey Park.'

'But you won't be going there?'

'No. It's boys only,' Frankie said. 'I don't know where I'm going yet. There's a private school for girls a few miles away and I might go there, just for the last year.'

'Oh.' Amy flushed, said nothing.

'I'd rather be staying here,' Frankie told her, anxious to make it clear. 'But it will only be for another year. Maybe we will both get places at Newcastle.'

Amy nodded, knowing that was extremely unlikely, knowing it was clutching at straws, knowing that things would never be the same again.

'The houses are grey except for our house . . . ' Frankie went on, wondering why she had called it 'our' house when it belonged to Granny.

'Is that why it's called Greysands because the houses are grey?'

'I don't think so. All the houses up there are grey. It's the local stone.'

'I'll miss you,' Amy said suddenly, a catch in her voice. 'There'll be nobody to talk to. Please don't go, Frankie.'

'I might have to,' she said, feeling tearful herself. She wanted to stay here where everything was familiar, with friends like Amy. Quickly, before she made a fool of herself, she leapt up. 'Are you ready? I've had enough. I'm starting to burn.'

She set off and, Amy followed, at a distance, dragging her feet.

6

Julia was not happy to be keeping a secret, a secret such as this, but she and Tom had agreed on a united front and were sticking to that. She hoped she could trust Frankie not to say anything either, for it would kill her granny if she were to find out. After all, Mother, despite her efforts to keep abreast of the times, had been born in the early part of the century and things had changed since then. Julia, if she dared think about it, would even say her mother had probably never enjoyed the physical side of marriage. It was never talked about, and as teenagers she and Nina had been left to fend for themselves, finding out what they needed to know from their friends.

She was nervous about this interview. It was all very well her mother saying it was already in the bag, purely a formality, but she was still nervous on Tom's behalf. Suppose Mr McKay, Jonty McKay, took a dislike to him? What then? He was the headmaster, the one who would make the final decision, no matter how much influence Clemmie might try to wield and it was possible he might choose to overrule her. It would cause an almighty stink if he did, for Clemmie still thought she ruled the roost, but perhaps it was time Jonty McKay applied his authority. In theory it was nothing to do with Clemmie now, whom he chose to employ. In practice of course, she could wrap Jonty round her little finger, just as she had done with Dad. She had once told Julia that there are people who manipulate and people who prefer to be manipulated.

Exactly.

She sighed and Tom glanced her way for a second, taking his eyes off the road. The motorway was quiet on this weekday afternoon and this stretch seemed longer than usual.

'You might look a bit more optimistic,' he said. 'Am I or am I not the most impressive English master around?'

'Of course you are,' she said. 'It's not that. I'm just worried that it might go wrong for whatever reason and I'm suddenly very keen for you to get it. Believe it or not, I think I actually want to move back. Maybe I've been kidding myself all these years. Maybe I've always secretly wanted to come home.'

'Wow! Change of tune,' he said drily, giving her a quick look. 'What's the matter? You don't look so good. You're very pale.'

'My stomach's playing up,' she told him, determined to play it down. 'Is it any wonder?'

'Are you like me? Thinking about Frankie?'

'Yes, of course I am,' she said. 'Although she's better off staying at home for a couple of days. There was no point dragging her along if — '

'If I don't get the job,' he interrupted. 'You're right, although Clemmie would have been pleased to see her. Clemmie's going to worm it out of her, you know. I wonder if it might be better if we told her the truth now and have done with it, otherwise we'll never hear the last of it.'

'Goodness, no,' Julia said at once, relaxing as he returned to the inner lane after passing a large lorry with European plates. 'She must never know, darling. She adores Frankie. And I want it to stay that way. She's getting on and I don't want to spoil things for her.'

She let him get on with the driving, closing her eyes even though that did not help. She was conscious only of the noise of the engine as Tom coaxed the big car up a dragging hill, hearing him curse softly as he got stuck behind yet another lorry.

'Your mother is no fool,' Tom said at last, apparently musing on the matter. 'I think she should be told, so don't blame me when it all goes belly up.'

'I shan't be blaming anybody. We're all in this together.'

'I wish Frankie would talk about it,' Tom said. 'Isn't that what they recommend? She hasn't said a word. I can understand her not wanting to talk about it to me but has she spoken to you?'

'I tried to bring it up but she clammed up,' Julia said, biting her lip, and staring out on to the fields that were flashing by. Frankie was so brittle just now and she worried that if she pushed her she might break and never mend. 'I don't want to rush her. She'll talk about it in her own time. I don't think there's any lasting harm done.'

He laughed shortly. 'Try telling that to Mrs Muncaster. I bet they divorce within the next year. Their relationship won't stand up to it. How the hell would you feel if I had an affair with a seventeen-year-old girl, a student of mine at that?'

'You don't have girl students,' she said, dismissing it. 'Anyway, you wouldn't be so stupid.'

'Too right. Tell you one thing though, we've made a balls up of this parenting lark, haven't we?' he said. 'Good God, we've only got the one child. It isn't as if we had a dozen to cope with.'

'It's worse if you've only got one,' Julia said. 'You've only got the one chance.'

'Yes, well — '

'I know. Don't blame me for that completely,' she said, casting an annoyed glance his way. 'We reached a joint decision on that, Tom.'

'It doesn't help. I wish we'd had another child now. It's putting all your eggs in one basket. And, if it turns out to be a rotten egg — '

'Hey! Don't say that,' she said at once. 'She's a golden egg as far as you're concerned. She always has been. You're always ganging up on me.'

'You're not jealous, surely? Jealous of Frankie?'

'Don't be ridiculous. Anyway, I don't know why we're saying this. She's a good girl at heart,' Julia said, defensive now. 'She was vulnerable and he took advantage and I'm never going to forgive him for that. But . . .' she adjusted her position in the seat, moving her legs, which were getting stiff. 'We've got to support her now, Tom. Moving up here is the first step. New school. New start. At least, this way we've got a good report from her year head.'

'If he only knew. I don't know how we've managed to keep it quiet. I know why you wanted to keep it to ourselves, darling, but what really gets me is that bastard Muncaster is going to get off scot-free.'

'Oh no, he's not,' she said, remembering the look in the wife's eyes.

'We have it on our conscience if he seduces another child.'

'She's not exactly a child. She's a young woman.'

'She's a child in his books,' Tom said. 'For Christ's sake, Julia, he was her teacher. In a position of trust. He should have lost his job. He would have if I'd had my way.'

'We've been through all this over and over again. Karen didn't want to give up on her marriage. She's giving him another chance. He won't do it again,' Julia said confidently. 'He has too much to lose. And you beating him to a pulp wouldn't have solved anything, would it?'

Silence thudded and she glanced at him but he was giving nothing away. It occurred that she wouldn't have minded if he had done just that but that was Tom. He never let his temper get the better of him and whilst that was a quality to be admired, nonetheless Frankie was his daughter and surely any normal father . . .

For a while longer they were quiet, Julia thinking about the interview that awaited them. She was to be interviewed too, for after all she would have to play a small part in the running of things as the wife of a senior master. The cottage did not come completely free in that sense but living in the cottage in the school grounds would be a weight off their minds for the time being and save them the necessity of staying with mother. Once they were settled they could think about buying another property, and when the sale of their house went through they would have more than adequate funds.

'I want you to know I'm doing this because we have to,' Tom said at last, voice earnest, as they came off the motorway. 'I'm in two minds about the whole set-up. I have some trouble convincing myself that Florey Park is such a good school — never mind that I went there myself.'

'What a thing to admit,' she said, cross with him, for he had never mentioned it before. 'I hope you're joking.'

'No. From things Clemmie has said I'm worried that it's going downhill. I don't believe Jonty McKay was the best man for the job. I know it was hard for anybody to replace your father, but from what I hear he seems to have been resting on his laurels these last few years. I've been doing some research, and whilst results have been adequate they are not exceptional. I think a bit of complacency has been settling in and I intend to get my department sorted out pretty damned quick.'

'That's good to hear. You must say that at the interview. As far as I'm concerned, he's doing a good job and, whatever we might think, Mother thinks he's wonderful. Let's not dwell on the negative side, darling. That's the one thing that will really put Jonty off. You have to be seen to be one hundred per cent behind him.'

'I know. Don't worry, I'm not going to do or say anything to upset him.'

★   ★   ★

Good-looking he might be but it would take some time for that nose to return to normal, Tom thought with satisfaction. He had not planned it but a couple of days ago he'd come across Muncaster outside the gym he frequented, coming out laughing and talking with some friends and Tom had seen all colours of red.

Thinking of that put-upon wife of his and the kids.

Thinking of Francesca, whom he had seduced.

On the spur of the moment, not waiting to analyse his feelings, he had followed him, waiting until the friends disappeared, then catching up with him in an alley. He was in such a fury that it never entered his head that the guy was a helluva lot younger and fitter than he was. Probably never smoked in his life.

But he had one advantage.

Surprise.

For a minute, he thought he might kill him.

He had caught up with him, called out his name. Hoisting his sports bag on to his shoulder, Muncaster had turned round. Recognition would come later for him. Tom hadn't said a word, just landed out and felt his fist hitting the soft facial flesh and the hard bone of his nose.

It was the first time he'd ever done it, hit a man in anger, and by God it felt good. The surprise in Muncaster's eyes was shuttered for ever in his memory. It hurt his hand. It had stung for days but he'd never said a word to Julia because she would be horrified at such an uncivilized action.

He had left Muncaster leaning dazed and bloody-nosed against the wall.

Bastard.

★ ★ ★

The westerly rain welcomed them as they headed for Carnforth, then Milnthorpe and the south lakes. Julia had been away too long, the last visit had been months ago, and it felt like coming home. Norfolk was lovely but this was home; a part of her would always be rooted here. If mother had her way, they'd all end up buried here in the windswept churchyard on the outskirts of town where Father's grave was. The funeral had been well-attended but it had been so cold, the winter wind whipping in from the sea with flurries of sleet. Appropriate somehow. Appropriate that they should all be so uncomfortable out there, but she had felt so sorry for Father, having to stay there, when they were all gone back to Rosemount for a welcoming glass of hot spicy punch.

She rarely spoke about it but she suspected that her mother would recall every detail of that day. At times, she could be fearfully morbid, making sure that they were all aware of her favourite hymns, the ones she wanted at her funeral. One was a rousing Salvation Army tune, the one Jean Simmons sang in *Guys and Dolls*. She had also requested Frank Sinatra singing 'How Deep is the Ocean'.

Then, a few days after the funeral, they were to have a quiet elegant dinner at her favourite restaurant over in Grange-over-Sands and set a place for her, toast her with champagne and wear beautiful bright clothes. Her jewellery was to be distributed evenly between the three of them, Julia, Nina and Francesca.

Julia sighed.

'I'm looking forward to seeing Nina,' she said. 'Poor love. I thought she did terribly well at Christmas but she was very down. It broke her heart, that thing with Harry. I know he let her down badly financially but I'm sure they could have worked something out. They were so good together. Don't you think?'

'Leave me out of it. I hardly knew him,' Tom said. 'Although I saw right through him. I did say we ought to warn her but you said she wouldn't listen.'

'And I was right.' Julia glanced his way. 'Women in love are a race apart.'

'Why did you make her wear that awful frock at our wedding?'

'What? What's brought that on?'

'Just thinking about it. I even remember what it looked like. Frilly thing. Burgundy. She looked a fright.'

'Goodness, you have a good memory.' She laughed. 'Not many husbands would know details like that. And I didn't *make* her wear it. We had to choose dresses for the three of them and it's really hard. I have to admit it flattered the others more than it did Nina. I felt terrible about it afterwards. She should have said something. I wish she had but she said she didn't want to upset me when I'd gone to such trouble.'

'Ah. So you didn't do it deliberately?'

'No. I did not,' she said, annoyed that he should think that. 'I love her too much to do that. Anyway, I wish you wouldn't say things like that about her. She's very pretty. She always has been. And not every man wants to marry a beanpole.'

'Sorry,' he said quickly. 'But you have to admit that she doesn't know how to make the best of herself, does she? Considering she has some sort of interior design diploma, she has rotten taste in clothes. Don't you think?'

'I'm surprised you've noticed.' Julia smoothed down her skirt, mollified to some extent, although the mention of the bridesmaid's dress was a sore point. She had worried about that for ages afterwards, annoyed with herself for not trying harder to find something more flattering for her sister to wear. Big mistake. But, making a huge fuss about it, apologizing for the gaffe, would have only made things worse so she did what she was best at.

Played it down.

Distracted, she took in the view as they

113

drove at last along the lower coastal road towards the river-mouth and Greysands. They passed the 'Greysands Welcomes Careful Drivers' sign and Tom slowed down without her reminder. He had a few points on his licence already and had to watch it.

'I hope it works out, all this,' he said. 'For all our sakes. And I hope you and your mother will have some time together before she dies.'

'For heaven's sake, don't say that. She's fit as a fiddle,' Julia said. 'She's never had a day's illness in her life. She'll live to be a hundred.'

'You reckon?'

She was suddenly nervous, urging Tom to slow down as they neared the hairpin bends on the peninsula strip. He understood at once, doing just that, taking it nice and easy, but she still found her eyes drawn to the tumbling cliffs at *that* corner, felt a shudder run the length of her. Silently, they completed the journey, edging through the tall elaborately wrought black gates hung between the stone piers, up the gravelled drive to the house beyond.

'Still as pink as ever,' Tom commented, pulling the car to a halt.

★ ★ ★

Clemmie watched from the window. She saw them climbing out, stretching their limbs, approving from a distance of the tailored cream dress and high-heeled shoes Julia was wearing. Julia was tall and proud of it, none of this nonsense about flatties and hunched shoulders. Luckily, Tom still towered over her, heels or no, and she was reminded for a moment, as Julia stood close to her husband, of herself and Anthony at that age. Oh how she wished she was forty-something again.

Anthony was like a Greek god. He should have been an actor, for he had that stage presence, that ability — wonderful in a headmaster too — of being able to walk into a room and have silence fall and people look his way. He'd had a deep, resonant voice — respectable singing voice too, in the amateur dramatic world they had once been part of. He'd always worn his hair just a little too long and had a habit of pushing it off his face. Dark hair that had changed to a very attractive silver in his fifties. He would never have gone bald. She just knew it.

She heard the telephone ringing and waited for Mrs Harrison to appear.

'It's that Mrs Plowright on the phone,' Mrs Harrison came in from the hall, wiping her hands. 'Do you want me to tell her you'll ring her back.'

'Please. My daughter and her husband have just arrived, Jean. Would you ask Joe to help with their bags and show them up to their room?'

Clemmie was unconcerned about missing Dilys's call. It would be nothing important. She had missed a lunch date today with Dilys Plowright because of Julia and Tom arriving, but she would catch up later.

She hurried outdoors to meet them. As she kissed them her daughter smelled of Dior and Tom of a rather nice aftershave. They seemed in no hurry to be indoors, taking off for a gentle stroll around the grounds, deliberately walking slowly for her benefit, she supposed, and that irritated her for she was more than capable of doing a trot. More so than Julia, who had a pasty look about her. It didn't look as if she was using the gym membership that Tom had bought her for Christmas. Strange gift — she would have flung it back in Anthony's face if he had ever done that to her, but then Anthony had been a jewellery man. And she had a safe full of beautiful jewellery to prove that. Gyms were the new dance-halls, Nina had informed her, the place where young women met their young men. Or, if not there, then the supermarket.

How very odd!

'Had to have the roof done last year,' she

told them as she saw them looking back at the house. 'Cost a fortune. Isn't it boring spending money on things like that?'

They agreed. They seemed tense, but that could be because of the interview and its importance. What had brought about the change of mind Clemmie had no idea but what did it matter? What mattered was that they were seriously thinking of moving back and the job was as good as Tom's. In fact, Clemmie could not think of any circumstance that would stop Jonty from offering it to him. His qualifications were excellent, he had attended here as a schoolboy and he was her son-in-law.

They walked away from the house towards the wild meadow and at this point Clemmie left them to it, saying that tea would be waiting for them when they were ready.

* * *

After the journey, the stroll in the warm, sultry air was welcome. Julia had forgotten how different the air was up here. It was very quiet with just the distant sound of waves breaking on the shore below and the occasional screech of gulls overhead. Northern air, yes, but oddly mellow and distinctly soporific.

To her surprise Tom took her hand, whispering that he loved her.

'Do you?' she asked, her head full of doubts these days. 'Do you honestly?'

'Honestly,' he said, drawing her closer. 'This feels like a new start for us too. You know how things have been lately. Well, this can only be good for us.'

'I hope so. It feels good to be back,' she said softly. 'Thanks for doing this, darling. I know you don't really want to and — '

'Ssh.' He kissed the top of her head. 'It'll be all right. You'll see.'

'I feel I've really let her down. She's only a child, Tom,' she said, against his chest, feeling *her* chest hurting. 'Just a little girl. I wanted her to stay a child a while longer. If only I'd talked to her but I thought there was plenty of time for that. She's never really had a boyfriend.'

'Come on,' he urged, checking to make sure there were no tears. 'Let's go and have that tea.'

7

Mrs Lawson lived in a proper farmhouse belonging to a working farm, a few miles inland, although as Nina stepped out of the car she could still smell the sea. The predominant smell, however, was a pungent mix of cowmuck and chemical fertilizer, which would effectively nullify her own brand of scent from a lavish bottle of 'Joy', a present from her mother. Mother often bought her presents — *for your birthday, darling*, she would say — and when Nina protested that it was not her birthday, Mother would shrug and say: 'Have it anyway, I might be dead by your birthday.'

Nina wished her mother would not joke about things like that. Mad as a hatter she might be but she loved her a lot and life would never be the same without her.

'It's you,' Mrs Lawson said, opening the door and looking at her in vague surprise, sniffing suspiciously as she did so. 'Sorry about this. Vile, isn't it? I don't know why it has to smell so foul. It lingers for days. I warn you, it gets on your clothes. I'll take those, dear, while you get the rest of your things. Cup of tea first?'

'Thanks.' Nina went back to the car, got out her little pair of steps and assorted tools needed for the pelmet and rail and carried them indoors.

The rambling, shambling house was, like its sixty-something owner, poshly chaotic, complete with a couple of overweight black Labradors. It took a moment for Mrs Lawson to make room on a chair for Nina to sit on, one of the dogs taking great exception at being told to move.

'He's an absolute pain these days. On his last legs, poor darling. Deaf as a post. Oh Lord, you don't mind dog-hairs, do you?' she asked, sweeping her hand forlornly over the seat. 'They get everywhere.'

'I don't mind,' Nina said, plumping her beige linen rear on the chair. 'I love dogs. I'd have one myself but it's a bit difficult being on my own.'

Mrs Lawson beamed. She was wearing the baggiest, shabbiest trousers Nina had ever seen, a hand-knitted, loop-stitched, coral sweater that had been washed too often and a double row of pearls.

'I'm so sorry to drag you out but we're having visitors this weekend and I really want to have the curtains in place for them.'

'No problem,' Nina said with a smile, although she had hoped for a quiet night in and, knowing how Mrs Lawson talked, it would very likely be late when she got back. However, she had been a very good client and there were a lot more rooms waiting to be decorated. Because Mrs Lawson was nervous about what went with what, she was to be given a free hand with them.

'I'm so excited about all this,' Mrs Lawson said, clapping her hands in her delight. 'Isn't the fabric fabulous? Now, dear . . . ' she glanced anxiously towards the door. 'If he asks, you're to say roughly two hundred. All right? He'll think that's exorbitant but then he doesn't have the faintest idea what things cost these days.'

Nina nodded, used to the conspiracy. She had done a lot of work for Mrs Lawson and it was always like this, a little game she liked to play. Nina suspected that Mr Lawson knew very well what things cost but she was more than happy to play along with them. When Harry had done the same thing to her, lied to her about money, it had been altogether more sinister, as he ploughed her money into propping up the furniture-building side of their business. His stuff was good, no doubt about that — modern antiques, he called them, but they were of necessity very pricey and it was a difficult market in which to make a breakthrough. Harry, brilliant creatively, had been hopeless with both money and marketing and, as she had now discovered, it was impossible to run a successful business with only one element of that combination.

The windows in Mrs Lawson's sitting-room were tall and narrow but the fitting was not straightforward, the new rail taking an age to screw in place. By the time Nina was finished her arms were aching from holding up the heavy folds of fabric and she was exhausted. Mrs Lawson's agitated hoverings and the dogs' boisterous assistance, one of them trying to scramble up the steps with her, did not help.

Thankfully, Mr Lawson did not appear, so it was not necessary to lie about the bill, but as she was packing up Mrs Lawson reappeared with a coffee tray and another man whom Nina did not recognize.

'Alex will take those out for you if you give him your car keys,' she said. 'One of my sons, Alex.' She waved a hand his way. 'This is the wonderful girl I was telling you about. She's called Nina Scarr and she's been helping me with the decoration.'

Nina put down the little set of steps and her tool-bag and smiled across the room at him.

Wouldn't you just know it?

Alex Lawson was lively-looking, fortyish she supposed, reminding her of one of those men in upmarket men's casual clothing catalogues, good-looking in a weather-beaten way. The sort of man who you wouldn't be surprised to find hanging resolutely by his fingertips half-way up a rock face and here she was, hot and bothered, dog slobber staining her trousers, her make-up shot to pieces and her hair anyhow.

'Hi. I don't normally look as bad as this,' she said, making it worse, she realized as she caught his amused glance. 'It's been quite a day. I've been at it from the word go.'

'Really? You look fine,' he said and smiled.

It was one of those sorts of smiles, those easy, lazy, male smiles, a smile that sized her up, a smile that reminded her instantly and regrettably of Harry, therefore striking an immediate warning. No way, José! She was in no mood to get tangled up again with another easy-going charmer, who thought that money, her money, grew on trees. Next time, if there was a next time, it would not be a carpenter who fancied himself as the modern day equivalent of Thomas Chippendale. Rather it would be a man of integrity belonging to one of the sober professions, a doctor, a lawyer, an accountant like Julia. Something like that.

An ordinary-looking man who adored her.

She would settle for that.

'Alex is just back from Australia,' his mother said, eyeing him fondly. 'It's wonderful to have him home again even if he's probably going to be off again soon. London, I expect,' she finished with a sigh. 'That's where all the jobs are, he tells me.'

She wondered if she should pass up the coffee but Mrs Lawson was already pouring it out into pretty china cups and it seemed churlish not to sit down as directed and wait for Alex to return from taking her things out to her car. The car was an absolute rubbish dump inside, a movable tip, and she wished, too late, that she had tidied it up a bit before coming out.

'Thanks.' Deciding to offer no excuses for the car, she took the keys from him, hardly daring to look at him because she felt so awkward, like a gawky teenager. She could think of nothing interesting to say, so fussed one of the dogs instead, who was leaning against her leg.

'Nina runs her own business down in Greysands,' Mrs Lawson explained, passing a cup to her son, a delicate cup that looked so small in his big hand. 'She's one of the Scarrs.'

'Is she now?'

124

'Her parents founded Florey Park, the public school on the headland . . . '

'Ah yes, I know it,' Alex said. 'A friend of mine's son is there. Reasonable listing in the school tables, he tells me.'

Nina managed a smile. 'Don't ask me. All I know is that it's doing terribly well.'

She had no idea if that was true or not but it was what mother said she ought to say if anybody asked. Exude confidence, she said.

'Nina's father . . . ' Mrs Lawson looked sympathetically at Nina, then soldiered on, determined to give Alex a potted history. 'He was a delightful man, I understand, although I never met him. Well, he was killed in a car crash, wasn't he, dear? In the seventies, I believe, before we were here.' She paused, aware of the silence. 'Oh, do forgive me. I didn't mean to drag that up.'

'That's all right. It was a long time ago,' Nina said politely, although the casual mention had shocked her. She still read about car crashes with a shiver. It had been winter. One of those crisp, beautiful mornings, the garden heavy with frost, the pond iced over, and Daddy . . . she recalled that he'd had to mess about with de-icing spray before he could set off that day. She happened to be upstairs, had heard the car starting up at last, rushed over to the window to see it going down the drive, going through the gates on to the lane. She'd watched its progress through the bare trees until it was out of sight.

She remembered saying: ''Bye, Daddy' and dropping the curtain as a feeling of complete misery overtook her.

It was almost as if she had known, but she had not liked to dwell on that since.

Her last ever glimpse . . .

She swallowed, fighting the sudden sharp memory, not looking at either of them as Mrs Lawson carried on, a little too brightly now.

'And Nina's mother — now I do know Mrs Scarr — she's a charming lady. She lives in the pink house. On the headland again. Wonderful views I'm told, although I've never been there.'

She gave Nina a quick glance as if expecting to be issued with an invitation to view. Nina did not respond as it was hardly her place to do that and her mother might well take umbrage. Rather a cheek actually, but the sort of cheek posh, dishevelled people like Mrs Lawson could get away with. Nina did not mind, was amused in fact, but what was rattling her now was the effect Alex Lawson was having on her. Dragging her attention back as he directed a sudden question her way, she found herself coming over all girly, which was utterly comic in the circumstances.

Steady on . . .

She was glad to get away eventually with a smile and brief handshake, glad that just Mrs Lawson and the dogs accompanied her to the car, the chemical fertilizer having dispersed in the air, leaving the still-strong sniff of cow-muck. As Nina drove off, the summer sun setting across the bay, the sky a painter's dream in shades of pink and gold, she sat up straighter.

With a bit of luck he would be off to London in a few days as his mother had hinted and that would be that. She had ascertained from Mrs Lawson that he was in 'property' whatever that might mean. It could mean anything. A jobbing builder or an entrepreneur.

Whatever. It was no concern of hers.

Although . . . she had no doubt that he would be a wonderful lover. He had that look about him, but he was to be avoided at all costs. She knew nothing about him. He might be married for all she knew. There might be some little Lawsons lurking about, although she doubted that. Mrs Lawson would have mentioned grandchildren and had photographs all over the place. If she wasn't mistaken, there had been a serious attempt back there at matchmaking.

Forget it.

A love life and the complications that followed was just not for her.

★ ★ ★

Tom retired to bed early, saying he needed to go over some things for the interview.

'How lovely! Just the two of us,' Clemmie said, coaxing Julia into the drawing-room. 'Sit down, darling, and we can have a chat. We hardly ever have time to chat.'

Julia, now wearing smart black skirt and camisole top, sat down as instructed. Something was wrong, of course; it had taken Clemmie all of five minutes to know that but it might be a little longer before she coaxed it out of her. Unfortunately, Julia kept her problems to herself, though maybe that was a family trait, for she was guilty of it too.

'Daddy's chair . . . ' Julia gave a huge sigh, running her hands over the arm of it. 'Who chose this?' she asked, frowning at the fabric. 'Nina, I suppose.'

'You suppose right. She uses me, I regret to say, as a sounding-board — I think that's what she called it — in other words I try out all the things she's not sure about.'

'She's right to be not sure about this.'

'Quite.'

'The cottage in the school grounds is furnished, as you know,' Julia said. 'Which means we shall have to put our furniture into storage until we find somewhere of our own. Assuming Tom gets the job of course. We mustn't count our chickens.'

Clemmie dismissed the doubts, not sure whether Julia was fishing to stay here at Rosemount instead of the cottage. Well, she could forget that. She had rooms galore but she would prefer them empty rather than occupied by her family. They were welcome as visitors, yes, but that was different. Living together now, at their ages, was out of the question. Nina had only stayed a few months when she returned heartbroken from London, but by the end of it they were both tearing their hair out.

The modern view was that they both needed their space.

Some might argue about what an old woman like her needed with *all* this space, but need it she did. All the rooms held some special significance for her, not least this drawing-room, Anthony's favourite.

'What a pity Frankie hasn't come up,' she said, eyeing her daughter closely. Julia was fiddling with one of her slides, a very characteristic gesture which meant she was nervous. Clemmie wished she would get her hair cut. Hanging on to the old style did her no favours, but it was probably to do with Tom. She herself had done lots of things to please Anthony.

'She will be here soon enough,' Julia said. 'Again, assuming Tom gets the job. Everything depends on that. You do think he will get it, don't you, Mother?'

'I've told you already. There is no doubt. I've had a word with Jonty. He was relieved. Saves him the bother of advertising and everything.'

'Does he think you're interfering? Most men would.'

'I don't care what he thinks, darling. When he took the job on, he knew perfectly well how things stood. I said at the time that I needed to retain an interest in Florey Park. I have money tied up in it and Jonty is under my thumb, whether he likes it or not. If I pulled the plug on him it would all go belly-up. As it is, he's always coming to me for what he calls topping up funds.'

'Which you give him?'

'Of course. I don't want to talk money, darling, but you know as well as I do that there is a considerable amount in the Forsyth trust fund. I'm not going to run out of money.'

'Is there a problem at school?'

'Nothing you should concern yourself with,' Clemmie said, looking beyond Julia and admiring the sunset through the window. 'I hope you will have time to see Nina tomorrow before you go back. She would have popped along this evening but she had an engagement at a client's house. She's making rather a go of it, you know.'

'Really? You surprise me. I'm not saying she doesn't have an eye for interiors but she doesn't know the first thing about business, does she?'

'Enough. She had a rude awakening with that fellow of hers. I could tell from the beginning that he was more interested in her money than he was in her.'

'I don't think so, Mother,' Julia said, jumping instantly to her sister's defence as Clemmie had half-suspected she would. 'You do him an injustice. I thought he genuinely loved Nina and I for one was very sorry to see it fall apart as it did. I don't think the money was an issue.'

'Don't you?' Clemmie sighed, wondering if she was being a little unfair. People were always quick to jump to that particular conclusion when money was over-valued in a relationship. They had said the same about her and Anthony — behind their backs of

131

course. It was preposterous in their case, for they had been head over heels in love and Anthony would have pursued her if she had been a pauper. That Harry fellow had been out for what he could get, a leg-up in business at poor darling Nina's expense and then, when it failed, he simply bailed out and left her to pick up the pieces. When it came to men, it had to be said that her daughters were singularly hopeless.

Clemmie did not care for Tom. She had buttered up his image for Jonty's sake but he was so ordinary, without fire. She could not for a moment imagine him doing what Anthony had done for her.

Never in a million years.

★ ★ ★

They were in a particularly large guest-room at the front of the house, a room that Nina had not yet got her hands on because it was wallpapered in a green-and-gold stripy wallpaper, with a dreadful, supposedly toning, carpet. The bathroom was down the corridor, miles away, but then Rosemount needed a thorough up-grading. Only one proper bathroom in a house this size was quite ridiculous, and the solitary extra lavatory in some vague corridor off the downstairs hall was no compensation.

Julia had no idea what they would do with Rosemount when Mum died. She had never discussed it with Nina because neither of them was happy talking about Mum dying.

But perhaps they should.

She could not imagine herself living here: far too big and draughty, the upkeep enormous, rates sky-high and they would have to employ some staff. Tom was no gardener and she no housekeeper, not on this level.

Tom was in bed, reading through some papers when she eventually excused herself, leaving her mother downstairs settling down to watch a late-night film on television. She had the stamina of a much younger woman, more stamina than she had herself, but then all this worry lately had knocked the stuffing out of her.

'It's like a fridge in here,' Tom said with a smile. 'Remind us not to come here in winter. I still have nightmares about what it was like at Christmas.'

'Bedsocks and hot-water bottles.'

'And you in your warmest pyjamas.'

Julia went across to the windows, looking out a moment at the darkening grounds. She could see the glimmer of dark water and the moon, a quarter of an orange tonight, suspended in the sky, more and yet more stars becoming visible to her as she stared. Looking at the night sky always made her reflective as she tried to take in — always failing — the vastness of the heavens. And, as always here at Rosemount, through the half-open window, there was the smell of the garden and the sea.

It was odd to think that soon they might be back here for good, staying at the cottage in the grounds of the school. Florey Park was on the wider spit of land nearest town, over the hump of the hill, not much more than a stone's throw from here. She had not been back there for years, although she would bank on its being exactly the same. Give or take. Tom and Nina had been over at Christmas, just to gaze at it from the drive, but she had known that it still had that special pull, just from their expressions when they returned.

Tomorrow she would accompany Tom. He would have the interview whilst the matron — still the same old title — would look after her until she was required. Her interview would be over tea and cakes and she knew precisely how to handle it. She had met Jonty McKay and liked him. She was going to be honest with him when she said that she was going to do her very best to support Tom.

Sitting down at the walnut dressing-table

with its three mirrors, an old design but so perfect for you could see three versions of yourself, she took out her slides and brushed her hair. Therapy. How could she cut it as Mum was always on at her to do when it was such therapy to touch it and brush it like this? To her horror, she could see, from these angles, that she was ageing. Past forty and her skin was already losing that lovely smoothness of the young. It was an awful thought and not one she cared to cling to.

Through the main mirror she could see Tom and, as if sensing her watching him, he put his papers aside, took off his spectacles, and smiled at her.

'Well, darling, here we are,' he said. 'I never thought we'd be doing this. We are doing the right thing, aren't we?'

'Don't let's have doubts,' she said, whirling round to face him. 'For Frankie's sake, we have to be as positive about it as we can. We *are* doing the right thing, Tom. We're giving Frankie the chance to start afresh, to forget him. And one day she will forget him. When it's the right time she will find somebody else. And nobody need know about it.'

'Clemmie was looking at you strangely,' he said, watching as she quickly undressed and slipped into bed beside him. 'I'm wondering how long it will be before she puts two and two together.'

'I can handle Mother,' she told him, although she was not sure that she could. You'd think that at her age she might be winding down a little but not a bit of it. She was as sharp as a razor, eyes still keen, although what went on behind those eyes it was sometimes difficult to tell.

She cuddled up close for a while to Tom, but they were both tired from the journey, nervous about tomorrow, and they quickly moved to their back-to-back sleeping position. She slept badly, dreaming about the interview which, in the dream, went horribly wrong.

★   ★   ★

Next morning, the sea mist extended to the gardens, draping them in a wispy veil of swirling cloud inches above the lawn. It would clear by eleven, it always did, but in the meantime it would make the journey along the coast road worse than usual.

Clemmie insisted on their eating a cooked breakfast in the dining-room, the windows closed to the mist. Of all the rooms in the house the dining-room had changed the least. There was the same furniture, solid and highly polished; the same dishes, exquisite willow-pattern, all matching, for mother cared for detail. Sitting there, trying her best to finish her breakfast under Clemmie's watchful eye, Julia tried to quell the rising panic about what was to come, the dream not helping. She worried that Jonty might be resentful of her mother's interference in the running of his school. From his point of view he had to keep the old dear sweet because she was a money-pot he could keep dipping into, but her constant visits must irritate him immensely.

She had settled on a neat summer suit, plum-coloured, dithering with a lightweight scarf before discarding it as too fussy. She tied her hair back and up, thinking it looked more appropriate. Tom was wearing his grey suit with white shirt. Interview gear for both of them, with butterflies in her tummy to go with it. The mist, drifting awkwardly over the coast road, meant that she clutched her seat with a sharp intake of breath as Tom negotiated their car round the hairpin.

'Sorry . . . ' she said, feeling she was being critical of his driving. 'It's just . . . '

'I know,' he said softly. 'It must be dreadful for you. And your mother. How must she feel every time she passes by? I did think it might be enough to make her move. She could have shaken off the memories then.'

'No, she couldn't.' Julia smiled at him. 'But she could have made it easier for herself. Now . . . ' she made a valiant effort to change the subject. 'Shall we go through it again? Are you sure you've anticipated all the questions he might ask?'

He nodded. 'You bet. I've sat in on more than enough interviews of this kind. I could answer the questions standing on my head. And I have a few to ask him too.'

She glanced at him, worried now that he might be over-confident. It did no harm to have a few nerves. Didn't they say nerves saw you through a difficult time? Nerves before you go on stage and then — wham. Complete confidence. The quiet confidence Tom was already showing was a little disquieting. If he didn't get it, what would they do? It would be back to the drawing-board with a vengeance and they were running out of time. The last-ditch scenario she had considered was to remain in Norfolk and send Frankie to a private boarding-school, get her out of Philip's way that way, but, now that the wheels were turning, she knew that *this* was what she wanted. To come home.

They turned into the school drive, through the gateposts under overhanging yews and then followed the drive past the sweep of lawn. The front of the building was clothed with ivy, getting rather out of hand, Julia thought, thinking of the beasties that would live in it and find their way through the windows.

She glanced at Tom but he just smiled, pulling the car to a halt and stretching his fingers.

'I need to go to the loo,' Julia said. 'I feel sick too.'

'Just nerves, sweetheart.'

'I know it's just nerves,' she snapped, stepping out of the car and smelling roses.

She was whisked away immediately as expected and would be joining Tom later, after his interview.

She couldn't resist a peep in his direction as he was led away by McKay's secretary. She wanted to offer a final nod of encouragement but Tom did not look back.

8

Clemmie had been having lunch on a Friday with Dilys Plowright for as long as she could remember. They always dined at the restaurant in Southwick's at the same corner table reserved for them. Southwick's was, as department stores go, small but sufficient for their needs, pounced on by visitors who did not expect such a thing in a town the size of Greysands. Perfumery, scarves and shoes on the ground floor, ladies' fashion and restaurant on the second, with a men's section, the caps-and-tweed variety, sandwiched between the toilets and the fire escape.

The restaurant had recently been refurbished, lightened, brightened, the new ash-coloured chairs with their chrome frames rather too fragile-looking for Clemmie's taste; the prints, splashes of orange and green, too modern.

Today she was just having a light lunch because she and Nina were invited to the cottage over at Florey Park this evening, where Julia was cooking them a splendid celebratory meal. It was a month now since the interview; Julia and Tom had been back to

Norfolk to sort out their house sale and now they were up here permanently, with Frankie.

'How lovely for you,' Dilys said warmly after Clemmie had told her the news. 'No more tiresome trips down to Norfolk.'

'Quite. It is delightful I must say,' Clemmie said, smiling at her friend. Dilys, widowed for years, had no children; worse, no grandchildren, and was only now, late in the day, resigned to it. 'You must come for coffee, Dilys. Julia will be so pleased to see you again.'

'Thank you. I look forward to that.' Dilys smiled, her blue eyes crinkling as she did so. 'Isn't it warm?' She leaned forward and lowered her voice. 'I felt quite faint, in fact, with the heat. I'll let you into a secret, Clemmie, I've just taken my vest off in the ladies.'

'Really?' Clemmie raised her eyebrows, although she was perfectly used to Dilys's quirkiness. 'And what have you done with it?'

'It's in my handbag, of course.'

'You ought not to be wearing a vest in summer, Dilys. You don't feel the benefit in winter then. That's what my mother used to tell me.'

'It's silk, dear. Blissfully soft. I bought a set of three with matching panties. From the lingerie department here. They have a

141

beautiful selection of nightgowns too, and I do so love pretty nightdresses. I always have a brand-new one ready in case I am whisked off to hospital. And new slippers.'

'So do I.'

That subject exhausted, they returned to the subject of Julia.

'She's not like Nina at all, is she?' Dilys said thoughtfully.

'Not a bit. Nina's a mess.' Clemmie sipped her tea and looked around, checking who was in the restaurant. 'She hangs on to life by the skin of her teeth,' she added, seeing nobody of interest.

'Guess who I saw as I was coming in?' Dilys said then, not waiting for Clemmie to try: 'Edward Grantham. Out on the sands with his easel. Far out. He ought to be careful. He doesn't walk fearfully well, does he — and it's a long trek back to shore.'

'Yes, he might get caught in the quicksands, although he would take some swallowing up,' Clemmie said, smiling to show it was a joke.

Dilys smiled too, thankfully not noticing the nasty edge to Clemmie's remark.

'He has put on such a lot of weight, hasn't he? He was so thin once upon a time. But then you remember him much more than I do, my dear,' Dilys added pointedly. 'After all, you were his fiancée, not me.'

Clemmie nodded. Dilys would never let her forget it. Indeed, they had been a foursome for a while, she and Edward, Dilys and Reggie. In fact, once upon a time she had thought that Dilys would be better off with Edward; she had certainly done her share of flirting.

But Edward only had eyes for her. In his twenties, Edward had been skeleton-like. In his thirties, he was merely thin and he had been at his peak in his forties. In his fifties . . . she sighed as she remembered him then. Anthony had been madly jealous, or rather, he pretended to be just to infuriate her.

'All right . . . ' she had once screamed at him. 'I did admire Edward once. And you know perfectly well we were engaged but it was all over as soon as I met you, as you well know. I certainly don't have any interest in him now. He hasn't a hair on his head.'

And now, in his middle seventies, he was also fat. Red-faced. Rude. Grumpy. And his feet . . . Clemmie shuddered when she thought about his feet. Adult feet were ugly things anyway, only babies had pretty feet, and hers would not stand close examination, even though she used a peppermint moisturizer every night and painted her toenails. She was proud of the fact that she could still bend her legs sufficiently to do her own toenails. But Edward's toenails were particularly repulsive and looked as though they belonged to an aged reptile. He had an unfortunate habit in summer of wearing tan leather sandals dating from the year dot and no socks, which meant your eyes were continually drawn to the dratted toes. Damn the man. She sometimes wished she'd never set eyes on him in the first place, certainly never shown an interest in him, for look where it had eventually landed her. Dependence on him like this at her age was wearisome.

'What's the matter?' Dilys asked.

'Nothing's the matter,' Clemmie said, seeking a diversion and reaching for her handbag and rummaging in it. 'Did I ever show you the birthday photograph of Frankie?'

Dilys admired it, returning it with a smile.

'Lovely girl. You must be so proud. I hope you live to see her married, Clemmie.'

'Of course I shall. I intend to live until I'm ninety-nine and then go peacefully in my sleep.'

'Why not a hundred?'

'Because you can't avoid the publicity then. And my publicity-seeking days are over, dear.' She glanced across the room just as Edward came in, holding the squashy sun-hat he wore

144

for outdoor painting, taking up his position in the small queue waiting to be seated.

'Oh . . . there he is.' Dilys said, smiling and waving.

'Not, alas, swallowed up by the sand,' Clemmie murmured, unable to resist the jibe.

'He must have finished his painting,' Dilys said, eyeing her with some exasperation. 'Shall we make room for him? I can give the waitress a call. Or will it be too embarrassing for you?'

'Embarrassing?' Clemmie asked faintly. 'What do you mean? I do not care one way or the other.'

'It's just that he . . . ' Dilys sighed. 'Goodness, surely you know, Clemmie. It's very obvious he worships the ground you walk on. I think he rather thought that, after Anthony died, you and he might get together again. After all, you were engaged once.'

'Why do you keep bringing that up? Yes, we were engaged but it was a mistake and even if Anthony had not come along, I would have broken it off. You're welcome to him,' Clemmie said, trying to keep this light. 'Look, ask him over if you will but I'm going to visit the powder-room and slip out by the other door.'

Dilys laughed. 'For goodness sake, Clemmie, he's not that bad.'

If only Dilys knew . . .

Clemmie stood up and slipped out, studiously avoiding looking in Edward's direction. Anthony had been right, the man was a swine, a slippery eel. She hoped Anthony would understand. She hoped that when they met up again she did not have to go into a convoluted explanation of why she had done it.

The answer was simple anyway: for the family.

★   ★   ★

Nina was having lunch in Valentine's, a little coffee-shop a stone's throw from her own shop. She normally ate on the hoof but today she had needed to get out for a while and Mary was happy to work through her lunch-hour.

'Take as long as you like,' she had told her magnanimously, as if she were the boss. 'You were working late last night.'

She slipped out then and, because she felt like it, took ten minutes out for a stroll along the shore. It was cooler now but dry after a week of almost continuous rain and she walked quickly, watching a boat bobbing about in water, far out, and by the water's edge, a lone fisherman, who should have known better. These sands were dangerous. Patchy. And the last thing you wanted if you ended up in quicksand was to have your feet stuck in a pair of fishermen's boots.

She was looking forward to Julia's dinner this evening. Julia was a good cook. Nina wished she could muster up some enthusiasm for cooking. Harry had been an energetic but splendidly hopeless cook himself, but he had never minded what he ate and they had lapsed into a far too easy way of life that involved eating out and takeaways. She had all the equipment, all the useless utensils, all the gadgets, but it made not a scrap of difference.

Julia cooked properly and that was why Nina was childishly looking forward to a home-made dinner. Mind you, Julia was looking rough these days. Maybe it was the move and the stress. Nina hoped so. She hoped Julia wasn't hiding something from them. She had the awful thought that Julia was ill. Very ill. That would explain the blank look, the fear in her face. That would explain her coming back, the suddenness of it, the abrupt change of mind. It puzzled Nina and illness would explain it. Julia wanted to be near them. Maybe she was terminally ill. Maybe she only had a few months to live.

The thought, though idiotic and thoroughly groundless, frightened her nonetheless. As she was fiddling with her cutlery her knife suddenly shot off the table and landed on the floor, practically stabbing a man in the leg in the process.

'I'm so sorry,' she said, feeling herself flush with embarrassment, reaching for the knife and slowly raising her eyes at the same time.

Oh, hell's teeth! It was only Alex, Mrs Lawson's son. Well, it would be, wouldn't it? She was sticky from the walk, her hair felt stiff, sprayed with salt water. She was wearing a top in baby pink which was the last colour she should wear, a disastrous impulse buy, but everything else was in the wash or waiting in eternal hope of being ironed. As if that wasn't enough, she was in the middle of eating a very gooey cake, so she probably had cream on her lips, or worse, the tip of her nose.

'May I join you?'

'If you want,' she said ungraciously, delighted to see as he put his tray down that he had an equally squidgy cake. She couldn't stand holier than thou eaters. This cream-cake, this temptation to which she had succumbed, was a rare treat, for normally she ate sparingly, too aware of calories to enjoy eating.

She loved her family, didn't she just, but it was irritating in the extreme that Julia could eat everything within sight and still not put on an ounce. Her mother was like a clothes'-horse and even Frankie was locked into that slim family shape. Anyway, as she saw it, she was OKish just now but there was no way she could afford many more ounces, for that would tip the balance between attractively curved and fat.

He settled himself opposite, taking his plate and cup off the tray and finding space for them on the small table.

'Where . . . ?' he waved the tray and she pointed out where to put it, watching as he carried it over. He was wearing a suit, on a sweltering day like today, a nice suit at that. An inconspicuous silk tie and an expensive shirt. God, the things she noticed in ten seconds flat. He had also cut himself shaving — the human touch — and the nick had caused a blob of blood to cake on his chin and a tiny bit had escaped on to the buttoned down collar of his shirt. She wondered if she should mention it but decided against it. After all, that would be a very wifely thing to do.

'I've been for a walk on the beach,' she told him, as soon as he was settled. 'That's why I look like I do. A bit windswept.'

'Stop apologizing for the way you look,' he said with a trace of impatience. 'You look fine.'

'You look very smart. Business?'

He nodded but did not elaborate and, bursting though she was with curiosity, she did not ask.

'My sister Julia is moving back home,' she said instead, searching for something to say. 'Coming up from Norfolk. Her husband's got a job at Florey Park. Senior English.'

'Good for him,' he said. 'You must be pleased.'

'Thrilled,' she said. 'We can get to know each other properly again. It's been so long. My niece Francesca is seventeen and we've got a lot of catching up to do. She thinks I'm decrepit,' she added with a smile. 'I don't know what she makes of Mother. She might act like she's middle aged — no, not even that — she acts sometimes as though she's young but she's actually seventy-five.'

'Oh, to be seventeen again,' he said. 'I couldn't get rid of my energy. Football. Cricket. Skiing.'

'Skiing? I tried once,' she said. 'Once only.'

She did not add that she had given up not because she had hated the skiing, but because of the clothes. Ski-clothes made her look like the Michelin man. Never mind the slinky

150

après-ski stuff when she could flaunt her generous breasts, the damage was already done on the slopes, the image difficult to shake off. Probably because of being self-conscious about her appearance, she had proved to be spectacularly bad at skiing. And spending the morning spread-eagled on the slopes was not her idea of fun. To cap it all, extreme cold made her skin go blotchy, so she really could not win.

Very aware of each other they finished their lunch and as he went to get a couple more coffees Nina glanced at her watch. Oh no! Mary would wonder where on earth she'd got to. But, providing she got back for three when she had a client coming to see her, there should be no problems. Mary was an oasis of calm, although she insisted that she wore a completely different hat at home.

'My mother loves what you've done to her dining-room, by the way,' Alex said, passing her a cup. 'She's ringing all her friends, telling them about you.'

'Good.' Nina sipped her coffee, glancing at him surreptitiously. 'When are you off to London?' she asked at last, curious enough to go for the straight question.

'London?' He raised his eyebrows. 'That was just Mum. It was never my intention. I'm hoping to get settled round here.'

'I see.'

'So, we might be seeing quite a bit of each other. I hope,' he added with a grin that told her a helluva lot.

She had to smile back, but she could not quite look him in the eye, not yet, for she didn't want to give too much away.

She loved this, the early sparring, the looks, the tactics, the anticipation. Of course they had only just met but that meant nothing, for they had hooked on to each other immediately.

Fact of life.

So, it was too late.

It was also much too soon.

'I've got to go,' she said, standing up and noticing that he half rose from his seat too. How nice. 'I have a million things to do at the shop.'

'See you around,' he said.

'Very likely.'

She tried her damnedest to sashay out, weaving her way past the tables. Realizing he was very likely looking at her rear view, she sighed. The cerise cropped pants were last year's and too tight and she was aware that the crêpe material was stretched to screaming-point across her bum and the pink top had shrunk in the wash and was riding up, allowing her midriff to peep out. Only seventeen-year-old midriffs, flat and bronzed like Frankie's, should be allowed to do that.

What was it with her and clothes? An incompatibility that verged on the catastrophic. The trouble was she had a mountain of clothes in her wardrobe, oddments and remnants, but nothing that went with anything else. Complete chaos in other words. Amazing. She could look at a room, see it exactly as it should be, clothe it beautifully, but when it came to herself, her own body, she was still searching for her 'look', and worse, still making monumental mistakes.

In a slight daze, remembering Alex's look, she hot-footed it back to the shop, panicking that poor Mary might be snowed under.

She was not, for the shop was empty.

'Sorry I've been so long,' she said, finding Mary in the workroom. 'I got side-tracked. Met this gorgeous man for lunch and we made love lying across the table. In Valentine's coffee-shop. Perked everybody up no end.'

Mary laughed. 'I see. That's why you look like the cat that's got the cream.'

Flushed and flustered, more like.

Feeling guilty for leaving Mary to cope on her own for so long, she took over Mary's work, telling her to go and have a coffee

153

herself. As always, the stitching, close, quiet work, calmed her down a little, the material soft beneath her fingers. She could do this in her sleep.

Her thoughts wandered. Next time, if there was a next time, she would make damned sure she was at her best. Something really glam. Make-up spot on. Hair fantastic.

What could he see in her?

But then, she'd always been at a complete loss to know what men saw in her.

★ ★ ★

The day started well for Julia. She awoke to sunlight streaming in, which was always a good start. They had made love last night, the first time for a while, and it had been extra special because she was feeling relaxed and comfortable with herself for once. Awake, she stretched out her hand for Tom but he was already bathed and getting dressed. He paused as he saw she was awake, came over to kiss her.

'You are warm and gorgeous,' he murmured. 'If I wasn't determined to make an early start, I'd get right back in bed with you.'

'Off you go,' she said, flopping back on to the pillows. 'I'll stir myself in a few minutes. I've got a busy day ahead too. You won't forget the dinner party this evening, will you?'

'How can I? Sure you don't want me to pick anything up for you?'

'No. Everything's under control.'

Over a leisurely breakfast she went over the menu for this evening. It would be a squeeze in the dining-room here but there were six matching chairs, and the in-house crockery, plain white, would look all right against her own scarlet tablecloth. Not having a lot of her own things was a nuisance but they would get by.

Tom was going into school most days, even though term had not started, to get the feel of the place, to read up on his new students, and for discussions with Jonty, who seemed permanently entrenched there. So that left her and Francesca free to do what they wanted. She was taking a break from her own work until they had settled but one of the bedrooms was to become her study for the moment. In addition to that, there was a room for Frankie. Their bedroom, half the size of their Norfolk one, overlooked the tennis-courts and the back of the school.

The cottage was furnished adequately if unexceptionally and Julia was determined that it would be temporary. There was no time limit on how long they lived in the cottage but she did not want to linger long and was keen to make a search for a new home. Their house in Norfolk was expected to go quickly with an offer already made, and that would leave them chain-free and in a strong bargaining position.

She had finished breakfast when Frankie wandered in, shuddering when breakfast was suggested.

'No way,' she said shortly. 'And I hate that bedroom. It's so small. And the mattress is hard. It's like sleeping on cement.'

'It won't be for long.' Julia assured her, tired of the grumbles but unwilling to argue at such an early hour. 'I'm going to visit some estate agents so that we can start looking. You can help me if you like.'

Frankie shrugged, although a tiny spot of interest showed in her face.

'I don't mind. Though it's not going to be my house for long, is it? I'm out of here as soon as I finish the sixth form.'

Julia sighed, controlling an irritation.

'I know that, but I would like some input. We want you to like the house as much as we do.'

'Why? Haven't you been listening to what I said?'

'Yes I have.' Julia heard her voice rise. 'And I'm getting a bit sick of all this. What's happened to you, Frankie? I don't think you appreciate quite what we've done for you.' Horrified, she heard herself saying the words she never meant to say. 'Your father was happy in Norfolk, I was happy there and you've forced us . . . '

'I did not force you,' Frankie yelled. '*You* forced us. Me and Dad. We didn't want to move, you did. You were frightened of people finding out. Frightened of what people might think. Well, tough. I don't give a shit what people think.'

'Don't say shit.'

'I'll say what I want,' Frankie said fiercely, although her lip was beginning to tremble and Julia knew she was close to tears.

'Oh sweetheart . . . ?' She ached to hold her but something in Frankie's expression told her to hold back and she allowed her daughter a minute to get herself together. 'I thought you might wear that blue dress from Next this evening,' she added, trying to make amends. 'You look lovely in it and Granny will like it.'

'Will you, please . . . ?' Frankie's face twisted, the tears held in place. 'Will you stop treating me like a child?'

And with that she shot off.

Julia knew better than to ask where on earth she was going.

9

'Auntie Nina . . . ?'

'Hello, darling.' Nina looked up from the fabric swatches she had been poring over. 'How nice to see you. Why didn't you come earlier? We could have had lunch.'

'Yes.' Frankie smiled, although she didn't look too thrilled with the idea. 'Are you very busy?'

'So-so. It's just pretty steady at the moment. Sometimes I wonder whether I should take on extra staff,' she added, almost talking to herself. 'Perhaps I will. Part-time anyway. Homeworkers.'

'Good idea. I'm glad it's going well, Auntie Nina.'

She was hovering in that guilty way she used to hover as a little girl. A little girl who wanted something. Nina took off the spectacles she wore for the extremely close work and grinned at her.

'Well? What do you want?'

'May I use your phone?'

'My phone? Why? What's wrong with your own? Don't tell me you've not got a mobile?'

'There's something wrong with it. It won't

work properly. The reception's lousy here anyway,' Frankie said. 'I want to ring Amy and the phone at the house is in the kitchen and mum will be there all afternoon. I suppose I could try the phone box,' she added with a frown. 'Do you need lots of change?'

'Don't be daft. Of course you can use my phone. Go upstairs.' Nina tossed her the flat keys. 'And try to keep it reasonably short if you possibly can. You'd think I spent all my time ringing Mars if you could see my phone bills.'

'Thanks.' Frankie managed another smile but she looked tense, unhappy. In fact, she hadn't looked really happy since she'd arrived. Seventeen was a bad age to uproot, to leave friends. Poor love. Although she was delighted that Julia and family were back, Nina sometimes wondered if Julia had thought it through, considered the effect it might have on Frankie at this stage in her life. After all, if they'd waited another year, she would have been at college and only home for holidays, already beginning to feel she was loosening the bonds. If they'd just waited another year it would have been so much easier all round.

Goodness, she had room to talk, for she had scurried home pretty damned quick

159

when things had gone wrong. Her little escape to the city had only served to show that she had made a complete mess of it. Back here it was all so much easier, and the business was thriving when the similar one in London had failed. It was the lack of competition, if she was honest, but she liked to think that it was not entirely that and that talent was in there somewhere. With women like Marian Lawson batting for her, she was gaining a worthy reputation.

'Do you like this?' she asked Frankie, holding up a swatch. 'A bit wishy-washy for me but the client wants a little rose pattern, so that's what I'm going to give her.'

'It's lovely,' Frankie said, having a good look at it. 'I have something like that in my bedroom at home. My real home that is, not the cottage.'

For a minute, her face dissolved and Nina thought for an awful moment she was going to cry. Just for a second Nina was reminded of a tough little two-year-old, jagging her knee quite badly on a rock on the beach, crumbling into tears but bouncing back quickly after a hug. Julia had gone daft when they arrived back, Nina carrying Frankie, which was not at all surprising because she was inclined to be over-protective.

'What the hell were you doing to let her

hurt herself?' Julia had said, which had only added to Nina's guilt. It was a nasty cut and had required two stitches. She found herself glancing at the knee now, where a thin white scar was just visible if you knew where to look.

'You won't be staying long at the cottage. I'm sure your mum will be on the look-out for something pretty special,' Nina said, trying to sound positive. 'And if you'll let me, I'll help you design your own room when you move in. How about that?'

'Please don't treat me like a child, Auntie Nina.' Frankie looked at her hard, with those Julia-like eyes of hers. 'I have enough of that from Mum.'

'I didn't mean to,' Nina said, horrified that she had come over mumsy. 'I just thought you might be interested in design that's all. Your mum said you were good at art.'

'Sorry.' Frankie cast her eyes down, looking suddenly very small and young. Nina reached across and pulled her towards her.

'Hey, what's the matter? You can tell your Auntie Nina.'

She felt the slim body shudder under her touch, kissed the top of Frankie's head before she gently pushed her away.

'Go and make your phone call,' she said. 'I'll give you half an hour then I'll come and get you, ready or not. What's for dinner tonight, by the way, or is it a secret?'

'A chicken dish, I think, one of her special recipes,' Frankie said, tucking her hair behind her ears. The short bobbed hair, Nina noted, was streaked. Red bits amongst the brown. A mistake but she had no intention of saying anything. She and Frankie had to ease into a relationship and now at last they had time to do it, but she was taking it carefully. They had to get to know each other first. She felt she did know Frankie but it was all to do with memories of the baby and the little girl and not so much with this young, very attractive woman.

★ ★ ★

Frankie unlocked the door and stepped into Nina's flat. She had been here briefly at Christmas when they had had to come back to collect some presents her aunt had forgotten. It had been completely chaotic then, with a Woolworth's silver-frost Christmas tree leaning by the window and a few bits of tinsel stuck half-heartedly here and there. She had made room on the mantelpiece for a sprig of holly. The decorations down in the shop were a whole lot fancier and in fact Scarr Interiors had won the

162

Greysands Christmas Window Competition, although Auntie Nina would take no credit for that, insisting that Mary had done most of the work.

'I know it's not very festive up here but I can't be bothered,' Nina had said, catching her gaze and having the grace to look a mite guilty. 'You feel you have to do something but it was Harry who used to be really keen on Christmas. Now that I'm on my own I can take it or leave it.'

She rarely mentioned Harry and hardly ever nowadays but Frankie was a little more aware of what it must have been like for her when the relationship disintegrated. Poor Auntie Nina. She was so very nice. She deserved better than that. She remembered Harry from a Christmas three or four years ago when he and Nina had been together. Grandmother had been stiff with him and so the rest of them had had to try extra hard to be welcoming. From what she could dredge from her memory, Auntie Nina had seemed very happy and Harry had looked at her with adoring eyes.

The room looked different today, with the summer light pouring in through the window, the forlorn tree returned to the attic. Happier somehow, as Auntie Nina herself seemed to be. Maybe she was getting over it at last.

Frankie liked the colours. Warm shades. Burnt sienna and hot pinks with splashes of red. A lot of satin throws with fringes and huge cushions. Big modern prints on the palest peach wall. Very exotic. She could see into the bedroom with its stripped polished floor and enormous high bed covered in patchwork and velvet. The bedhead was wrought iron and a garden-type matching chair stood in a corner, festooned with a colourful display of knickers and bras. Frankie smiled, thinking of her mother, whose underwear was so unadventurous, just plain white, athletic style. These looked altogether more glam, were very Auntie Nina.

Her mum would go all sniffy at this, the slight scruffiness, but then Mum liked things to be just so, spent her life tidying up after Dad, always aware of what other people might think. Down in Norfolk, Julia had been part of the small community, roped in to be treasurer of various organizations, grumbling about it a bit but pleased underneath. Part of the community, merging quietly into it, respected and respectable. Frankie felt an unexpected twinge of guilt that it was she who had ruined it all for them, ruined it by falling in love with a married man, her teacher at that.

Philip . . . she smiled a little as she thought

about him, aching suddenly to be with him, held in his arms. She was seventeen, not fourteen, and there was an important difference. If he had not been her teacher, if he had not been married, then it might have been different. He was seventeen years older, yes, but that didn't matter.

She had fallen in love with him at the start of the sixth form term, when they split into small discussion groups and the teachers lost some of their mystique and became much more approachable, treating them, as they needed to be treated, like young adults. He was a good teacher, passionate about his subject and, as it was one of her pet loves too, she was soon lapping it up, confident that she would do very well when it came to exam time. But falling in love took away some of her concentration. Before long he was all she could seriously think about. She began merely to sit in on the lessons, watching him all the while, scarcely taking in what he was saying, the notes she was meant to be taking almost indecipherable later.

She had caught one or two glances from him, interested glances, she now realized, but she had not been aware at the time that she was sending out signals.

She had overheard him telling somebody that he was going to visit the modern art exhibition in town, so it was simple enough to make sure that she was there too. She watched him going in, alone, waited a while before going in too. So it was surely quite by chance that they came to be standing side by side looking at an exhibit. Soon, they were having a rather heated discussion, although they both admitted they knew precious little about this kind of art. And then . . . then he had asked if she wanted to adjourn to the coffee shop to take their discussion further. If there had to be a defining moment, it was then. That was the moment when they were no longer teacher and pupil but two people who wanted to talk to each other.

All the girls fancied him. Well, they would, wouldn't they? A young teacher, a handsome man, and they were mostly appalled that he only ever saw them wearing uniform. They knew it was out of the question, of course, for anything to happen. The young male teachers were pretty wary about the sixth form girls, knowing that with one false move they could be up for sexual harassment and dead in the teaching dust.

That day in the gallery, she had been in civvies: jeans and sweater, the sweater a flattering blue in angora wool and, being out of school, she was wearing her then long hair fastened up. A hint of lipstick, a dash of her mum's perfume, her silver earrings and she knew she looked good. Older.

And he noticed. *How* he noticed. Although she had seen that in the coffee-shop he took a quick glance round, as if checking if there was anybody they knew there, as if he was suddenly aware that this was already edging into something dangerous.

By the time they finished coffee, he had arranged to meet her again.

Poor darling, he never knew what hit him . . .

She would ring Amy soon but not yet, not until she felt better about being up here, maybe when term had started and she was caught up in work. Then, she would ring Amy. Amy's proposed visit was cancelled, the excuses Amy presented paper-thin. She suspected that Amy was washing her hands of her, knowing that things would never be the same again and maybe not able to cope with that.

In any case, Amy belonged down there. She would be like a fish out of water here and things would turn awkward. It was probably best to leave it at that.

Frankie sighed.

Picked up the phone.

Dialled.

Her heart seemed to miss a beat as she

waited for him to answer.

'Philip, it's me,' she said at once. 'Can you talk?'

★   ★   ★

Mr Harrison was driving Clemmie round to the cottage.

Seven-thirty for eight.

It took an age to decide what to wear. She felt this dinner party was important, a pointer to how things would be between them all. The problem was that she felt a little agitated as a result of seeing Edward Grantham this afternoon. She would not feel truly at ease until he was dead. If there had been a way, she would not have hesitated to kill him herself, but being branded a murderer, having the family live with *that*, was worse than the other thing.

Strange to think that she had once thought Edward a pleasant young man, but that changed for ever, of course, when she dumped him and turned to Anthony. He soaked up the bitterness he felt, soaked it into his body like a sponge and hung on it thereafter. He ought to have spat it out, of course, and got on with his life, but not Edward.

He waited a very long time for his revenge.

168

He had always stood on the sidelines, watching her and Anthony. It was a nuisance having what amounted to a lovesick puppy forever looking at you with imploring eyes. Drat the man. He had been insanely jealous of Anthony but it was hardly Anthony's fault that he went off to war and returned a hero whilst Edward, with some sort of heart stutter, failed his medical and never got the chance to prove his mettle.

Things were never the same again after a man kissed you.

It was remembered. Always there. The memory ignited whenever a glance was exchanged. It was like that with Edward, the visits he insisted upon were such a nuisance. She had paid her debt to Edward several times over.

This evening she would wear the grey silk with the black and grey fringed stole. Charming. Very French. Understated. And with it, her shiny black stockings and high heels because she would only be teetering a short distance and everybody was appalled that she wore them at her age.

It was difficult to imagine that, if he had lived, Anthony would have been seventy-nine and an old man. In a way that made it easier, for he would have hated that. He had gone out in a blaze of glory, such a dramatic exit, and left behind for his family, his beloved girls, only good and great memories. A man who had done his bit in the war, and, in peace, a headmaster much respected by his pupils, a wonderful husband and father.

The obituary had been glowing.

And that was how it would remain. The secret was shared now between herself and Edward and she had made sure that Edward kept his silence.

What a price to pay!

She picked up her small evening bag, slipped a handkerchief and a tiny bottle of perfume into it and hoped to goodness it would not be chicken or anything sweet and sour.

★　★　★

'It's chicken, sweet-and-sour apricot chicken,' Julia told him as he popped into the kitchen asking what were they having and belatedly offering a hand. 'Chilled soup to start and a choice of summer pudding or mixed berry icecream. Cheese to follow, of course.' She smiled at him, spoon in hand, and a juicy stain on her white top. 'I know,' she said, catching his glance. 'I should have worn an apron but it doesn't matter. I'm going to wear the red dress and put my hair up. What do you think?'

'I think . . . ' he put his arms round her, squeezed her, heard her delighted squeal of protest that she would spill something. 'You are beautiful, my sweet,' he said, giving her a quick kiss. 'And I love the red dress. You'll look great. Hang on, I've got something for you.'

'Flowers!' she exclaimed as he handed over the bouquet of yellow roses. 'Oh Tom, they're gorgeous. Thanks, darling. I'll put them in the dining-room where we can all see them.'

That meant a hunt for a vase. He watched, leaning against the work surface as she cut and trimmed the flowers and arranged them. She was good with her hands. Cooking. Flower arranging. Good with her head too. Hence the accountancy. Not so good, though, with her heart, her emotions, not so good with dealing with Frankie.

'What have you persuaded your daughter to wear?'

'Oh, she's *my* daughter now, is she?' she said with a smile, putting the finishing touches to the display and holding it aloft. 'I don't know where she's got to,' she told him. He followed her as she went into the dining-room. 'She went out in a bit of a huff after lunch. Told me to stop treating her like a child. Maybe I was doing that but to stop is

171

easier said than done. After all, she is my little girl still.'

'Exactly. Just like you are your mother's little girl still,' he reminded her, wishing he hadn't thought about Clemmie coming along this evening. He liked Clemmie, in a way, sympathized with her that she had coped so admirably since Anthony had died at a relatively young age. That was not unexpected, for she did not strike him as the sort of woman who would fold under those circumstances. There was a strength about her, a resolve, that was somehow missing in Julia. He worried about Julia. Wondered how on earth she would cope if he were killed in a car crash. She would have her work, of course, which would help and she would have the family close to her now.

A great wave of affection for her rose up, coupled with desire, and he would have liked to take her to bed there and then but it was out of the question with the guests due in a couple of hours and with no sign yet of Frankie. She knew how much her mother was looking forward to this meal, how much preparation had gone into it, how she wanted it to be a success, a lovely family gathering. She had better not spoil it or he would really have to tell her off.

The problem was he found it difficult to

172

tell her off. Always had. In fact, he had put the burden of that, the telling-off, very much on Julia over the years. Frankie had only to gaze up at him with those blue eyes and he was lost. And that was why he hated Muncaster for doing this to her. He ought to have insisted, never mind what Mrs Muncaster and Julia thought, he ought to have made him suffer for that. His career would have been ruined, for as a teacher you were in a position of trust and you bloody well resisted temptation, even if it came in the form of lovely seventeen-year-old girls.

'I hope she'll behave herself this evening,' Julia said. 'She knows that we want to keep it to ourselves but things slip out sometimes and I just hope mother doesn't start quizzing her about boyfriends. She's got it into her head that she's the person Frankie needs to talk to but then, you see, she believes that Frankie is an innocent little girl still. And she's not, is she?'

'Frankie won't say anything,' he assured her, although he was not absolutely sure about that. He still held on to the belief that they should have come clean, told the truth within the family at least, so that they weren't constantly on edge about it. Clemmie would have accepted it, probably better than they thought, and it wouldn't matter a toss to

173

Nina. If it had been some spotty youth she had been involved with it wouldn't even matter much to them. It would be regretted but put down to experience. But a married man with a family, his wife pregnant at that, now that was entirely different. That tossed it suddenly into the realms of adultery and unacceptable behaviour, leaving an unpleasant taste in the mouth.

The cottage was ready for visitors, cushions plumped, furniture polished — Clemmie would notice that — a few of their personal belongings had been set out. The sooner they got their own house, reclaimed their furniture out of storage the better. Things were moving down in Norfolk and, providing there were no last minute snags, it should all go smoothly.

With Julia saying that everything was now under control he ran a bath and relaxed in the warm water. Julia had laid out clothes for him, smart casual she called them and he would happily don them later. He had no interest in clothes, other than looking reasonably OK. He was feeling much happier about this whole set-up now that he was up here. In fact, it was during the interview itself that he had first been touched by a genuine enthusiasm. The school was everything he could wish for, the changes both subtle and

174

major. A new gymnasium block, improvements to the swimming pool, and an IT department to die for. Money had been spent and it was no secret that much of it came from Clemmie, so it was no surprise that Jonty liked to keep her sweet.

He heard the door downstairs and voices. Ah good, Frankie was back. Now all that remained was for Julia to persuade her to wear something reasonably smart, pretty up her hair a bit, and they were all set.

Sweet-and-sour apricot chicken — sounded good.

10

Nina, mindful that her mother would dress up to the nines, rescued one of her more partyish frocks from the wardrobe. Peach. Calf length. Not unlike a nightdress with its pretty bodice and shoestring straps. She would have to wear stockings because mother abhorred bare legs at the best of times and it would be unthinkable this evening. Stockings, then, and some strappy shoes. Unfortunately she realized too late that her suntan was distinctly blotchy and the dress would look heaps better with a uniform tan. Also, to her irritation, she seemed to be clean out of mascara, which normally resided in a sponge-bag together with masses of half-used lipsticks, sample bottles of this and that. She must have a sort-out, she vowed, throw half this stuff away and start afresh. Some of this dated back to Harry and it was high time she got rid of it. So, no mascara and she felt naked.

Ah well, it wasn't as if there would be any interesting men tonight, because you couldn't count Tom. Oh God, she had to face up to this and it was better to get it over with, let him know once and for all that there was nothing doing. Absolutely zilch. She remembered the walk last Christmas in that cold crisp Boxing Day air, their feet crunching on the remains of the frozen snow. A little nostalgic ramble over to Florey Park, which had looked so beautiful in the snow. And then, on the way back, her feet had shot from under her and all he could do was laugh as he tried to hoist her up again.

But . . . and this was what rattled her. As he pulled her to her feet, holding her close a moment purely from necessity to steady the pair of them, she had made the mistake of looking into his eyes and seen what was there. She knew that look.

Her schoolgirl crush was long gone, flattened by time, nor could she raise an iota of interest in him these days, belonging as he did to Julia. No, that wasn't quite true. Even if he did not belong to Julia he would not interest her.

But he obviously had a little hankering after her, very likely because she was out of reach and in the danger zone, and she hoped it would not create problems now that they were back for good. She was settled here and she was not being hassled into moving for anybody, least of all him.

She hoped it would not come to the point

where she had to spell it out to him. She hoped he would get the message long before that was necessary. And it might be a good idea, just to be on the safe side, to avoid being alone together for any length of time.

Oh hell. Why her love life had to be quite so complicated she had no idea. It was not fair.

★ ★ ★

'Darling, you really should wear sleeves,' her mother said, when she arrived at Julia's, later than everybody else.

'Thanks. And you look great too,' she said, annoyed because Mother made no attempt to keep her voice down, might as well have announced it on the Tannoy that she possessed arms that needed covering.

'There's no need for that tone, Nina. If I can't tell you these things who can?' Clemmie persisted, in a stage whisper now, as Julia went to pour her a drink.

'You look lovely, Nina,' Tom said, coming to her rescue. 'Belting dress that. How's the decorating going?'

'Pretty good,' she said, having no choice but to sit beside him on the sofa. 'I'm learning how to listen to my clients, sympathize, and then do precisely what I want. It works.'

'Good. Thanks, Julia,' she said, taking her drink. Julia returned to talk to Clemmie, leaving her marooned with Tom on the leather chesterfield. 'Congratulations on the job by the way,' she said. 'It's great to have you back.'

He nodded. 'I can't say I'm exactly thrilled . . . ' he stole a glance at Clemmie, lowered his voice, 'with the string-pulling but yes, it is good to be back. And Julia's delighted.'

'And Frankie?' she asked with a wry smile. 'Not quite so delighted. Am I right?'

'You know teenagers. Nothing ever pleases them.'

'Talk of the devil . . . ' Nina murmured as Frankie came into the room, defiantly underdressed in jeans and white T-shirt.

Julia looked as if she was about to say something and Nina hid a smile as she caught Frankie's look. If you couldn't do your own thing at seventeen, when could you do it?

'There you are, darling. Now, if everybody's ready . . . Frankie, help your granny to get up.' Julia smiled. 'Let's go through.'

Clemmie was already up, not requiring assistance, kissing Frankie on the cheek and smiling as they went into the dining-room.

★ ★ ★

Nina took one middle-sized potato, a generous portion of carrots and string beans, pleased as she looked around that she seemed to have less than everyone else.

'This looks great,' she said, waiting whilst Julia finished serving. She looked round the dining-room which, for a rented place, was rather nice. 'And it's not at all bad, this cottage, is it? For starters anyway. Where are you going to look for a house, Julia?'

'Something in the country but not too far away,' Julia said, checking that everybody had sufficient before sitting down and urging them to start. 'There's no point in Tom's having to commute a long distance — or any distance on these roads. Finding somewhere where he can walk to work is probably optimistic . . . ' she laughed. 'But he may get a bike.'

'Good idea,' Tom said. 'That'll keep me fit. We've picked up details of various properties and we'll make a start this weekend. A couple look good on paper.'

'I should hate to have to look at houses,' Clemmie said, fiddling with her food prior, Nina knew, to leaving most of it. 'Such a bore. Thank goodness, I will never leave Rosemount, not until they carry me out in a box. And when I say a box, I use the term loosely. I mean . . . well, you know very well what I mean. Top of the range coffin for me, girls. And burial. Absolutely not cremation.'

Nina exchanged a glance with her sister. Not again. Not a reminder of the arrangements.

'I've left a list of instructions in the safe,' Clemmie went on, unperturbed. 'They are finely detailed so please take time to read them properly. And remember, you won't get away with palming me off. I shall be up there, watching your every move.'

'You might be down there, Granny,' Frankie said, watching her grandmother closely.

'I shall not. I have lived an exemplary life,' Clemmie said, smiling too. 'I shall cut a dash in heaven, I tell you. And I will have so much to say to Anthony. Poor darling, it's such a shame he never knew you. You would have been such a joy to him.'

'I wish I had known him,' Frankie said, looking round at them. 'He sounds just great.'

There was a short silence until Julia broke it by offering the dishes around once more. The glance she exchanged with Nina told her to change the subject — fast.

'I've met a man,' Nina said, gathering their attention in one go. 'He's called Alex Lawson and he's the son of one of my clients. A Marian Lawson,' she added, looking at her

181

mother. 'She says she knows you.'

'Never heard of her,' Clemmie said with a sniff, arranging her cutlery artfully so that it did not look as if she had left very much on her plate. 'Delicious, darling,' she said to Julia. 'I adore chicken.'

'A man, eh?' Tom glanced at her, raised his eyebrows. 'This sounds interesting.'

'Only marginally interesting,' Nina told them.

'What's he like?' Julia asked. 'Oh come on, Nina, you can't leave us in suspense.'

'Let me see . . . ' Nina pretended to consider. 'He's tall, dark, fairly good-looking. Looking to stay round here too, so he'll be on the look-out for a house as well.'

'Now that is interesting. What does he do, darling?' Clemmie asked. 'I do hope he's not a joiner,' she added, referring of course to Harry.

'Harry was a furniture craftsman,' Nina said quickly. 'A bit more than a joiner. Not that there's anything wrong with being a joiner,' she added, feeling she was talking herself into trouble.

Clemmie shrugged. 'Still an artisan, darling, whatever the title.'

Nina caught Tom's look, saw the warning nudge Julia gave him before he started.

'What *does* this new guy of yours do?' Tom

182

grinned, thankfully deciding to let the 'artisan' business go. 'We're all agog.'

'I've only just met him,' Nina said. 'It's not the sort of thing you discuss when you've just been introduced.'

'It most certainly is,' Clemmie went on. 'Didn't his mother tell you? I would have thought it would be the first thing she would say. Mothers always do.'

'Oh, all right . . . ' Nina saw them all looking expectantly at her. She knew the 'something in property' that his mother had indeed mentioned would not go down well with *her* mother. 'He's a doctor,' she said, saying the first thing that came into her head. 'He's a surgeon in fact,' she added, embellishing it further, deciding she might as well go for gold. 'He works over in Lancaster.'

There was an immediate buzz of interest as she had wickedly anticipated.

'Gracious me.' Clemmie perked up as Nina had known she would. 'How interesting! What kind of surgeon?'

'Orthopaedics,' Nina said wildly, mentioning again the first thing that came into her head.

'I see. Orthopaedics. That's wonderful,' Clemmie said.

'Yes.' Nina beamed round the table. 'That's right. Hips and knees and things.'

183

'We've never had a medical doctor in the family,' Clemmie continued happily. 'And a surgeon too. That *is* fascinating. You must invite him to tea, Nina.'

Nina shot Julia a glance, raising her eyebrows as she did so. It was all the two of them could do to stop from giggling and Nina was reminded instantly of their girlhood, when they had cooked up little things between them.

No harm done and it served mother right. Nina had no idea what the hell Alex Lawson did exactly but she rather hoped it was something her mother would disapprove of.

'It's time you got married, Auntie Nina,' Frankie piped up, catching her mother's eye and starting to clear up. 'I can be a bridesmaid, although I'd like to choose my own dress. Something sophisticated and not at all bridesmaidy. I hate frills and stuff like that. Did mum *make* you wear that awful dress at her wedding? Why do brides do it? To make themselves look prettier by contrast?'

'No, they do not,' Julia said, voice tight. 'Her dress was lovely. And she looked lovely. Didn't she, Tom?'

Tom smiled. 'Now what am I supposed to say to that? Should I be noticing the bridesmaids on my wedding day?'

They laughed, even Julia.

184

'If I get married,' Nina said, 'it will probably be a quick dash to the Register Office.'

'It most certainly will not,' Clemmie said, pushing her glass towards Tom for a refill of red wine. 'Not if you marry this lovely-sounding man it won't. It will be the full works, darling. We've always been rather big on weddings. Mine was perfect and yours, Julia . . . ' she raised her glass, 'yours was a splendid occasion. Such a pity your father was not there to see it. Having somebody else give you away was not the same. You, Tom, would have to give Nina away.'

'Oh, I hardly think . . . ' Tom blustered, looking at Julia to help him out.

'No buts. The decision is made,' Clemmie said firmly, taking a decent slug of wine. 'I have to say that I felt your father's presence very strongly at your wedding, Julia. He was beside me in spirit.'

Nina sighed, caught Tom's bemused look. Her mother seemed to be worse lately, always on about Father. Of course she would never forget him, how could she, but Nina worried that her mother was retreating into her shell these days, preferring to revisit the past rather than plan for the future which on reflection, at seventy-five, did not amount to a lot.

Perhaps that's what you did when you reached a certain age. Reflected on what had gone before.

Julia went to get the desserts, apologizing that the ice-cream was a little sloppy.

'None for me,' Nina said smugly, refusing the choice. 'Must watch my weight.'

'Yes, you must,' her mother said shortly. 'Especially for your new man. It is a fallacy that men like large ladies. Isn't it, Tom?'

'Don't drag me into it,' he said. 'I think Nina looks great these days anyway.'

Nina flashed him a glance before turning to Frankie.

'What about you? Do you have a boyfriend?' she asked, wishing she hadn't mentioned Alex Lawson, wondering what had possessed her to do so. 'Or have I put my foot in it? Did you have to leave him down there?'

'No, she did not,' Julia said hastily. 'Now, who wants what?' she added, brandishing a serving-spoon and looking at Nina with, for some reason, an edge of irritation.

'Don't lie, Mum,' Frankie said, looking at Julia intently, with such a flash of venom that she caught everyone's attention. 'I'll tell you the truth,' she said. 'If she won't do it, I will.'

'That's enough, Frankie,' Tom said, voice tight, lips compressed with his anger. 'How dare you accuse your mother of lying?'

186

'She *is* lying,' Frankie said with a short grim laugh. 'Do you want the truth?' she asked, looking round the table.

Clemmie looked at her coldly.

'I want to enjoy my dinner in peace,' she said. 'I do not approve of hysteria at the dining-table.'

'The truth is I was dragged up here when I didn't want to come. Dragged up by them,' Frankie went on, unstoppable now, scraping her chair away from the table and standing up, blue eyes flashing with her annoyance. 'And I had to leave him behind, didn't I? Well, you needn't think it worked,' she added, looking at her parents. 'Because I'm seeing him again. Soon. And we are going to carry on where we left off. So there.'

And with that, she threw her napkin on the table and departed.

'Leave her,' Clemmie ordered, as Julia stood up too and looked as if she was about to set off in pursuit. 'For goodness' sake, leave her. Tantrums! I've heard it all before.' To everyone's surprise she suddenly smiled. 'I'm rather pleased actually. She shows a bit of spirit. I was fearfully spirited when I was her age. Born ahead of my time. I think they call it being feisty now. It was considered unladylike then. Showing off, my mother said. She used to tell me to count to five

187

before I introduced a new topic of conversation and then, when I had considered whether or not it was appropriate, only then, might I speak. Frankie would do well to take heed of that. Or Nina,' she finished, looking pointedly at her younger daughter.

'Would you like me to go up?' Nina looked at Julia who had sat down again but was looking anxious. 'She might talk to me.'

'No. Leave her as Mother says,' Julia said. 'I'll talk to her later.'

★ ★ ★

Clemmie had spoken briefly to Jonty McKay following Tom's appointment. The school was officially on holiday but, as he lived locally and had no family commitments of his own, he was around a good deal, catching up with work and getting the odd jobs done that were so difficult to do when the school was buzzing with boys.

She was invited for tea with him this afternoon and, feeling tired after the dinner party, she asked Harrison to drive her the short distance and drop her off at the gates, so that she could at least enjoy the walk up the drive. She was not expecting to see Julia this afternoon, for she was house-hunting.

She stood at the gates a moment after

188

Harrison had left, getting her bearings and simply admiring the building. Next to Rosemount, which was her absolutely favourite building, Florey Park rated an excellent second. She knew its history as well as she knew the history of Rosemount and she liked to think that she had rescued this house from becoming derelict, for a building this size was too large for family occupation. It might have become a hotel, she supposed, but this area was too much off the beaten track, and had never fared as well as the opposite shore of the bay. She did not mind that in the least, for they had quite enough visitors, thank you, for three seasons of the year. If Florey Park had become a hotel, she suspected it would have died a death.

As it was, as a good private school in a spot that appealed to parents, it was flourishing. And it was all down to Anthony and herself. He had had the expertise, the contacts, the ability to turn the near-derelict building back into a sound one and the foresight to see what it might become. She had had the money to realize his dreams.

The drive swept grandly to the right and Clemmie made her way, in more sensible shoes today, up and round, feet crunching on the corn-coloured gravel. The edges of the lawns were smooth and uncluttered following the curve. Nearer the building there was a series of wide, paved terraces, their symmetry broken up by herbaceous plants and shrub roses. There were thirty-seven shallow steps and she felt every single one today, pausing half way for a breather, looking out across the bay as she caught her breath.

There were sweeping views, views she never tired of, for this was home, always had been, this sleepy-bay-air was the air she had first breathed as a baby. Walking as she often did in the gardens of Rosemount, the memories, good and bad, came flooding back, remembered voices were at every turn in the path, in every rustle from the leaves in the trees, visions past and present and sometimes future glimpsed in every evening shadow.

It was inconceivable that the family would ever move from here and she deliberately chose not to enquire of Julia and Nina what their plans for Rosemount might be. From this high point at Florey Park she could see the wide expanse of sand and mudflats.

As a young girl she had been guided across the bay at low tide but it was an experience she did not care to repeat, for out there in the squishy sands, following a path only the guide knew about, she had felt small and vulnerable, her survival out of her hands and in his. That was the reason she did not fly because it was putting too much trust in another person. She liked to control her own destiny, as Anthony had controlled his, although she doubted she had the courage to do what he had done at the last.

Closer at hand she could see mossy patches in the lawns, the roses had not been dead-headed and there was a build-up of last term's litter against a wall. Unforgivable. She would mention it to Jonty, for they must not become complacent. First impressions were vital if they were to draw parents in. After all, they were in competition with like-minded schools.

Clemmie breathed a sigh of relief as she stood at last on the well-trodden paved area fronting the school with just a few thankfully level yards remaining across the hallowed forecourt into the building itself.

There was nobody about; silence bounced off the hills and from across the bay. She loved it like this, pre-term. A few boys were here, boys whose parents, for whatever reason, wished them to stay on during the holidays, but it was all free and easy and they seemed remarkably unconcerned to be thus abandoned.

As she neared the entrance Clemmie saw that the window in Jonty's study was open, so at least there would be some respite from the cigarette smoke that inevitably accompanied him. She pushed open the heavy door and wandered into the hall, feet tapping on the floor, pausing a moment to glance at the picture of Anthony with its little inscription beneath: Anthony George Scarr, co-founder of Florey Park School, a loyal and beloved headmaster, 1916–1971. *We owe you so much.*

The picture was of Anthony, roughly the same age as Julia was now, and he looked so handsome and self-assured, seated at his desk, his ready smile contained because it was meant to be a serious study.

Beside it, in the trophy cabinet, were displayed the sporting cups, school rolls and assorted memorabilia. Briskly now, not allowing the picture to upset her, Clemmie walked up to the dark panelled door, labelled HEADMASTER, the very room Anthony had occupied for so long, the room she still felt was theirs.

'Clemmie . . . ' Jonty's voice sounded as she tapped on the door. 'Do come in.'

There had been few changes to the room over the years: a burgundy and grey scheme, touched up frequently but always remaining the same colour choice, reflecting the school colours. There stood the old highly polished desk, there hung the vast, gilt-framed busy and bloody Battle of Trafalgar painting — truly awful — that Anthony had loved for some reason, pouncing on it a very long time ago in some nondescript gallery and paying over the odds for it, thirty pounds, which was a lot of money in the sixties.

'It's my money. From my salary,' he had said when she complained. 'And if you don't want it in the house, I'll put it in my study at school.'

And there it had stayed. Perhaps Jonty had not the heart to sling it out. Perhaps Jonty liked it. After all, it was very much a man's painting, thunderously grim, brimming with fresh detail every time you cared to glance at it.

Thank goodness, the computer and other modern equipment were housed in the secretary's office next door, although there was a cream push button telephone now in a prominent position which jarred, in Clemmie's eyes, with the old beauty of the desk.

'Sit down. Take the weight off your feet,' Jonty said, his opening gambit never changing. 'Good chap, that son-in-law of yours, by the way. I think we've made an excellent choice there. Florey Park old boy, as you well know, which has to rate for something. I've had a word with his head and he's very sorry to see him go. He notched up a good record there. The boys thought highly of him.'

Clemmie murmured appreciation. A teacher of Tom's calibre was a treasure. She thought she had done Jonty a favour and not the other way about.

Jonty smiled, showing his poor set of teeth. He had a housekeeper to look after him at his home in the town but her duties obviously fell short of helping him choose his clothes. They were dreadful, his suits ill-fitting, off the peg from a chain-store, his shirts unironed and his shoes unpolished. When Clemmie thought of Anthony and how much attention he had paid to his appearance she was appalled. However, Jonty ran the school well, was kind to the boys, properly respectful to the parents and, all in all, they could have done worse. And sometimes, parents took a shine to a little eccentricity in a headmaster. She hoped Anthony would approve her choice, the first decision of any consequence she had had to make herself.

'I'm glad you've come today, Clemmie,' Jonty said, pushing his chair to one side and stretching out his legs at the side of the desk. The trousers were just that important half inch too short, brown socks visible. Brown socks with black shoes! 'I wanted to talk to you privately before we get the rest of the board together. Fill you in on what's

194

happening.' His sudden fidgeting and opening of a desk drawer signalled what she had known was coming — a cigarette. 'Do you mind?' he asked, waving the packet at her.

'You know perfectly well I do mind,' she said with the slightest of smiles. 'But you may smoke, Jonty. I know it relaxes you.'

'Thank you,' he said with relief, lighting up. His tie had a greasy stain on it, she noticed, and was unable thereafter to take her eyes off it. 'How long have I been headmaster, Clemmie?'

'Very nearly twenty years,' she said at once. 'Atkins was acting head for a while after Anthony died and then we appointed you. Atkins never got over it, did he?'

'Indeed not. Good man, greatly missed.'

'How time passes.'

'Twenty years,' he echoed, as if not believing it. 'A long time. Things have changed a great deal.'

She nodded, waiting for the point of all this. He was apt to go round in circles.

'I was going to give you a ring,' he went on. 'As I say, it's important that you find out from me before the rumours start up.'

'Rumours?' She gave a sigh. 'About what? You're not leaving us, I hope?'

'No. I'm here to stay, Clemmie. No, the point is, I have no idea how rumours get started but, as often as not, it's the wrong end of the stick. However, it's best you know now.'

'Oh come on, Jonty, you are being very mysterious,' she said, unable to stop a glance at her watch. For some reason, she found her eyes drawn to the Battle of Trafalgar painting in all its gory glory and it made her shiver. Why did she have the feeling that Jonty was about to pierce her heart with a sword too?

Jonty looked at her anxiously. 'Very well. I'll come straight to the point if I may.'

'You may,' she said, feeling a dread in her bones.

'We're thinking of going co-ed,' he said. 'Co-educational,' he amplified, as if she might not know what it meant. 'Not until a year next September. These things take time to organize. We've got to go for it before it becomes imperative. As I've explained to you before, Clemmie, we're losing revenue each year as we lose boarders and if we start to take in girls we will be able to hang on for a while to come. We believe we could attract a lot of new boarders, poach some from one or two of the Lakes schools. It'll be more convenient for a lot of parents to be this side of the bay.'

'Girls?' Clemmie waved away his cigarette smoke impatiently. 'What are you talking about? You know my feelings on this. Anthony and I founded it as a boys' school and that is the way it will continue. We will weather the storm. There's no need for panic.'

'There's every need,' he said, all attempts at jollity gone. 'We might have to close in three years if we don't get more pupils. The finances are finely balanced as you know, Clemmie. And I don't intend to ask you for any further subsidies. We can't have you propping us up any longer. We need a radical rethink.'

'Remind me what the shortfall is,' Clemmie said, taking a pen from her bag and reaching across the desk for a piece of paper. 'Write it down for me.'

He scribbled a figure, passed it back.

She put on her spectacles, looked at it, returned the paper to her handbag without a word.

'A lot of money,' he said, allowing her a moment's thought. 'And the bank's starting to be damned awkward. Asking questions, wanting a future prediction or some damned thing.'

'Just fifteen new boarders will guarantee that income, sufficient to satisfy the bank I should think,' Clemmie said. 'A good publicity campaign, a grand open day ought to bring in that number. If it's tackled properly that is. You could leave that to me.'

'Perhaps it might be better left to a marketing man,' Jonty said, looking just a little shifty. 'It needs the right packaging.'

'We are talking about Florey Park, Jonty,' she reminded him. 'Not a jar of jam.'

'I bloody well know we are talking about Florey Park,' he said, cheeks dangerously flushed, which meant he was close to an explosion. 'That's my whole point. It means a lot to me, Clemmie.'

'I will not allow the school to close,' she told him, eyes blazing in matching anger. 'Anthony would turn in his grave if he knew we were having this conversation. If it's purely a matter of money and you object suddenly to my giving you any, then I suggest you turn to the parents. We have some very wealthy parents and a word or two in the right ear . . . '

'No,' Jonty said, stubbing his cigarette out on to a wobbly metal ashtray. 'I have no intention of doing that. Worse possible scenario. It will just get their backs up and make them very nervous. They would remove their sons by the bucketful. No, this is the only way. A positive solution. There's a whole new crowd of folk out there we have to impress. Parents with *daughters*. Sixth form only to begin with, to see how the young ladies fit in.'

'This is a recipe for disaster,' Clemmie said. 'I shall oppose it vigorously at the meeting of the board of governors. And my views hold weight, Mr McKay . . . ' she realized she had childishly dropped the Jonty but was so annoyed with him that she could not bear to call him by his Christian name at that moment.

He raised his eyebrows, the point taken.

'You are not thinking clearly. Look at the positive side. It will do the boys good,' he said, blowing smoke towards the ceiling. 'Competition. Girls outstrip boys in academic achievement these days.'

'They always did,' she said drily. 'But they didn't get the opportunity in the old days. You are making an enormous mistake and I want my feelings to be taken into consideration. Young men and young ladies together . . . ' she shuddered her distaste. 'I don't need to tell you. It's asking for trouble.'

'Don't worry. When the girls arrive we intend to keep a close eye on them, Clemmie,' Jonty said, suddenly noticing the stain on his tie and rubbing at it. 'Matron will act as chaperon. We're simply going co-educational, not into the knocking-shop business.'

'I beg your pardon.' She regarded him coldly. 'You won't get sufficient votes to get this through. I will see to that personally. A word in a few ears will work wonders.'

'I wish I shared your faith in words in ears,' he said, baring his teeth.

'Scoff all you like but I have considerable experience, which you would be unwise to discount,' Clemmie said, firing on all annoyed cylinders now, determined to leave him in no doubt as to where she stood. 'You seem hell-bent on this but let me tell you, there are alternatives. I've saved the school's skin once before . . . ' she stopped, before she became completely indiscreet, for Jonty knew nothing of the circumstances of his appointment. 'I would suggest a small sherry party for selected parents. Discretion, that's what we must aim for.'

'Clemmie . . . ' Jonty sat down again. 'Don't think I haven't been grateful for your support and encouragement over the last twenty-odd years. Of course I have and I couldn't have continued without it but I feel now that the crunch has come. I have to learn to stand on my own feet, make the school pay its way with the help of the governing body. We cannot rely on your handouts any longer. I'm seriously thinking of appointing a marketing man, or woman. We need to sell ourselves. That's the only way to succeed in business these days. You have to have aggressive marketing. We'll be producing a glossy brochure. It will cost us but it will be worth the expense. The old-style words in a few ears that you're so keen on is no longer viable, my dear Clemmie.'

'Why this change of heart?' she demanded, feeling her own heart pound at the injustice of all this. God in heaven, she hadn't kept the school afloat, steered it through choppy waters, lied like the proverbial trooper, to have it cast down as casually as this. 'You were more than happy to accept my financial help in the past. Let's see what the board of governors has to say.'

'I've already done some sounding out,' he said. 'Had a look at some other boys' schools that have gone this route. You don't imagine I'd go into this cold, do you?'

'A little spying, Jonty?'

'Not spying. I made no secret that we were considering doing the same. Look, the last thing I want is to hurt your feelings,' Jonty said, and she saw that his eyes had developed a steely glint now. 'But you really must learn, Clemmie, to let the rest of us make the decisions now. Your feelings on this matter will of course be taken into account but I believe I can carry the majority support. You have done outstanding work for Florey Park . . . ' he continued pompously. 'You and

201

Anthony founded the school, got it off the ground, made it what it is today but Anthony is gone and you, dearest lady . . . '

She bristled as she turned to go.

'Don't you *dearest lady* me,' she said quietly.

'Oh come, you must learn to relax,' he said with a smile. 'It's time you retired.'

'Retired?'

'Get yourself a hobby. And perhaps, might I suggest that, when school reconvenes, you restrict your visits to one or two a term?'

That did it. A hobby!

Speechless, Clemmie took her leave, doing her very best to maintain her dignity even though she felt like collapsing into a little helpless heap.

She was not wanted.

No longer needed.

So, what was the point any more?

11

Frankie's outburst had worried Nina but after a quick word with Julia she was told to leave it for the moment. Julia looked as if she was going to tell her something — gave her that secret look that she knew well — but Mother had interrupted them and put paid to whatever it was she was about to confess.

Nina had a bad feeling about it. She didn't know Frankie well enough yet to come to any conclusion, but the visit here to use the phone took on a new meaning. She had probably been ringing the boyfriend, very likely someone she had met at her old school, and Nina knew that Frankie might have to face the fact that absence, rather than making the heart grow fonder, usually spelt the end. This whole thing would have to be approached with tact. Nina recalled how devastated you were at seventeen when you lost a love.

It seemed like the end of the world.

Remembering how she had felt when she broke up with Harry, she knew she had to treat Frankie very tenderly just now, try to show her that if she needed a shoulder to cry on she was there.

She was surprised that Julia had not seemed more sympathetic to her daughter's disappointment, but Julia could be like that sometimes, in such tight control herself that she extended that tightness to others. Much as she loved her, she could see that she might seem a shade off-putting. For once, Nina was with her mother on this. It sounded daft but it was the extremely long hair that did it. Extra-long hair in a woman of her age said something, made a statement. She should get the damned hair cut and with it she might discard some of the burden she seemed to be shouldering.

'I'm off, Mary,' she called, picking up her folders. She was off to visit a new client, a lady who had recently moved to the area and desperately wanted advice on decorating. Blank canvas time, free rein, and boy, was she looking forward to that. Second home stuff and no shortage of cash either. 'Shut up shop early,' she added, knowing Mary was going out tonight. 'Put your feet up, have a bath, relax.'

'Chance would be a fine thing with my two,' Mary said with a smile. 'Thanks anyway, Nina.'

Smiling, arms full, Nina side-stepped out

of the shop and nearly fell over Frankie, who looked as if she had been hovering on the pavement.

'Oh! You're not going out, are you?' she asked. 'I was just coming to see you.'

'I'm just off to a client's,' Nina told her, struggling to reach her car keys in her pocket. 'Want to come along?'

'May I? I promise I won't get in the way.'

'Of course you can come along. I'll enjoy the company.' Nina glanced at her, at the still-tight expression, deciding she would make no mention of last night's little outburst unless Frankie did. 'Do you need to ring your mum? Tell her where you are?'

Frankie shook her head, walking beside her in silence to the car.

It was cloudy with just a few patches of blue, the sun hidden. Nina was wearing her client-visiting gear, designed to make an impression on them: smart black trousers, flat shoes, scarlet jacket and a black top. Frankie did not look too bad, wearing a skirt for once, long and cream, and a skimpy blouse. She also had a little butterfly tattoo on her shoulder, which Nina did not enquire about. She looked older than her age, somehow. Yes, that was it. Since the last time she had seen Frankie, nearly nine months ago, she had suddenly grown older and it was something more than just the calendar ticking along. It was a blossoming that could only mean one thing. Oh God, she didn't feel up to this, to a possible confess-all situation. She would be embarrassed to talk about sex with Frankie.

'Sorry about last night,' Frankie said, once they were on their way. 'I got a bit fed up, that's all. I shouldn't have spoilt the party.'

'That's OK. It livened things up. As a matter of fact, your granny was completely unfazed, delighted in fact. She said you reminded her of herself when she was young. Spirited, I think she called it.'

'Did she? Did she honestly? That's all right then. I thought she would be really cross. I don't like to upset her. I can't imagine her young. She was very good looking, wasn't she. In the old photographs.'

'Oh yes. And so was your grandfather.'

Frankie sighed. 'I wish I'd known him. I feel really cheated that he died before I was born. Although I bet he would have liked a grandson, after two daughters.'

'Not a bit. It's girls all the way in our house,' Nina told her. 'Daddy always said he was glad he had girls. He had quite enough of boys at school.'

'He looks like he smiled a lot. He's always smiling in his photographs,' Frankie said with a sudden unexpected smile herself.

'He did smile a lot,' Nina said, the memory hurting, surprised that it could still hurt. Grief was still capable of hacking at her, after all this time. It was impossible to live for ever in that grief-contained world of the newly bereaved, but just when you thought you were getting over it you found it still had the power to stab at you. She had been only sixteen when he died and the shock of that day was still vivid. One of those days that were imprinted, almost minute by minute, on your memory. The other day was that hot day in Venice with Harry.

All the memories of her father were happy. He had been a fantastic father and she and Julia had been very lucky to have him. And he was a wonderful headmaster. The funeral had been such an occasion, some senior boys lining the route from the road to the church, her mother pale but composed in a gorgeous brand-new black outfit. Edward Grantham had supported her, a well-known local figure, an accountant, president of the golf club, universally respected, Nina imagined, though scarcely liked. She had always detected a coolness between him and father. Not surprising, for Clemmie had once been engaged to Edward, many moons ago, but then she married Father and that was that. Edward Grantham had apparently given in gracefully but he had never married, was always there, somewhere, in the background and they, she and Julia, thought that he had never got over losing mother.

It was rather a romantic notion, even though it was difficult to see Edward as a dashing young man. Nina found him faintly repulsive in fact, and it was nothing to do with his appearance. Mother, in spite of their history, seemed ill at ease with him, too, but still found time to visit him for tea and, very likely, stilted conversation. Who knew what they talked about? They could hardly talk about the past and their future was limited, so what *did* they talk about? Mother always seemed anxious when she returned from the visits, so why on earth she kept on going was a mystery.

'I was younger than you, when Daddy died,' Nina said, breaking a little awkward silence, hearing her voice shake. 'Sorry, it still gets me.'

'I'm sorry to have reminded you. It must have been awful for you. I can't think what it would be like to lose Dad,' Frankie went on, noting her distress. 'Oh shit, I am sorry. I didn't mean to upset you.'

'You haven't,' Nina said quickly, dragging her attention back, shocked but not exactly surprised to hear the word 'shit'. That was youngsters for you. 'And you can drop the auntie bit if you like. Isn't it about time you just called me Nina?'

'I'd rather not if you don't mind,' Frankie said, a shyness surfacing. 'You'll always be my auntie to me, no matter how old I am.'

'OK. As you like,' Nina said, rather pleased in fact.

'Would you teach me to drive?' Frankie asked, watching her as she negotiated the narrow lanes. 'Mum won't. And Dad says I have to have proper lessons.'

'He's quite right. You should have lessons,' Nina told her, feeling like a staid great-aunt. 'Otherwise you'll pick up all sorts of bad habits. But I don't mind giving you the practice in between the lessons. Tell you what . . . ' she braked sharply at a junction, thinking ruefully that she was a fine example. 'I'll pay for you to have some lessons for your birthday.'

'My eighteenth? It's not for ages yet,' Frankie said doubtfully.

'An advance present then.' She dared to glance her way. 'You'd better accept them because I'm a bit flush at the moment and it might not last for ever. Your mum won't mind, will she? She won't think I'm pushing my nose in? I suppose we should ask her first.'

'I don't think she'll mind. She knows I will learn to drive, even though she'd rather I didn't. I know why, of course. She's very nervous herself when she's driving.'

'Well yes . . . ' Nina checked the signpost, one of the old variety, signalled and carried on. 'It is bound to shake you, but then most families know somebody who's had a serious road accident. It happens. But it's never happened to me or your mother and it won't happen to you either. You look as though you'd be a natural.'

'You think so?'

'I do,' Nina said confidently. 'I'll book you the lessons when we get back. I know just the person.'

'Great. Thanks. That will be fantastic. I'll be able to drive myself all over the place.'

'Hey, steady . . . one step at a time,' Nina said, smiling slightly and wishing she would stop talking like a forty-year-old. She was not forty. Not yet.

'This boyfriend of yours . . . ' Frankie asked. 'Is he nice?'

'He's hardly a boy,' Nina said wryly. 'I'm not into the market for toy-boys, sweetheart. He's about my age, a bit older I think, but yes, he does seem nice.'

'Is he really a surgeon? Or were you just making that up?'

Nina laughed. 'How did you guess?'

'You looked shifty.'

'I always do when I'm lying. Isn't that maddening? The truth is I don't know what he does. I don't know him very well. We've just had coffee, that's all, but I think we might get along very well together.'

'Oh. I see. I thought you meant that you'd slept together,' Frankie said. 'That's what it usually means when you say boyfriend.'

'Does it?' Nina asked, the words squeaking out in her surprise. She had not expected Frankie to say that, and that did shock her. Because of the big timegaps in seeing her niece she supposed she still thought of her as a little girl, and she was not. She was seventeen. And, from the way she talked, Nina would not put money on her still being a virgin.

'I'm not a child any more,' Frankie said, reading her mind. 'I'm completely grown up, Auntie Nina. You shouldn't be surprised. Things are different these days.'

'You talk as if I'm eighty,' Nina said, slightly affronted. 'You can always phone him up, you know, this boyfriend of yours. And, although Norfolk is a long way away, it's not that far. You can meet now and again and who knows, you might end up at the same college and, even if you don't, who's to say

211

what will happen? Look at your mum and dad — they met when they were young and managed to keep it all going, despite being apart for long stretches. If it's the right person then it works out,' she added, thinking bitterly of Harry.

'You don't understand,' Frankie said. 'It's a delicate situation and I've promised Mum, hand on heart, I won't tell you.'

'Oh come on,' Nina turned up a steep lane, realizing she was a little lost as the expected house had not yet materialized. Bugger. She might have to ring the woman up, tell her as much, but she did not want to do that because it got things off to a bad start, looking as though you were inefficient. 'You can tell me anything. It'll be between the two of us. I shan't tell your mum or your granny. I might be able to help. I am very experienced, Frankie, in love affairs that go wrong. I have this knack, you see, of always picking the wrong men.'

'That's where I get it from then,' Frankie said with a short laugh.

'Seriously. I'd like to help.'

'Nobody can help,' Frankie said defiantly. 'Is that it? That house over there?'

'Could be.' Nina glanced at her, realizing she was not going to get it out of her, not at this moment. The only thing she could think of, the really bad thing, that Julia would be terrified of leaking out, was an abortion. Frankie had got pregnant with this boyfriend of hers and Julia had arranged for an abortion and that was why they'd had to come up here, to get Frankie away from him. My God, Frankie pregnant.

It *was* the right house, a grand Victorian villa with wonderfully huge windows which she was already aching to dress.

And the client was anxiously waiting for her at the door.

★ ★ ★

Julia was viewing a converted chapel, the estate agent having thrown in the particulars on the off-chance, because it did not quite match up to what they had asked for. For a start, it was further out than they intended, a good half hour's drive from Greysands, and it was almost beside the shore, when they had really set their heart on a property further inland. Julia knew what the winters could be like here and being adjacent to the shore meant it would be no picnic during the long winter months. Swirling sea mists were chilly in a specially sinister way. She had had more than enough of swirling sea mists down in Norfolk. They might be fine for dramatic

213

effect but in reality they were cold and miserable and the days were spent clothed in thin droplets of water.

So she was less than enthusiastic when she set off. But as she approached it, seeing it from a distance through a gap in the trees, her heart soared and she knew, even before she stepped through its door, that this was to be their new house, give or take the usual hassles and waiting time.

The particulars informed her that it had been deconsecrated as a site for religious meetings in 1970 before being converted into a family home, although to Julia, it would always retain that holy feeling, a bit disconcerting in some respects but also comforting. The conversion was sympathetic to the original chapel, and its heart had not been ripped out. The cupboards and bookshelves that lined the hall, for instance, were of appropriate ecclesiastical style, the hall even boasting a magnificent chapter door. The sitting-room, beautifully proportioned, would be an ideal focal point and just looking out of the window — for the sitting-room was part of the original main body of the chapel — produced a wonderful calm in her.

She found herself standing looking out of the window, just in front of what would have been the altar. The sun shone in and flooded the room with light. Foolishly, she felt like dropping to her knees, realizing it had been a very long time since she had prayed. Not since Frankie's birth in fact, which was a disgraceful state of affairs. She had thanked God when it became clear that Frankie would pull through, then promptly forgot Him. Oh well, she supposed He was used to that. Closing her eyes, clasping her hands, she breathed in the warmth of the sun, the feel of this place and felt the peace closing in on her.

She stepped outside, after a brief tour round the upstairs rooms, taking some steps down into what would be the garden. It was shamefully neglected but she had already formed some ideas of how she would renovate it. Tom would adore it, she felt sure, but it hardly mattered what he thought.

She had made up her mind and that was that.

12

Clemmie was busy dressing for a funeral. At her age there was always somebody of her acquaintance passing on and her favourite little black outfit was much in demand: a sharp black suit, very French, worn with her black highish heels and a neat hat.

Her hair was newly done so she left the hat at home, beginning to regret it as Harrison drove her to Dilys's house where they were to pick her up. The recently deceased, a female friend with a penchant for gin, bridge and Yorkshire terriers, had adored hats. She had also requested no flowers and no mourning-clothes, both of which requests Clemmie was choosing to ignore.

How perfectly ridiculous!

She had sent an enormous wreath of lilies and Hilda, the deceased, was hardly in a position now to take exception to that thought. As for no mourning clothes, she for one was not attending a funeral dressed in anything other than black. And Hilda could lump that too. She could see her friend now, eyes flashing with annoyance, the little fond memory having the unfortunate effect of

216

making her own eyes prickle with the threat of tears. Hilda had been a woman after her own heart, also the mother of daughters and all that that involved.

Edward Grantham had offered to bring her along today but she had refused. She would see him on Tuesday as per their arrangement and had no wish to see him before then, but that could not be avoided with today's sad event, for he was sure to be there to pay his respects. He was much respected in the community, his podgy fingers being in various local pies.

She had not told anybody about Jonty McKay's outburst the other day. She had no intention of taking the slightest notice of it anyway. How dare he tell her that she was no longer required, how dare he toss aside her ideas for a reception to boost funds. If he had suddenly got on a high horse about asking her for subsidies, he ought to think more carefully before dismissing her imaginative ideas for alternative ways to raise money. They had some wealthy parents, including a lottery winner, and all it needed was a delicate touch to prise extra cash from them.

There was no need for panic. No need to start talking about going co-educational.

Over her dead body.

'There's Dilys,' she said to Harrison as they

217

neared her house. 'Waiting for us. Are we late?'

'Exactly on time,' Harrison said firmly. He drew to a halt and stepped out so that he could open the passenger door.

Dilys was likewise in black from head to toe, Clemmie noted with satisfaction. So much for Hilda's wishes, although it sadly reinforced her own belief that one couldn't rely on people to do what you wanted once you were dead. So infuriating.

'Did you send a wreath?' she asked, as Dilys, in a cloud of her habitual Coty *L'Aimant*, settled herself.

'Pink roses,' Dilys said. 'I know it said no flowers but . . . '

'I want none of that nonsense at my funeral. I have requested flowers, masses of them,' Clemmie told her, not for the first time. 'I am relying on you, Dilys, to uphold my wishes. I can't rely on my daughters. They will go to pieces if I know them and forget everything. And you must tell the vicar that, in addition to the hymns I have requested, it was my last wish that he plays a CD of Frank Sinatra singing 'How Deep is the Ocean'. Julia seems to think I am joking and I am not.'

'I will do my best but what if I go before you, dear?' Dilys asked, turning to smile at her. 'I am older than you, after all.'

'Yes, but you have all the ailments under the sun and I am perfectly well and it's often the fit ones who surprise everybody,' Clemmie said.

'Good job we don't know, ladies,' Harrison chipped in cheerfully, as was his way. 'Like I said to Mrs Harrison, you have to live for the day because you might not be here tomorrow. For instance, we could turn this bend and wham . . .'

There was a silence. Oops.

After a while, Dilys, rather desperately, began to twitter on but Clemmie let it wash over her. This road was so familiar, she knew every inch of the town, and that made it worse in a way, for memories lurked round every corner. Even if things had changed — and there had been many changes over the years — she could still see what had been, point things out if she cared to. Just now she did not.

She must remember to tell Frankie — when the time was right for their talk — that, when you were considering a young man, you simply had to look at his father to gauge what he might be like in years to come. A good reliable indicator and, if you did not like what you saw in the older man, then you might well reconsider.

Of course, at seventeen you were reluctant to look into the future. The future stretched ahead into the far far distance; it was only as you grew older that it shortened considerably and you dare not look too far ahead for fear of what you might see.

Edward Grantham had been a fool. He ought to have seen it coming. She knew she had his ring on her finger, that they were betrothed, but as soon as Anthony appeared on the scene — *as soon as* — then the writing was on the wall. Never mind the serenading, the roses, the scribbled verse that Anthony said he had written himself when she knew perfectly well he had copied it from a book of old romantic verse. Never mind all that. She fell in love instantly and wondered how on earth she had ever imagined herself to be in love with Edward. Even in his twenties, he had been plodding. Earnest. Of course it had been an anxious time during the war when Anthony was away and Dilys was quite right to say she had dangled Edward on a string. She was ashamed that she had kept him in reserve during that time, with just the right amount of teasing, allowing him to live in hope. During the war was not the right time to be married, she told him and he believed her.

After all, on a purely practical level he was

better than nothing and men would be in short supply by the end of the war. Luckily Anthony was spared and it was only then that she — and she cringed even now at her timing — that she gave Edward his ring back and terminated their engagement.

He made a blessed fuss at the time. No backing off gracefully for him. No *may the best man win*. No indeed.

'You won't get rid of me,' he'd told her, stuffing the ring in his pocket, blazingly angry. 'You needn't think you'll drive me away from here. I'm staying in Greysands. And so are you. So you will never get rid of me, Clemmie. And one day, when he tires of you, you'll beg me to take you back.'

Words.

'We're here,' Harrison said, parking beside the church. 'What's happening afterwards, Mrs Scarr?'

'A reception at Hilda's elder daughter's house,' Clemmie told him. 'There'll be no shortage of offers of lifts back but I'll ring you later, Joe, if I need transport.'

They alighted from the car, she and Dilys, and, composing their features, walked towards the church. Some woman, Clemmie noted, was looking perfectly miserable in scarlet but the others had blissfully ignored Hilda's last request.

Clemmie usually got Harrison to drop her off in town when she visited Edward, on the first Tuesday in every month, kept free for him for the last twenty or so years, the date religiously adhered to, give or take special holidays and the odd times when one or other of them was unwell. Edward lived in a splendid town house, opposite the church, in whose graveyard her friend Hilda now lay buried. It was where she would rest too, one day. With Anthony. In adjacent plots.

She always visited Anthony's grave first before she went to Edward's house. It seemed right and proper to do so and she always took a posy of flowers for him. Strange to think it was where she would end up too, a bag of bones beside him. But that was how it should be and her instructions were specific. She had been facetious when she talked to Dilys of living until she was ninety-nine. Sometimes it was such an effort these days and some days she quite simply did not wish to wake up but rather stay in that dream state with Anthony.

Edward looked after his home himself and kept it neat as a pin. It was a large house for a single man, a warren of rooms which were full of furniture, good solid pieces he had inherited from his parents. In Clemmie's eyes it lacked the little touches to make it a proper home, his few plants were dusty and neglected. He ought to have married. Good lord, he had had ample opportunity once upon a time, for there were more than enough women out there willing to take on a man with money and a respectable job. She knew there had been the odd dalliances but they had never come to marriage. Of course, he said he had not married because he still loved her, would always love her. A funny way of showing it then, and her once-vaguely held affection for him had been cut off like a limb after Anthony died. To have to cope with bereavement *and* blackmail had made it a very difficult time.

'I saw you at Hilda Perkins's funeral,' he observed, taking her coat when she arrived and hanging it on the coat-hook by the door. The hall was narrow and dark and one of his water-colours, a local scene, hung there in a frame that did nothing to flatter it. 'I thought it a bad show that nearly everybody wore black,' Edward said, putting on his pompous air. 'When the dear lady specifically requested otherwise.'

'Oh Edward, don't be such a bore.'

She sniffed, recalling that he had been in an ill-fitting check sports jacket that would have been more suitable for a bookie. That and tan trousers that did not go with the jacket. But then, that was the way with unmarried gentlemen — nobody to say *My God, you're not going out in that?* Anthony had always sought her approval but it was scarcely necessary because he had an eye for clothes.

'I wouldn't dream of wearing anything other than black to a funeral,' she told him sniffily, looking up at him. He was considerably taller than Anthony, if a little stooped these days. 'If I go before you, Edward, I very much hope that you will not come to my funeral. The girls will wonder why, of course, but you will think of an excuse. I don't want you to be there.'

'Really, Clemmie . . . ' he clicked his tongue and looked as if he was about to argue but she waved a hand at him and he shut up.

'I trust also that you will honour our agreement and destroy the evidence.'

'You won't . . . go before me, that is,' he said with the hint of a smile. 'I am living on borrowed time, according to the doc. It's got considerably worse lately and I could go any time. I keep having these pains. Severe. They double me up.'

'Have you never heard the saying about cracked pots?' she said, following him into the sitting-room, where there was a small tray with tea and biscuits. Always the same custard creams because she had once said she liked them. For a man who was artistic, he could be rigidly unimaginative. 'Jonty McKay wants Florey Park to go co-educational,' she said, changing the subject and instantly regretting unburdening herself to him. 'Silly man. I shall oppose it fiercely. He's also being very snooty suddenly about my donations. Says he wants to manage without them. He won't even ask one or two of the wealthier parents to help out when I know they would be more than willing. That lottery winner, for example, won six million. Thick as two short planks, unfortunately, but we shall have to see what we can do with the boy and you have to admire his efforts to bring the child up a notch in the social scheme of things. Of course the boy won't thank him for it and in time will come to ridicule him but there you are — ours not to reason why, ours to take the money and do the honours.'

'Clementine, you are all heart. When will you learn that Florey Park is not your business any more,' Edward told her, passing her a cup. Despite the ridiculous sun-hat he wore when he was out painting, the top of his head was flaking from the recent sunny weather and his wispy hair, what he had of it, curled round his collar. 'Forget it. Let him get on with it and if he makes a balls-up of it, then it's his fault not yours.'

'That is not the point and you know it,' she said tartly. She flicked an imaginary speck from her pale-blue skirt and looked at him. Living on borrowed time, eh? Well, she for one would lose no sleep and shed no tears when he went, but she would, of course, do the decent thing and organize the funeral because, so far as she was aware, there was nobody else to do it. She might, however, wear scarlet on that occasion as a celebration, not of his life, but of his passing.

'You ruined my life, Clementine,' he told her. She ignored him for he always said this and more. He would never ever let the subject drop. Here was a man who had chosen to submerge himself in self-pity, resentment, revenge and it showed in his tense, unforgiving features. 'You told me you loved me. We were to be married, live here in this house,' he continued sulkily. 'You were to become my wife, have my children.'

She said nothing, merely fixed her eyes on the window, through which she could see the church opposite and hear the chimes of the quarter-hour. Discreetly, she checked her watch as Edward rattled on.

'And then he . . . that bastard Scarr.' He balled up his fist. 'It wasn't my fault I didn't get any action in the war, although he always looked at me as if I'd done it deliberately, as if I was a conchie. This bloody heart condition . . . '

She smiled a little. Sipped her hot tea.

'Edward, you will have a seizure if you carry on like that,' she told him mildly. 'Think of your blood pressure.'

'To hell with it. Marry me now,' he said. 'Give me that last small pleasure. It's not too late. People would understand.'

'No. Certainly not. Look, Edward . . . ' she lifted her sleeve, glanced at her watch. 'Edward, I need to talk to you. This has gone on quite long enough.'

'There's nothing to say,' he said hastily. 'You forget I risked my professional career all those years ago, just to protect you. We made a bargain and you must stick to it, Clementine. Anthony would have wanted that, wouldn't he?'

'He would have wanted the family reputation to stay intact,' she said reluctant to agree with him.

'Exactly,' he said, triumph in his eyes as at last he looked directly at her. 'Do you remember when we were engaged? Before he came along?'

'Of course I do. But, as I have told you a thousand times, I was never in love with you,

227

Edward. I thought I was but I was just a young girl and you were quite handsome in those days. And from a good family. You fulfilled all the criteria for my mother. We were all worried about a war and I was pushed into an engagement. It was a mistake, I'm afraid.'

'A mistake? I seem to remember . . . ' his eyes narrowed. 'I remember one occasion very well when I deflowered you.'

Despite everything, she laughed at that.

'Deflowered? What an extraordinary thing to say, Edward. All right, I accept that I lost my virginity to you but afterwards sex with you was a rare occurrence because, quite simply, you don't enjoy it, do you? And frankly, I don't see how we could ever have had children if we had married because you never wanted sex. You get your thrills in other ways, don't you?' She sighed, seeing him look her up and down and knowing she could not put this off much longer. 'I was pleased to be asked to do it once upon a time. I thought it was sweetly risqué then, but now . . . ' she shivered. 'Now I see that you are a pervert.'

'Pervert?' He grew redder than ever, eyes aflame. 'What the hell are you talking about? I paint you, that's all. That's all that ever happens. How dare you call me a pervert?'

'You paint me entirely against my will. I am

228

sick of doing it. Sick and tired of it. At my age it feels disgusting. Who would ever want to look at a painting of a naked old woman? If you were ever to sell them that is.'

'I told you I will never sell them. They are for nobody's eyes but mine. And, if you do die before me, then yes . . . although it will break my heart, I will destroy them. I've promised that.'

'Why, Edward?' she asked, close to tears suddenly, because sometimes she got an inkling of why he did what he did. She had been incredibly unpleasant to him over the years and yet he still persisted in this ridiculous pretence of loving her. 'Why do this to me?'

'You cannot know what pleasure I get from my painting,' he said. 'Maybe it is my sexual outlet, I wouldn't know. Painting was all I ever wanted to do but I was forced into accountancy — a proper profession, you see. But I know I have talent. Not only that, I know, in my heart, and I can tell you this, Clemmie, that I am a *great* painter. Not the sand pictures,' he said dismissively. 'Not them. My greatness is in painting the human body. You have seen the paintings. Surely you can see that? I could have been famous. People would pay a fortune for an Edward Grantham. It's all I ever wanted out of life and I was denied it and the world was denied a great painter.'

'You are certainly confident of your abilities, Edward. You should have stood up to your parents, told them to stuff the accountancy,' she said bluntly, knowing even as she said it that it was not so easy in those days to rebel against what was planned for you, particularly in the kind of families they were from. That was why she had gone ahead with the engagement. As for his being a great painter, she had no idea. If she looked at them with a dispassionate eye then yes, they were very good. They looked like her, that was all she knew. Very like her. The likeness was as clear as a photograph and now, in the later paintings, he was capturing her very soul, the pain in her eyes as her body collapsed around her. She hardly dare look at the earlier paintings now, when she was beautiful. Nobody would ever see them. That was her side of the bargain. She sat for him. He painted her. And nobody would ever see them. Least of all her family.

'But haven't you done enough?' she pleaded. 'I know it takes you an age to do one but you have so many now.'

'Thirty-six. All of you but all very different. Sitting. Standing. Reclining. Looking this way or that. Hands folded or outstretched. Each time your expression as unfathomable as the *Mona Lisa*. I shall never do enough,' he said. 'I am still searching for my masterpiece. I am still trying to capture that elusive something. And I shall know when I have painted it. When that happens, then it is finished. I shall kill myself then.'

'Don't be so melodramatic.'

His face set into that little boy look she knew well. 'If he can — '

She held up her hand. 'No. Don't say it. I don't want to do it any more, Edward. I really don't. It makes me feel dirty.'

'Why? It's art. There's nothing dirty about art. I find the human body endlessly fascinating and painting it is what I was meant to do. Painting you, the woman who would have been my dearest wife, the woman I have always loved.'

'Anthony would be appalled.'

'I know.' He smiled.

'Appalled but proud of me,' she continued, taking a deep breath. 'Proud that I should do this for him. His daughters are proud of him. The whole family is proud of him. And they will never know the truth. None of them. He must be remembered as a perfect gentleman.'

'Which is why you must continue to sit for me, Clementine. If you refuse then I make the facts known to your daughters and destroy all their illusions,' he told her crisply. 'It's up to you.'

'Do you hate me?' she asked. 'Because if you love me as you say, you would never do this to me.'

'You humiliated me, Clemmie,' he said, quiet and still. 'You never realized how much you humiliated me by dumping me and going off with him. You must see how it looked. You, going off with the war hero, people shaking their heads, being very kind and understanding. And other women looking at me with pity. That's what you did to me.'

'And now you humiliate me,' she said sadly. 'I have no choice, Edward, because the girls must never know, but you must know I hate you for this.'

As they went upstairs to the room he used as his studio, she could heard the sound of the tune she also hated now, the one that he insisted was their tune, one that had been playing in the background when he asked her to marry him.

Another of Frank Sinatra's tunes.

They Can't Take that Away From Me.

'Warm enough in here?' he asked, slipping on his painting overall.

The room smelt of linseed oil.

Turning away from him, she began to unbutton her blouse.

13

They were going ahead with buying The Old Chapel. With everything as straightforward as could be, it would be theirs directly the paperwork was sorted out. In the meantime, although they couldn't actually put any furniture in, the estate agent with a cavalier disregard for legalities had given them a key, purely for measuring purposes.

It seemed churlish not to ask Nina for some help with the proposed decoration, even though Julia felt sure she could do it herself. However, she knew that she and Nina were treading carefully just now, getting to know each other properly at last, and with Frankie so on edge, Julia's nerves were stretched to breaking-point.

She had tried to talk to Frankie about the outburst at the dinner party, asked what she meant about seeing Philip again, but Frankie would say nothing. It made her uneasy, this disinclination of Frankie's to face up to the facts. Philip was trying to steady his marriage, there was a new baby now and Frankie just had to keep away.

She had said all this, trying to make

Frankie see the sense of it, was halfway through it all when she realized that her daughter was not really listening, looking at her with pity. With *pity*.

'You are wasting your time, Mum,' she told her coldly.

Julia wanted to hit her for that. The smug look, the knowing eyes infuriated her. She wanted to shake the sense back into her but she saw how useless that would be. She had never hit Frankie, not once, and it was too late to start now, but she wished at that moment that she had retained the right to do it. A short sharp slap was just what she needed.

On top of all this there was the added stress of her health. She was not feeling well, hadn't been feeling well for weeks, months in fact, which was hardly surprising given the stress she had been through. She was putting off going to see the doctor for two reasons. Firstly, they were not actually registered yet with a new practice, which was no real excuse and secondly, she did not want to hear bad news. Better to postpone it a while. A few weeks would make no difference. She could not feel any lumps anywhere but then sometimes, if it was deep inside, they couldn't be felt anyway. Tom called her a hypochondriac, laughed at her, and yes, it was true that when she had a bad headache, she immediately thought *brain tumour*.

She did not tell Tom this time. There was no point in worrying him too and she knew he would have her at the doctor's straight off.

Nina had been to see The Old Chapel, loved it, and this afternoon, Julia was going to the shop to look over some patterns for the furnishings. It had to be a professional relationship, Julia insisted; she wasn't after a freebie but an equally determined Nina said no. She would be happy to do it for nothing. Well, maybe a huge box of chocolates, something dark and delicious and forbidden.

They struck a deal and Julia, rather to her surprise, had been impressed by the expertise and flair that Nina displayed as she took measurements, made suggestions, and looked out at the views.

'It will look a million dollars,' she assured her. 'Take it from me. And just imagine waking up every morning and looking out at the sea. Fantastic.'

So now, even though her stomach was playing up, Julia was in the workroom with Nina, looking at fabric swatches and wallpaper patterns.

'We'll let Frankie choose her own for her bedroom,' Julia said, as Nina spread them round the big bench. 'We're keeping most of our furniture so we'll have to work round that. It's all pretty neutral if you remember.'

Nina nodded, head bent over the samples.

'I think we'll carry the sea theme indoors,' she said. 'Greens and blues. Something like this for the lounge. What do you think?'

'I think . . . ' a wave of dizziness overcame Julia and she closed her eyes, dropped her head and breathed deeply. When she opened her eyes, Nina was looking at her anxiously.

'Are you all right?' she asked. 'You look pale. I'll get you some water.'

'Thanks.' Julia waited for it to appear, drinking it greedily before Nina told her to slow down. 'I think I'm sickening for something,' she said. 'It'll pass.'

'Come on . . . ' Nina pushed the samples aside. 'You can tell me. What's going on?' she looked at her, saw her expression. 'Oh my God, I had this feeling. Something's wrong, isn't it? Are you not feeling well?'

'Well, no. I don't know if it's serious or not,' Julia said, catching the anxiety. 'I daren't go to the doctor, Nina. Just in case it is.'

'That is daft,' Nina said. 'You'd be the first to tell me that if it was the other way round. I knew there was something up when you decided to come up here to live. There had to be a reason, a good reason. I know Tom. He liked it in Norfolk and so did you. You drag

236

poor Frankie up here, take the poor girl away from her boyfriend, and for what? Look, if you're feeling off, and it's not a cold or flu then there has to be a reason for it. We have to know, love. One way or the other. I'll come with you. There's no point in worrying Mother.'

'Or Tom,' Julia said miserably, although she did feel a little of the burden shifting on to Nina. 'Oh Nina, if you knew what we've been going through these last few months with one thing after another. I keep trying to put it to the back of my mind, this little health problem. I want to move to the chapel, it's so beautiful, but how much time will I have there? I'm only forty-two for heaven's sake. It will kill Mother.'

'Then you *do* think it's serious?' Nina asked quietly, reaching over the bench and taking her hand.

Julia nodded. 'Just a feeling. I'm normally so well, give or take the odd cold. But I've got this awful dragging feeling deep down. Something's there that shouldn't be there. I just know it.'

'Why didn't you tell me before?' Nina asked, exasperation showing. 'Surely you can tell me anything? I'm your sister. I happen to love you, you big twit.'

Julia managed a smile, surprisingly moved by that.

'It will probably be something and nothing. Just a minor stomach thing,' she said, trying to be positive. 'After all, you know me, I worry about anything. Tom says if they had a National Worry-Yourself-Sick Day, I should be president.'

Nina laughed but her eyes were deeply concerned.

It was agreed that an appointment would be made at the doctor's and that Nina would accompany her in case a bit of hand-holding was called for.

★ ★ ★

'You look like my son when his team's lost,' Mary told her, snipping at the cotton and holding up her material. 'What's up?'

'Nothing. I'm just knackered, that's all. And bored rotten.'

'We all get bored,' Mary said, in the voice she might use when talking to her son. 'Life's pretty boring when you get down to it. Same old routine. You slip into routine without realizing what you're doing.'

'Thank you very much for those pearls of wisdom,' Nina said sharply. 'Will that be ready for tomorrow? I've promised the client it will and we need to check it over yet.'

'It's very nearly ready now,' Mary said,

suddenly flustered. 'It's awful material to work with. You can start checking if you want.'

Nina sighed. 'Sorry. I didn't mean to snap. I need to do something, Mary. Go shopping. Spend money I can't afford. Buy myself some really expensive, totally useless shoes maybe.'

'There is something up,' Mary said. 'I can always tell. I'm a mother, Nina, and you develop this instinct. We could shut up shop. I'll come shopping with you if you like.'

'Oh no. Not here. Somewhere with lots of shops. Paris or Milan.'

'Can't help you there. I know, why don't you come to my evening class tonight?' Mary said. 'It's a course for stress relief. It's been going for weeks but you can join in any time. All you need is a mat to lie on and comfortable clothes. It will loosen you up.'

'Stress relief?' Nina grinned. 'I don't need any of that counselling stuff. I had enough kind offers after I split up with Harry. It's best, Mary, to cope alone. Do it your way.'

'OK. Don't come then.' Mary said. 'Sit at home alone this evening. Wallow in your troubles. Cry into your cocoa.'

'Don't get cheeky with me.' Nina laughed. 'I pay your wages, remember?'

'Of course.' Mary looked a little more serious. 'It will be good for you though. You

239

feel great afterwards and I always sleep like a log.'

Sleep like a log, eh!

That was all it needed really, the possibility that she might actually get a good night's sleep. Worrying about Julia was driving her mad and she had woken up last night in the very early hours, wide-awake, staring into the darkness, listening to the sounds of the sea washing on to the beach. Funny how sounds like that travelled.

She had made herself a cup of hot chocolate eventually but even that had failed to relax her sufficiently and counting sheep had never worked for her.

'What time?' she asked Mary, reaching a decision. 'And who else comes to this class? It's girls only I hope.'

'Oh yes,' Mary assured her. 'You can't relax with men about, can you? I'll be here at seven and we'll walk round. It's at the United Reformed Church hall, by the way.'

★ ★ ★

Candles and a sweet smell and the woman's mesmerizing voice were just the start of it. The woman was called Belinda, had masses of red curly hair, and was as thin as a rake. Her enthusiasm was catching. Nina was told

240

it might be difficult to let go, this first time, but not a bit of it. Within minutes of lying on her mat, taking notice of her breathing — funny, you normally just took it for granted — allowing herself to become deeply relaxed, she was soon feeling pleasantly drowsy.

Belinda's lovely warm voice soothed on.

They were to imagine they were stepping into a beautiful garden, feel the soft grass on bare feet, smell the flowers, see the colours. Select a favourite colour — blue for Nina — and bathe the garden with your chosen colour. She led them gently along, step by fragrant step, looking and listening at each step, and Nina, deciding she was brilliant at this, followed her, the voice gradually almost melting into the background, as she saw for herself the flowers at every turn in the path, the views of purple-edged hills in the distance — she was good at hills — and then the sound of the sea. Rhythmic surge of the sea.

Belinda led them down shallow stone steps, warm with the heat of the day, to the bottom of the garden to a secret place and then, as they turned the corner, she left them there.

See what you will now, she said gently, *see what or who comes to meet you*, and then there was silence, broken only by the conscious sound of breathing.

Unaware of the others now, Nina was in the garden, in that secret place, within sight and sound of the sea, the colours whirling in her mind and he was sitting there, on a bench, waiting for her. Smiling at her. Holding out his arms to her.

Harry!

Feeling as if her feet were walking on air, springing along as in a dream, she smiled too and edged forward. She had so much to say and so little time to say it.

'And now, ladies, may I bring you back into this room?' the woman's soft voice droned. 'Back through the garden and into the room. Stay still a while, let your senses recover, and then, in your own time, slowly sit up.'

Nina was one of the last to emerge from the 'garden', sitting up and blinking, seeing the others, all looking bleary-eyed, as if emerging from a sleep.

★ ★ ★

'Well . . . ?' Mary asked, when they were on their way home.

'Great,' Nina said, still thinking about it.

'Sets me up for a few days,' Mary said happily. 'Until the kids start to get to me again. I love them to bits, don't get me wrong, but you know what teenagers are like.'

242

'Vaguely,' Nina said, thinking of Frankie.

If Mary thought she was unusually quiet that was too bad. The evening had disturbed her in a way, ultimately settling some thoughts for her, showing her — if she needed to be shown — exactly where her heart lay.

With Harry of course.

This was not going to be easy.

★ ★ ★

In the bright light of day, it all seemed a bit daft. There was no point in trying to manipulate the future, veer it in a certain direction when you damned well knew it would just go its own sweet way. Better to go with it. Let it be. There was no future with Harry and she would be a fool to think there was. He would never change. He would be a liability for ever.

'Sleep well?' Mary asked with a grin.

'You bet,' she said. 'Off before my head hit the pillow.'

No dreams either. No visions of men waiting on benches for her.

Knowing that there was a danger today of being hemmed in by delivery vans, she parked her car in the interests of a quick getaway in the awkward little hilly car park off Market Place.

On her way to visiting a client, she noticed Alex Lawson hovering by the pay-machine.

'Hi there,' he said with a smile, putting aside any thoughts she might have of sneaking past unseen. After last night's little episode, this man now felt very much like second best, which was such a shame because there was a little spark somewhere between them.

'Oh hello,' she said, marginally happier anyway, because for once she was dressed reasonably and had just refreshed her make-up and tidied her hair, prior to coming out. 'How are you?'

'Fine.' He had a handful of coins, jingled them. 'I'm just getting a ticket,' he said, stating the obvious, and she warmed a fraction to him, at the slight confusion she seemed to have caused. 'Scraping the barrel for change. You don't have twenty pence, do you?'

She dipped in her purse, found him a coin.

'There you are, but you needn't bother,' she told him. 'The traffic warden's got a bad knee and she never bothers coming up to this car park. The locals never buy a ticket.'

'Famous last words,' he said, as the ticket popped out anyway. 'Look, Nina . . . say if you're busy or you don't want to but I'd like to take you out for dinner.'

244

'Would you?'

'Yes I would. It's ages since I've taken a beautiful woman out to dinner.'

She hesitated. Fool to herself or what?

'I'd like that too,' she said carefully. 'Sometime.'

'How about tonight?'

Oh no. Pressure.

'Sorry. I'm off to see a client and I don't know how long it's going to take.'

'OK. Some other time then?' he asked and she saw from his face that he wasn't sure if her refusal had been genuine or an excuse. What the hell! What harm could dinner do?

'Next week maybe,' she said. 'Mid-week. Tuesday or Wednesday. I'm usually free then. Give me a call.'

'Great.'

She watched him striding off into town. Liked the way he walked. Confident but not over-confident. And that relieved smile as she asked him to call her had been genuine.

So, maybe he did care. Maybe she should give it a go.

She found she was smiling as she drove to her client's. A date. How exciting. And, at her age it was a bit daft to feel quite so pleased about it. After all, this was going no further. But dinner would be pleasant and he would be an interesting man to get to know.

And, to top it all, it would be an excuse to buy something new.

She would ask Julia to come and help her choose something.

She wished she'd not thought about Julia. They were seeing the doctor on Friday. Ten-thirty at the surgery on Heatherbarrow Road.

No point in panicking until they found out what was what.

If it was serious, though, they would have to do a lot of reorganizing of their lives. And if . . . the thought had to be faced . . . if it was really serious, if Julia was terminally ill, then she would have to take on responsibility for Frankie. She would be a poor substitute for Julia but she would not shirk it if it came to it.

Mother would have to be told then. And Julia was right, she was bound to take it badly.

Her mood dipping, she concentrated on her driving.

14

'Now, listen to me ... ' Nina said as they approached the doctor's surgery. 'No matter what, we're all here for you so it won't be the end of the world. You won't be on your own. Do you want me to come into the doctor's room with you?'

'No. Stay in the waiting-room,' Julia told her, smiling her thanks.

She was glad now that she had told her sister what was wrong. Nina was being fantastic, calm and controlled, helping to keep the panic from rising. Julia had not slept properly for nights now. Lying awake, staring into the darkness, thinking. Even during the day it would hit her from time to time and send a cloud over whatever it was she was doing. If it was something serious, and she could hardly bring herself to think the word *cancer*, then it would be most unfair at her age, at only forty-two. But then, when was life fair? It had snatched Dad from them, far too young, and sometimes people even younger than he, children even . . . she could not bear it if Frankie died. She really could not. Frankie had fought so hard to survive, overcome one crisis after another when a couple of the other babies in the neo-natal unit had lost their fight. That had been hard. Giving comfort to the other mums, whom she had come to know, and feeling guilty because she was so glad it was their baby and not Frankie who had died.

She knew she ought to have talked to Tom about all this, about her being unwell, but she couldn't bring herself to do it. If it was something unimportant, something that could be sorted out with a few pills, then so be it. Then she might tell him how worried she had been and how bad she had felt, which might explain her short temper of late.

The waiting-room was full and they were asked to take a seat if they could find one. Seeing that they were together, some people helpfully did a bit of jiggling around, so that they could sit side by side.

The usual mix. Coughs. Sneezes. A child with a rash who was quickly dispatched to a private waiting area. A perky pregnant woman. All the usual waiting-room stuff.

They sat, facing the reception desk, eyes drawn to posters for the morning-after pill and sexual advice for teenagers. Bit late for that with Frankie, Julia thought bitterly. An affair with a married man! She still could not quite believe it. She hoped that it had been just talk about her seeing him again. There was no point in rekindling anything, for it would all end in tears.

'I hope you don't mind about the driving lessons for Frankie,' Nina said, in a vain attempt to take her mind off it. 'Sorry. I should have asked you first before I rushed into it. It's just that Mary's husband runs this driving school and I knew he had a vacancy. Anyway, they're booked now and she starts next week. I know you're not keen and I understand that. But what happened to Dad . . . ' she lowered her voice. 'It was an accident. Black ice, that horrible hairpin. The point is, Julia, she'll have to learn to drive sometime. You won't be able to stop her and she'll be perfectly all right. She's very sensible and I think she'll be a natural. She's not too clumsy. She looks as though she's got excellent co-ordination.'

'Do you think so?'

'Absolutely.' Nina said. 'Is that butterfly tattoo the real thing by the way?'

'Yes. I'm afraid so.'

'I think it's pretty.'

'You would. Oh Nina, you'd have a lot to learn if you had a daughter.'

'Yes, well . . . ' She bit her lip and Julia was sorry she'd mentioned that.

'So long as Frankie doesn't expect a car of

her own at the end of it,' she said, taking the conversation back to the driving lessons. 'I worry that we spoil her and she's definitely not getting a car, not until she starts college, anyway, and maybe not even then. Tom will want to buy her one but — '

'Look, I know I have no experience with children but why are you so hard on her?'

'Hard? I'm not hard,' Julia lowered her voice too, aware that people in doctors' waiting-rooms had nothing better to do than listen in. 'I've always been very conscious that she's an only child and tried not to spoil her, that's all.'

'Very commendable. But you've gone to the other extreme.'

'She just doesn't talk to me, Nina. She never has. I can't get through to her.'

'Isn't that what all mothers say about their teenagers? Did you talk to mother? Did I?'

'No, but . . . ' she paused, very nearly ready to blurt it out.

'What was all that about? At the dinner party? Who is this boyfriend? I've asked her but she won't say. What she did say was that she'd promised she wouldn't talk about it. Promised you that. So, what's the big deal? Has he got two heads or something? Don't you consider him *suitable*?'

'I'm not like that and you know it,' Julia

250

said, sounding so unhappy that Nina took her hand and squeezed it in apology.

'Sorry. Although Mother was always a bit like that with Tom, wasn't she?'

'Well, yes. I don't think she entirely approves of him even now, but he doesn't mind. He likes her.' Julia listened for her name, as the buzzer sounded but somebody else rose to their feet and shuffled off. 'Look, I will tell you about Frankie but not now. It was stupid to think we could keep it quiet. Although I think we'll have to keep it from Mother. I can't make her out. I don't know how she'll react. You know what she's like when it comes to family standards. We have a lot to live up to, with Dad.' She sighed, that instant happy memory flooding into her brain. 'We were lucky to have such a wonderful father, Nina. He was very nearly perfect, wasn't he? Always ready to listen. Cheerful. Patient. And he liked Tom. That meant a lot to me, having his approval before he died. And, do you know . . . ?' she hesitated. 'Remember what mother said about him being there at my wedding? Well . . . I felt it too. His presence. It was very strong. It wasn't Uncle James holding my hand at all as we walked up the aisle, it was Daddy.'

Nina managed a nervous smile, squeezed her hand.

'Sorry.' Julia muttered, feeling herself flush

with a sudden embarrassment at what she had said. She had never meant to say that to anybody, but Nina was so sympathetic and she needed sympathy. 'Can I say something?'

Nina nodded. 'Fire away,' she said.

'It's just that . . . I need your promise, Nina, that you'll be there for Frankie if I'm not around.'

'Oh, come on, let's not start on that,' Nina said briskly, taking a careful look round. 'For God's sake, be positive.'

Easier said than done.

Julia swallowed nervously, wishing this was over. She would have to be brave, face up to it, if it came to it. *After a long illness, bravely fought*, wasn't that what they always said in the obits? And look at Daddy, snuffed out in the few minutes it took the car to fly over the edge and on to the rocks below.

Positive thoughts. Positive thoughts.

'I've got butterflies.' Nina's voice at her side was gentle. 'Must be sympathy pains. Now, let's get this show on the road. Have you written down your symptoms? You don't want to forget anything. Tell him exactly how you've been feeling. Tell him about those little pains and the dragging feeling. Are you sure you don't want me to come in with you?'

'I'll be fine on my own. In any case, if I know doctors, he won't know exactly what is wrong, not without tests and things. So, maybe I won't know for sure today. It's the not knowing, Nina. I should have come before. I would have but I've been so frightened. You know me, I've had every ailment under the sun. In my mind. It might be IBS, I suppose. A nuisance but not life-threatening.'

'What's that?'

'Irritable bowel syndrome,' she said, warning her with a look not to repeat it out loud.

'Oh, right. Sounds horrific. Very unromantic. On the other hand, it might be just nerves. Stress. Whatever that problem with Frankie was . . . ' Nina eyed her shrewdly. 'You look a bit better today and I'm not just saying it. You've got a bloom in your cheeks.'

Funny that. Yes, she did feel a bit better today, but she had put that down to making an appointment to see the doctor and having her symptoms suddenly disappear on her. She hoped she was not wasting his time, as she would hate to do that. On the other hand, that churning feeling was never too far away, on the fringes, and she needed to know if there was a physical reason for it. If there was something nasty lurking, then it could not be avoided any longer.

'Mrs Julia Vasey . . . Doctor Armstrong. Room Seven.'

'Yes, that's me,' she said, comically announcing it to the people around, grabbing her bag and setting off, looking back and seeing Nina sitting there, looking absolutely wretched.

★ ★ ★

Alex picked her up at six the following Wednesday. He had booked a table at a wonderful hotel over on the shores of Ullswater and it would take a while to get there.

Nina had gone to town on her outfit. A little black number, the back scooped away, and, underneath it brand-new black undies. Her shoes were hellishly uncomfortable but very sexy, entirely unsuitable for a stroll along the lakeside but she was hoping they would arrive barely on time and be shooed into the restaurant pretty quickly.

'You look lovely,' he told her as she prised herself into the passenger seat of the Japanese sporty car he drove.

'Thank you,' she said, trying to calm herself down.

Despite her efforts, she did not feel particularly lovely. She had had a row, a humdinger of one, with Julia this afternoon and it was such a rarity that it had taken both

254

of them by surprise. It had been left in a very unsatisfactory state with neither of them prepared to apologize. Nina almost groaned aloud at some of the things she recalled saying.

'You look as though you've had a tough day,' Alex said, knocking the nail neatly on its head.

'Fairly tough,' she said, not wanting to talk about it, not with a man who was as yet almost a stranger. 'It's probably lack of food,' she told him, trying to make light of it. 'Saving myself for this meal. It had better be good. I hope you don't think you can palm me off with something under par.'

'It will be good,' he assured her. 'I've been there a few times and that's how I managed a table. They're like gold-dust, the good ones that is, the ones with a view of the lake.'

'I see. Are you trying to impress me by any chance?'

'Absolutely.'

He was a good driver, confident but not over so, and she allowed herself eventually to relax, although she dared not close her eyes in case she dropped off. Julia's nightmare of the last few days, until the results of the tests were through, had been her nightmare too. She had imagined the very worst because then it might not be so bad if they had to face it. She had gone through some sleepless nights.

'You're quiet,' Alex said and she roused herself, feeling guilty for neglecting him.

'Sorry. I've a lot on my mind,' she told him. 'Family crisis.'

'Oh hell. I thought it was just my lot who had family crises. Mum's found a lump on George so we won't rest easy until we find out what it is. He goes in on Tuesday for an exploratory op.'

'I'm sorry to hear that,' she said, not sure who George was. 'That's awful. It makes my problem seem trivial. I'm sorry, who is George?'

He laughed. 'One of the dogs. Sorry, I should have made it clear. Mum thinks the world of him, so it's not really trivial.'

'I see.'

'Do you want to talk about it? Your problem?'

'Not yet. I've promised Julia to keep it under wraps for the moment,' she said. 'But thanks anyway. Tell me, Alex . . . ' she drew the conversation round to him. 'It's time we knew a bit more about each other. What exactly do you do? Incidentally, I was so fed up with Mother trying to prise information out of me that I told her you were a surgeon. Orthopaedics. That's hips and knees and things.'

He laughed. 'Whatever did you do that for?'

'Because it shut her up. She's a bit of a snob I'm afraid. Now if you were a teacher of course, that would be different. She adores teachers.'

'I'm a property developer,' he said. 'I don't suppose she'll be too keen on that.'

'God, no. It sounds dubious,' Nina told him with a laugh. 'Sounds like you do something infinitely devious and end up making a fortune. Do you do that?'

'Not quite. But yes, my business partner and I do try to make money. That's the name of the game these days. We've just sold off some property in London, made a bomb on our investment so we're teaming up with a builder and are on the look-out for some land, although we've got tough planning regulations to cope with up here and of course we have to take every care that whatever we build slots into the environment. They're keen on that.'

'So they should be. I can see we're going to get on just fine,' she said, glancing sharply at him. 'I have to tell you that I hate new developments and nothing will persuade me otherwise.'

'I think I could persuade you,' he said with a quick confident grin her way. 'I work with a terrific architect. You'll change your mind when you see our designs. Sympathetic yet sensational.'

'What on earth were you doing in Australia?'

'Holiday. I haven't had a holiday for years and decided I needed one.'

'Know what you mean. I haven't had a proper holiday for years either,' she told him. 'The last was in Italy . . . ' She paused, remembering Venice. It took nothing to remind her of that. 'I don't fancy going on my own and the idea of a tour with other singles makes me feel quite ill.'

He laughed. 'We're two of a kind. I suppose it's easier for me to go it alone.'

'Oh I see. You were alone in Australia?'

'Yes. I'm divorced, Nina, in case you're wondering.'

'I wasn't,' she said quickly. 'But I thought you might be. At your age, you're bound to have been in a relationship.'

'At my age?' He groaned. 'I am forty-three, Nina, and it feels pretty old sometimes. I wanted it to work with Sheila but it didn't. She left me for another man.'

'That must have been hard for you,' she said, wishing he had not told her that because it made her terribly curious as to why this Sheila had done that. Alex did not look like the sort of man you would leave, rather the sort you might run to.

'Tough, yes. It was hard but she must have had her reasons. I'm still trying to figure it out.'

'And I'm still reeling from a serious relationship, so we've both been hurt, haven't we? It's a bugger, isn't it?'

'Yes. You could say that,' he said cheerfully. 'You get over it. Have to.'

'I've had all that from Mother,' she told him. 'Pick yourself up, dust yourself down . . . she even sang a song about it. She means well but it did not help at the time. You need to be allowed to wallow in self-pity for a while.' She glanced at him, wondered if she should ask, decided to do it anyway. 'Do you have children?'

He nodded and she felt her heart sink.

'Two. Two boys. Eighteen and fifteen. They live with their mother up in Scotland. I see them from time to time but it's all a bit difficult. Not surprisingly the new man resents me and I can't say I like him either. The boys have been a bit anxious the last few times I've been up.'

She caught the sudden edge in his voice, gave up on it before it spoilt the evening.

Complications. She was not getting into a possible stepmother scenario. That was a

259

no-win situation. And if he already had children he would not be desperate for any more.

So, all in all, a bad bet.

Pity though . . . she did like the look of him and he was nice. Never mind, they would enjoy their meal and they were at that wonderfully early stage when it was easy to step away without too much agonizing.

★   ★   ★

The rest of the journey passed pleasantly, no pressures, their conversation relaxed, the feeling growing that they would get on very well together. She fancied him and she presumed, as he had asked her out this evening, that the feeling was reciprocated. She hoped so or all this effort would be for nothing. Julia had told her to be careful, not to rush into another relationship on the rebound but, as she had told Julia, it was a long time since Harry and she had to get herself back into circulation or it would just get harder.

She must not compare. She must not compare.

She found she was reciting this mantra to herself as they drove up to the hotel at last, although she saw, as an attentive waiter settled them in the bar for pre-dinner drinks, that this was exactly the sort of place Harry hated. He would have had everybody within sight down as pretentious twits.

Funnily enough, she thought she might rather enjoy this.

* * *

It was a very dallying sort of meal. The view across the lake as sunset approached was softly beautiful and she could barely take her eyes off it. She was used to water views, living where she did, but this lake view was different from her punchier, wind-rippled bay. Mellow, darker water, lapping softly to the shore, the hills a perfect backdrop.

'Isn't it gorgeous here?' she said. 'It kept me sane when I was away from it, just thinking about it. I suppose I'm just not a city person. There are advantages of course but on the whole I think I'm glad I came back.'

'Are you trying to justify yourself?' he asked, amused.

'Maybe.' She looked at him, not hiding the fact that she was studying him closely. She liked the way he looked. She liked his hands. Nicely cared for and that was important to her. To hell with a man thinking there was something wrong, something faintly feminine, about caring for his appearance. Scruffy chic had never been a turn-on for her. Alex took care and looked good in casuals or the more formal attire of this evening.

On the way back, pleasantly relaxed now after a couple of glasses of wine, she found herself thinking — annoyingly — of Julia and the row they had had. Before she knew what was what and much against her better judgement she found herself telling him about it, thinking maybe that a stranger might have a different slant on it, come up with some answers. She dared not tell her mother they had had an argument because she would insist on getting the pair of them together and make them feel ten and six again.

'Can you believe this?' she started. 'Can you believe my sister?'

'Try me,' he said.

'The thing is I've been trying to get her to move back up here for years,' she began. 'I kept thinking how nice it would be if we could just call on each other casually if we felt like it without the hassle of a long journey, staying over and everything. Go shopping together, just the two of us. Pop over to each other's homes for a coffee and a chat. We used to chat. Once upon a time. And now . . . ' she glanced at him. He was concentrating on his driving but she knew she had his attention. 'Now she *is* back. For good. And it's all gone wrong. We've had a helluva row this afternoon. She has a vile temper when she gets started. All calm and quiet normally but you should have seen her. She threw a vase at me.'

He laughed. Apologized at once.

Nina laughed too. 'I know, it does sound ridiculous. She was arranging flowers, you see, she's very into flowers and the vase just happened to be handy. A beautiful vase at that. Smashed to smithereens. And the flowers flew all over the place too. Not to mention the water.'

'Wow. What happened for her to do that?'

'Well, I think I might have told her that her husband fancies me,' she said. 'Awful, isn't it? I should have kept it to myself but I was so pissed off . . . sorry . . . but I was,' she finished. 'She has it all. A job she likes. A husband and a lovely daughter. She's going to buy this wonderful old converted chapel. She's beautiful and she can eat whatever she likes and never puts on an ounce.'

'I see. One of those thin sorts eh?' Alex said. 'Not my type.'

'If you dare say you like your women with a bit of meat on them, I shall kill you.'

'OK. I shan't say it then.'

'Anyway, the point is . . . ' She sighed. 'She's pregnant and from the way she's reacting, you'd think it was the very worst thing in the world to have happened. I know she's forty-two but she ought to be thrilled to be given a last chance. I told her that and that's when she threw the vase at me.'

'Hormonal,' he said mildly. 'That's all it will be. My ex-wife was exactly the same. She will be fine as soon as it's sunk in. And you're right, you should have kept quiet about the husband. Big mistake, darling.' he snatched a glance at her. 'Is it true? Does he fancy you?'

'Sort of,' she said, uncomfortable to have mentioned it, as if she was somehow fishing for a compliment which thankfully he had not taken her up on. 'I think Julia's giving him a hard time just now and maybe he's just after some sympathy.'

'Careful.'

'I know,' she said, faintly irritated that he had felt the need to say that. 'Nothing will happen, not with Julia breathing down my neck. But I'm a bit stumped, Alex. I know you don't know Julia but what do you think I should do. Shall I apologize? Ring her? Or shall I let her stew for a while? Give her the chance to apologize to me?'

'In my capacity as agony uncle,' he said lightly, 'I suggest you buy her a new vase and stick some flowers in it.'

'Oh. So, you think it was my fault then?'

'I wouldn't presume. But, if she is going to stay here for ever as you say she is, then it's best that you be friends. These little misunderstandings can fester and the longer you leave it, the worse it will be.'

'You're so sensible, Alex,' she told him, a faint rebellion in her nonetheless. Why the hell should she apologize for having a vase thrown at her? And she *had* been right. A child was a gift, a gift from God if you wanted to be like that, and Julia ought to be grateful instead of muttering dark threats. What she would give to have the chance of a baby? She was very nearly at the stage where she would have the IVF and go it alone.

'You're not getting broody, are you?' he said, reading her mind. 'Biological clock, all that nonsense.'

'No, of course not,' she said hastily. 'I'm happy as I am. After Harry, I realized what was important to me. My career. Living here. That's what's important. I don't need anything or anyone else.'

There was a short silence.

Well, that had done it. Made it plain where she stood.

'Here we are,' he said unnecessarily, drawing to a halt outside her flat.

The night air was cooler and she shivered as it slid through the open window of the car.

'Thanks for dinner, Alex. It was great. Do you want to come up for a coffee? And I do mean just a coffee,' she added.

'I know that's what you mean,' he said, a little aloof suddenly. 'And no thanks. It's late and you need your beauty sleep. I'll give you a ring in a few days.'

He insisted on getting out of the car and escorting her the few yards to her door, giving her a quick kiss on the cheek, thanking her for the lovely evening.

'We must do it again sometime,' he said lightly.

She did not bother to answer, suspecting a brush-off.

Well, honestly . . .

Miffed, she let herself in and went upstairs.

The flat was spotless on the surface, all the things that usually lay strewn about were now stuffed in drawers and cupboards, for she had anticipated him coming up for a coffee.

Although, if she *had* meant just a coffee, why the hell had she gone to the trouble this afternoon of putting out fresh towels in the bathroom and changing the sheets?

15

'It isn't the end of the world,' Tom said, bringing her a glass of water. 'Come on, sweetheart, calm down.'

'I seem to remember you saying that once before,' Julia said, snatching the glass from him with a pained look.

'Exactly. And look what we have. Frankie. We wouldn't be without her for anything, would we?'

'No, but I was young then. I'm forty-two now in case you'd forgotten. Far too old to have a baby. I'm going to be a laughing-stock at the clinic.'

'Now hang on. You're having one, so how can you be too old? And it's no big deal, your being forty-two. Lots of women are having babies at forty-two these days. Forty-two is the new twenty-one.'

'Says who?' she asked, with no trace of a smile.

'Read it somewhere. Anyway, it'll be great. I'm looking forward to it. It might be a boy this time. Not that I mind either way,' he added swiftly. 'What do you want, darling? Boy or girl? Any thoughts on names?'

'For goodness sake, Tom . . . '

'OK.' He held up his hand, acknowledging she was not ready for that. He tried smiling at her, desperate to elicit some sort of positive reaction. She had just told him that she had feared she was seriously ill and had then been told she was pregnant, so she ought to be bloody relieved.

He was.

'What will Frankie say?' she wailed, holding her hands up to her face. 'What will she think of us?'

He laughed. He couldn't help it. 'She'll probably be shocked that we ancients are still having sex but I bet she'll be pleased. A brother or sister. I know there's going to be a big gap but that's how it is with some families. She'll be a big help to you. I don't see the problem.'

'You never do,' she said, face fixed. 'And while we're on the subject, what on earth are you playing at with Nina?'

Taken aback at the switch of conversation, he stared at her, wondering what to say.

'Don't deny it,' she said crisply. 'I might have known when you came back from that walk together at Christmas that you'd been up to something. She says you fancy her.'

'Well, she's got the wrong end of the stick,' he said. 'Bloody hell, she's got a high opinion of herself. I'm married to you. Why should I look at her?'

'I don't know. She seemed sure,' Julia said, a blessed doubt in her eyes now.

Even if he'd had a few thoughts about Nina, nobody was to know that and now that Julia was pregnant they had to get their act together. He saw it as being given a second chance at saving their marriage. It was the best thing that could have happened. Oh sure, it would mean the old routine again, nappies, sleepless nights, all that jazz, but just look at the positive side.

Another baby.

'She was going on and on about how selfish I was, how I ought to be glad I wasn't seriously ill, how she would give her right arm to be pregnant and then she said you fancied her anyway and I ought to be doing something about that. It was then that I threw the vase at her,' Julia said. 'That lovely green one. I'm sorry I did that and it wasn't as if it was ours either. We'll have to replace it.'

He laughed. 'God, yes. We can't be a vase short on the inventory when we leave. What will they think of us? As for Nina, well, I'd just ignore it. She's a bit uptight with this new guy she has and everything. Her mind is playing a few tricks.'

He went over, drew her to her feet, held her

in his arms, hoping for a smile, an acceptance but there was none. He was waiting for the breakthrough, the little chink in the armour, but he saw he would have to wait a while longer.

'You don't understand, do you?' she told him, drawing away impatiently. 'This is absolutely the worst possible thing to happen to me.'

'Worse than being told you have cancer?' he asked. 'Oh come on, Julia, pull yourself together. Most women would be delighted.'

'How dare you tell me to pull myself together. It's me who's having this baby with all the problems attached, and you should know by now that I am not *most* women,' she told him and her eyes were cold. 'I would have aborted it, Tom, but it's too late for that. How the hell can I have missed it? I thought it was the menopause for heaven's sake. A few missed periods signified nothing. I've always been haywire where they are concerned. I'm nearly five months pregnant. Do I look it?'

'No. But then you never looked pregnant last time either.'

'You'll have to tell Frankie,' she told him. 'I can't face that. It's bad enough having to admit it to Mother. Goodness knows what she will say. I think I'll phone her, then I can't see her face.'

270

He sighed. It was new, all this, and it would take time to come to terms with it. Once she had, then they could start to plan and he knew it would be all right. As soon as she showed the slightest interest in the planning, then he would know it would be all right.

'We'd better kit out one of the rooms at the chapel as a nursery,' he said, watching her closely. 'Will you need help? Somebody to help you with the baby. I know you didn't have help with Frankie but . . . ' He stopped dead.

'Of course I shall need help,' she said. 'I shan't be able to cope on my own, not this time. Heavens, Tom, some women my age are grandmothers. I don't know how you could have let it happen. If you'd bothered to have that vasectomy, this wouldn't have happened.'

He knew that.

He didn't need her to say that.

He wanted to draw her into his arms, have her soften and see that it was a wonderful thing, this last chance they had been given, but he caught her expression and knew it would be a grave mistake.

★ ★ ★

It was a glorious day and Clemmie and Dilys were taking tea on the terrace at Rosemount.

271

Butterflies were bombing the buddleia, the large pots that lined the terrace were brimming with trailing fuschia and the stone arch leading through to the vegetable plot was covered with orange honeysuckle.

She and Dilys were doing their best to be as bright and cheerful as the flowers. Clemmie's mythical arthritis was troubling her, her knees aching like merry hell and she felt stiff as a board, and Dilys had admitted to having problems with her hearing.

'Nonsense. You never listen, that's all,' Clemmie told her.

'It's you who never listens, Clementine,' Dilys said with a smile, adjusting the bodice of her printed dress. She dyed her hair ash-blonde, but since she was fair originally, it didn't look so bad on her. 'I've been pondering about whether to have an operation. I'd cherish your opinion, Clemmie.'

'Operation?' Clemmie was startled. 'Heart?'

'Goodness no. Plastic surgery. A second face-lift.'

'You are joking, surely? They can't work miracles.'

Dilys bristled, before relenting and managing a tight smile.

'You're quite right. If I wasn't so terribly ancient, I do believe I would consider having breast implants, dear.'

'Whatever for?'

'To make my dresses fit better,' Dilys said. 'I've always had a flat chest. Such a bore, isn't it. Yours is better. More of it. Do you think a surgeon would do it, at my age?'

'I doubt it. And it would cost a fortune.' Clemmie eyed her shrewdly.

'There's nobody to leave my money to.' Dilys said. 'Other than charity. And I can't decide which one. I find myself spending money, Clemmie, on the most ridiculous things these days. Gadgets, that sort of thing. Things I never use. It's such a waste. And plastic surgery seems so grand an option.'

'And dangerous at your age. You would probably peg out under the anaesthetic. I don't know why you talk about such nonsense. You know perfectly well you won't bother. It's too late, darling, for all that. Sadly, the body reaches a certain stage when nothing will help. I'm in the same boat.'

'Don't be such a misery,' Dilys said. 'A little make-up works wonders. And it's not as if anybody sees our bodies these days.'

'Quite.'

'I'm almost glad Reggie is not here to see me like this,' Dilys went on. 'He was always so dashing. Just like Anthony. I suppose you could say they went out in their prime.'

Dilys folded back into her chair, gazing out

273

over the garden and thinking about the past.

'Do you remember, Clemmie, back to the time when you were toying with both Edward and Anthony? Promised to Edward yet only able to think of Anthony. I did warn you that Edward would take it badly.'

'I never toyed with *both* of them,' Clemmie said. 'Not at the same time.'

'You jolly well did. You knew full well when Anthony was away at war that you would pack poor old Edward in, directly he got home, *if* he got home. You dangled Edward on a string for years. Getting him to escort you here there and everywhere. I shall always remember one moment at that summer dance to celebrate your birthday. You were wearing blue, a midnight blue dress.'

'Oh yes . . . '

'And you suddenly disappeared for a moment, leaving poor Edward standing there clutching your evening bag, waiting for you to come back, like a lovesick puppy. I should put that down, Reggie told him, give it to Dilys. She'll hang on to it. But no, he wouldn't part with it, as if I was going to run off with it. I can see him now. He worshipped you, Clemmie, and you treated him like dirt. You always have. I feel quite sorry for the poor man.'

'You needn't. It was a kindness to set him

free. That's how I saw it. I was in love with Anthony. Just as you were in love with your Reggie, Dilys.'

'Yes but Anthony was away and Edward should have used that to his advantage. Why on earth he didn't persuade you to marry him during the war is a mystery.'

'He did try but I refused. I told him it was the wrong time. Indelicate of us. And he quite liked the idea of a long engagement.'

'Why did he never marry?'

'I have no idea. That's his business.'

'Did you know he is planning an exhibition?' Dilys asked, before sinking her teeth into a cream cake.

'An art exhibition?' Clemmie asked, feeling her heart thud.

Dilys nodded, trying not to talk with her mouth full. She was in pink today, a silk dress with a sweetheart neckline, a deeper-pink cardigan draped over the cane garden chair. Dilys had little hands with stubby fingers, upon which Reggie's diamond engagement ring stood out boldly, and she fluttered every bit as much as the butterflies on the buddleia. She always had.

'Where?' Clemmie asked sharply. 'In Greysands?'

'Yes. At that new gallery on Hall Terrace.

They are opening with an exhibition of local talent.'

'He's got a nerve. Exhibition indeed! Who does he think he is?'

'Quite a good amateur painter actually,' Dilys said, putting a napkin up to her mouth to wipe away the excess cream and a good deal of her shiny red lipstick. 'They're his sand pictures. That's what he calls them. Pictures of the beach. Commendable but boring I should think. I suppose we ought to pay a visit. Show willing. How much do you think they'll be?'

'The ones he has in Nina's shop are outrageously expensive. About a hundred pounds.'

'He can forget that. I'm prepared to pay up to twenty-five pounds but no more. I mean, it isn't as if it's for charity, so we ought not to feel obliged but I would hate it if he sold none of them.'

Clemmie relaxed a little. Sand pictures. That was all right. But she would not be buying one, would not accept one if he was *giving* it away.

Dilys said yes to another cup of tea with a smile before leaning forward conspiratorially.

'Clemmie, my dear, have you heard the rumours?'

'About what?'

'Your school of course. Florey Park.'

'Oh.' Clemmie sighed her irritation. How ever did rumours get started unless, on this occasion, Jonty McKay was deliberately leaking them? 'I have no comment as yet, Dilys,' she said, anxious to nip this in the bud before Dilys managed to draw forth her feelings.

'You surprise me. I thought you would be up in arms. I am. The grounds are beautiful, special, and several houses, no matter how tasteful, would spoil them. And just think of the work involved. Builders. Machinery. Bricks. And the only access is from the school. Those beautiful grounds would be completely churned up. No indeed, I am thinking of organizing a protest group. Goodness, Clemmie, have you given your approval to this?'

Clemmie very nearly spilt her tea. It was so unexpected. She had thought that somehow Dilys had got wind of the co-educational idea but this was a completely new can of worms. New houses? Never. The grounds were superb, the *pièce de résistance* for the parents, and they must not lose a square inch of them. Having new houses sited there, with, as Dilys pointed out, the absolute horror of all the building work that would entail was out of the question. Jonty McKay must be going senile even to consider such a thing. Good gracious, what was wrong with the man? He hadn't had an original idea in twenty years and now he was falling over himself with them.

'I can't think where that rumour started,' she said firmly. 'But you can rest assured, Dilys, that it is merely a rumour. The school is doing very well indeed. We have an excellent staff. And — do keep this to yourself — we have a lottery winner amongst our parents, although we have instructions to keep the child's identity a secret. We are in a very sound position. There's no need whatsoever to sell off any land.'

'Good. I'm glad about that,' Dilys said, eyeing her calmly but a little suspiciously before turning to look at the gardens, which were looking particularly lovely. A man came in three afternoons a week and that was enough to keep them in tip-top order. 'I hear Julia is buying The Old Chapel?'

'Tom-toms in action again,' Clemmie said, irritated that the entire town should know. 'She is and they are delighted. So am I because it's quite charming. Not that I shall be completely comfortable about it though. After all, it was a chapel, a holy place, and I don't see how it can ever not be a holy place. If you see what I mean.'

'I do. My sentiments exactly,' Dilys said. 'But I'm told it was a very sympathetic conversion and the views of the bay are outstanding. I'm glad Julia's got it and not somebody wanting a second home.'

'With a bit of luck it will settle her down,' Clemmie said, flicking away a bee that was attracted to the remains of jam on the plate. 'Julia I mean. Moving is so stressful and Frankie is at that awkward age.' She peered into the distance, across the expanse of lawn towards the gates. 'Oh, there she is. How delightful! I wasn't expecting her.'

'I must go,' Dilys said, taking her cue. 'Will Harrison drop me off in town, dear?'

'Of course. And you needn't disappear so promptly. Do stay and have a word with Frankie.'

'No. I would be in the way. After all, you've only just got her back,' Dilys said with a smile. 'You must have so much to talk about.'

★　★　★

Frankie could see her grandmother and that dippy friend of hers taking tea on the terrace. She should have rung first because she really did not fancy sitting there, sandwiched between the two of them, being treated like a little girl.

Thankfully, by the time she got there, Dilys had already taken her leave and, with the sun skulking behind a bank of cloud, her grandmother had gone indoors into the cool quiet of the drawing-room.

Frankie had decided to apologize about the dinner party and her behaviour. It was entirely her own decision, for her mother, perhaps wisely, had not put her up to it. Looking back she felt ashamed of herself, acting like a child when she wasn't a child, and she needed to talk to Granny and explain as much as she was able.

She knew some people regarded her grandmother as formidable, particularly Mrs Harrison, but Frankie had never found her so. She liked the spark of mischief in her grandmother's eyes, bright eyes still, and she kept reminding herself of the lovely photograph of her grandmother when she was a young girl. There was one with Edward, the ex-fiancé apparently, although, for whatever reason, his face had been pencilled over. Why keep the photograph then? Perhaps because it was a particularly flattering one of grandmother herself. She had told Frankie that she was wearing an emerald-green dress, even though the sepia photograph kept that secret.

In his photographs Grandpa Scarr looked wonderful in his uniform. How awful it must have been for him, and for grandmother waiting at home, when he was parachuting out of his aircraft during the war. He had done all sorts of clandestine things in France that her mother said he did not like to talk too much about but he must have been brave because he was 'mentioned in dispatches', something that was an honour apparently, although Frankie was vague as to its meaning.

A hero, her mother told her. Her grandfather was a hero and she must never forget it. They had something, everything, to live up to.

What must it have been like to be married to a hero? She supposed Philip was the anti-hero in some eyes, in most eyes, because of what he had done but was he to be condemned to a life of misery and what-might-have-beens just because he had married the wrong woman?

As she walked up the drive, taking her time, it was almost as though she was seeing the house for the first time. She was surprised as always by the pinkness of it, a pink that seemed to change colour depending on the time of day. Today it was softly rose-pink in the sunshine, like blusher on a woman's cheek. She slowed her steps, taking her time, taking in the detail of it that usually escaped her. It was just grandmother's house, had been ever since she had first set eyes on it, but this time she was looking at it afresh.

Her grandmother was delighted to see her, although she said Dilys had tired her out. Sometimes it was hard to remember that she was as old as she was because she usually had such energy.

'Now, what's all this about a boyfriend?' Clemmie said brightly when Frankie was settled at last, choosing to sit on the floor. 'Who is he and have you a photograph to show me?'

'Did you fall in love with Grandpa straight away?' Frankie asked, bypassing the question with another. Good strategy, and one she was good at. 'Do you believe in love at first sight, Granny?'

'Absolutely. It was all very romantic in those days. The songs helped,' Clemmie told her with a smile. 'Such words. 'I've Got my Love to Keep Me Warm', 'Pennies from Heaven', 'In the Still of the Night' — now that is a particularly beautiful song. I always cry when I hear it. You don't know what I'm talking about, do you darling? Haven't heard of any of them. I believe it's the single most important difference between the generations — the songs of the young.'

'I know the Beatles' songs,' Frankie said with a smile.

'So much has changed during my lifetime,' Clemmie said, fingering the gold chain round her neck. 'It will be the same for you. By the time you're my age, you'll wonder what's what. You'll be talking about *your* past then . . . as if it was yesterday,' she added quietly. 'It's so vivid, Frankie. And in here . . . ' she touched her chest. 'I'm still young. Or at least, I'm the age I want to be. Forty I think. That was a good time for me. You can be any age you like, inside. But only when you've passed that age. You couldn't be forty, darling. You can only be twelve. Or seven.'

'Or two. I was a terror at two apparently.'

They laughed, Clemmie apologizing for twittering on.

'What did you do in the war? When Grandpa was away?'

'Haven't I told you? I was fearfully busy in the WVS, voluntary work. All sorts of things. Useful things. I could have learnt to drive but I didn't. And afterwards I never got round to it.'

'I've started lessons,' Frankie said. 'Auntie Nina's buying me them for my birthday. An early present. I've had two lessons already.'

'Splendid. I shall buy you a car, a small red one, when you pass your test but don't tell your mother. She's so afraid of my spoiling you. As a matter of fact, I think it's time you knew that I have been putting a little money aside for you ever since you were born. It's for your eighteenth birthday. It will help with your tuition fees at university.'

Frankie, expressing surprise, thanked her. She knew about it because her mother had told her but it was supposed to be a secret and she was happy to keep it that way. Things wouldn't be too bad then, with granny's help. A car and money to help her through. If she ever went to college that was and it was by no means clear that she would.

'Now, will you stop pretending to me that this boyfriend of yours does not exist and tell me about him,' Clemmie said, eyeing her shrewdly. 'And from your face, I see that you love him. How very sad to leave him. But at least he hasn't gone off to war. Can you imagine how unbearable that was? Not knowing if he would come back. Your mother and father managed a separation, after all, when they went off to university so I don't see it will be any different for you. So, for goodness' sake, cheer up, darling. I hate to see you looking miserable. You have a lovely smile and it's so sad not to see it.'

'He's married,' Frankie said, surprised at how easy it was to say it.

'Married?' Clemmie echoed, the dismay instantly displayed on her face. 'Oh, I see.

Well, this puts a completely different complexion on things. Married?'

'He has two children,' Frankie went on. 'A little boy and a baby girl. He was my teacher.'

'Teacher?' Clemmie shot a hand to her chest, her rouge showing as two bright spots on her cheek. 'That is deplorable. What can he have been thinking of? What does your father intend to do about it? Or does he intend to do nothing at all? Good Lord, your grandpa would have had him hanged, drawn and quartered. Nothing less would do.'

'They've hushed it up,' Frankie told her. 'His wife wants to try again. Sort things out. But they won't. He's called — '

'No.' Clemmie put her hands over her ears. 'I do not wish to hear his name.'

'It wasn't his fault,' Frankie said miserably. 'Not completely. I seduced him, Granny.'

Clemmie laughed, a hard sound, her eyes devoid of humour.

'Do you know what you are saying, Francesca? I would advise you strongly not to repeat that statement to anybody else. Whether or not it's true — '

'I fell in love. Is that so bad?'

'In this case, yes. We've all had crushes on our teachers, darling. But we shouldn't take it any further and it was very remiss of him to do so, whether or not you flashed your eyes at

285

him. That is beside the point.' There was a hint of a smile now. 'Extraordinary. I very nearly did the same thing when I was seventeen. Not my teacher, but an older man, a married man. I think my mother suspected and she very quickly put a stop to it before anything happened.'

'Mum didn't have any idea,' Frankie said quickly, feeling a sudden need to defend her. 'I used to tell her I was going to see my friend but she was having her driving lessons and Mum never once checked it out.'

'That's because she trusted you.'

'I know.' Frankie fiddled with a stray thread on the hem of her jeans. 'I know I let her down. I know that. But she did overreact. I could have coped with staying down there. I would have switched subjects. But they wouldn't have it.'

'Quite right too. Far too much temptation.'

'As soon as we knew it was serious he was very worried because of his wife and everything.' Frankie continued, desperate now to tell all. 'But I persuaded him that life was too short to have doubts. And that we should be happy while we had the chance. He was wonderful with me. Very sweet.'

'Are you telling me that you are no longer a virgin?'

Frankie felt herself blush, astonished that

her grandmother should say such a thing, not daring to look her in the eye.

'It's different these days,' she muttered, head down. 'I know that, in your day — '

'You know nothing about my day,' Clemmie said brusquely. 'So do not presume. At seventeen, my dear child, we are merely experimenting with love. You will meet someone else some day and wonder what all the fuss was about. You will forget this . . . this *man* but you will take the experience with you, so all is not lost. Do you see?'

'Don't lecture me, please. Mum does that all the time.'

'But you need lecturing, darling. You need to be made to see sense as I had to. People are far too lax nowadays about standards. Nothing surprises me, Francesca, I have seen everything, done everything, so don't assume for a minute that I do not understand. It's such a pity that experience comes to us when it's almost too late.'

'What shall I do, Granny? I'm so miserable without him.'

'I was miserable for four years, darling. When I was not much older than you. Miserable waiting for Anthony to come home. And the point was I did not know for sure he would be coming home.'

'How awful.'

'When I was young we had the devil of a job finding time to be alone with our sweethearts,' Clemmie continued. 'And that's how it should be. It is bad if it is too easy. I would willingly help you to see him, darling, you know that, if the boy was suitable, but this is a married man and he clearly is not.'

'I've spoken to him on the phone. He's miserable too. Without me. I would love to talk to him one more time, Granny.'

'For heaven's sake . . . ' Clemmie was clearly exasperated. 'What is there to talk about? It is over. You said yourself his wife wants to try again. Well, then. You have to leave it, darling. Nothing is to be gained by talking. You say the same things over and over again when there is nothing to say.'

'I want to see him one more time,' Frankie said, feeling small and defenceless as she caught her grandmother's steady stare. 'As soon as it was out, they wouldn't let me see him. And he refused to see me — she must have got at him. So the last time I saw him I didn't know it was going to be the last time and I want . . . ' she heard her voice crack, felt the tears she had bottled up beginning to loosen inside. 'I want to say goodbye. That's all. I want him to hold me one last time.'

'Oh dear, you are a romantic like your grandfather. Shall I tell you something,

Frankie? I watched him leave the house on that winter morning,' Clemmie said, after a short painful silence. 'The day he was killed. I watched him leave. He was wearing his camel overcoat over his grey suit, a blue shirt and the cuff-links I gave him for his fiftieth birthday. He popped his head round the door of the drawing-room just before he went out, and said goodbye.'

'He said goodbye?'

She nodded. 'He normally said something like 'checking out, Clemmie, see you later' but that morning he said 'goodbye'.'

'As if he knew?' Frankie said quietly, uncomfortable with the pain on her granny's face. She took a deep breath to control herself; for now was not the moment to burst into tears for it looked as if her grandmother might join her.

'Yes. As if he knew.'

'Did you say goodbye too?'

'Only when he was gone, after he had fussed around with the car, scraping the screen. It was very cold. The snow was packed solid. Not nice snow. Not the soft kind of snow when it's fresh. Well, after he'd done all that, he got in and he didn't look back, although he might have known I was watching from the window. And then he drove off. And that's when I said goodbye. He never heard me say it.'

'But you didn't know what was going to happen. Did you?'

Clemmie smiled. 'Enough of that for now. You have to put all this behind you. I know it will break your heart but we all suffer that. For your mother's sake — '

'Do you know she's expecting a baby?'

'Yes. What a surprise! I think it's wonderful even if she does not. Do you know what she said to me? 'You're never going to believe this, Mother,' she said, 'but something terrible has happened. I'm having a baby.''

'She's giving Dad a hard time.'

'She'll come round,' Clemmie said firmly. 'One has to. You must help her, Frankie. Be nice to her, for heaven's sake. Just now, she needs your support and now you are grown up . . . ' she smiled wryly. 'You are just the person to give her that support. She thinks I'm ready for the compost-heap and Nina desperately wants a baby of her own, so she won't have the patience to cope with it. Your father is too close to her, too guilty, so that leaves you. This is something you have to do. Do you see?'

'But we're . . . ' Frankie pulled the thread completely loose at last, seeing the hem unravel. 'She's not forgiven me for what I did.'

'I'll help you all I can,' Clemmie said. 'But I really am relying on you. Help her through this and she'll see what you did in a different light. It might very well bring you closer.'

It was a nice thought. They needed to bridge that little gap which had always existed between them. Frankie knew she was being selfish these days — it was so hard not to be, but now it seemed that her mother was miserable too, for a different reason, so you could say they were for once in the same boat.

Bobbing about. Adrift.

'I'll try,' she said, standing up and going across to Clemmie as she opened her arms to her. 'Oh, Granny, I'm so unhappy . . . '

'I know, precious. I know,' Clemmie said, feeling her own tears welling up as Frankie sobbed on to her shoulder.

16

One of the local craftsmen was carving seagulls from driftwood. After they had been languishing forlornly in the craft area of the shop, there had been a sudden rush on them. Nina would have to order some more. Edward Grantham's oil-paintings were still sitting there, four in all, and were quite nice if you liked that sort of thing: a series of views, from varying angles, of sand and sea. He had priced them at one hundred pounds each, which Nina thought a bit steep but he had refused to reduce them, had been rather offended, in fact, when she gently suggested it. She was only taking a five per cent commission if she did sell any, so it hardly mattered to her.

She was closing the shop for the afternoon. Mary was laid low with flu and Nina needed to get on with some sewing without constant interruption. The truth of the matter though was that she was feeling very fed up because Alex had not yet rung. What was the matter with him? There was no need for him to feel miffed because she had acted somewhat coolly. There was no rush, despite what people would have you think, to get into bed. She needed time, if she was honest with herself. Time to think about it. Sometimes, thinking about it could be better than the actual doing.

The shopbell jangled and she looked up, wishing she'd put the 'closed' sign on the door.

To her surprise, it was Tom.

'Hi there,' he said cheerfully. 'I was just passing. Thought I'd drop in. I thought you might like a spot of lunch.'

'Why not? I'm busy as hell but I'm still shutting up shop for the afternoon,' she told him, putting her work aside reluctantly. 'We could have a walk on the beach if you like. I'll just have to put some proper shoes on first.'

He waited in the shop whilst she dashed upstairs and tidied herself up. She did not quite believe the 'just passing' business. He was obviously here with an ulterior motive but she felt sure that he was not about to seduce her. Not now. That moment, if it had ever been, was past, although she would be wise not to engage in too much deliberate eye contact.

He was handling one of the driftwood seagulls when she came down again.

'I'd like to buy one,' he said. 'It'll look good in the house. It'll give Julia something to think about, deciding where to put it. She needs things to do. How much?'

'Twenty-five quid. Have it as a present.'

'God, no. You're running a business, Nina. I'll pay the going rate.'

'OK. If you insist. And then, as a very special treat, you can buy me fish and chips.'

'Great. I didn't really fancy Southwicks.'

★ ★ ★

They chose to eat the fish and chips sitting on a bench in the Floral Gardens. A vast array of regimented bedding-plants filled the flower-beds. In addition, there was a crazy golf course, a children's play area, an aviary, bowling green and tennis courts.

'So . . . ' Nina blew on the steaming-hot, vinegary chips, broke off a piece of battered fish. Salty and flaky and quite delicious. She'd forgotten how good they were. In front of them was a view of the bay sands and the purple-edged hills on the opposite shore; a gentle breeze rippled across the tidal water. 'How is Julia?'

'Julia is worrying me sick,' Tom said. 'I know she's not so young to be having a baby but she'll be fine. The doctor says that. They'll monitor her carefully because of last time but things have improved since then, advances have been made, and she'll be whisked into hospital if they think there's going to be a problem. She's acting as though she's got the very worst disease possible. It's driving me nuts. I'm trying not to lose my temper but I feel like shaking her.'

'I *would* talk to her, Tom,' Nina said, watching him as he attacked his little pot of mushy peas with a plastic spoon. 'But she threw a vase at me last time I saw her. And, after all, what do I know about having a baby? Zilch. How the hell can I offer her advice?'

'Do you think I should ask Clemmie to have a word?' he said thoughtfully. 'I'm not sure whether that would be a good idea.'

'How did Mother take it?'

He shrugged. 'She didn't help much. For a start, she was cross because Julia phoned her and didn't tell her face to face. She rang me later, told me she hoped we'd considered the problems attached to childbirth in women over forty.'

Nina laughed. 'Not very helpful.'

'At least Frankie's taken it well,' he said. 'She says she's looking forward to it and she hopes it's a boy. We can find out at the scan, if we want to know in advance of course. I would like to know but I haven't been able to get a response from Julia. It's getting to the stage when I daren't mention the baby.'

'She always did like a bit of drama,' Nina said, realizing she did not often criticize her sister and feeling guilty to be doing so. 'I suppose it's come at the wrong time. With you just moving and everything. One thing on top of another. Julia doesn't like things happening unexpectedly. She likes order.'

'I know that. You needn't tell *me* that.'

They finished their chips in silence, tossing the papers eventually into a wastepaper basket adjacent to the next bench before leaving the gardens and making their way across the road to the promenade.

The sand up at the top near the shored-up banks of pebbles was firm and dry underfoot and they kept close to the wall. Loose strands of glossy knotted brown seaweed and broken shells littered their path. As they walked Nina remembered their last proper walk together, at Christmas, remembered suddenly how he had looked. They were more relaxed now and she knew why. It was because the sexual tension had dissolved. It was there with Alex but, thank heavens, no longer with Tom.

'How's your love life?' Tom asked lightly, almost as if she had spoken her thoughts aloud. 'I hear from Clemmie that you've been out to dinner with this new guy.'

'Indeed I have. A posh hotel on Ullswater,' she said. 'The full works. He was driving so I was forced to drink most of the wine. Forty pounds a bottle and he didn't bat an eyelid. But you needn't worry, I did not get sozzled and he was very sweet. Dropped me off at the door, would you believe?'

'And? Has he rung you since?'

'No. And I'm not sure I want him to, Tom. I'm fed up if, you must know, with always picking the wrong men. He's divorced but he has two children and I don't know if I can cope with that. Do you see me as a stepmother? Wicked or otherwise?'

He laughed. 'Why not? I suppose it's your relationship with him that counts. You're not marrying his kids.'

'Don't you believe it.'

'What does he do? And don't tell me he's a surgeon.'

She laughed. 'Mother, bless her, still believes that. I must get round to telling her the truth, if I ever see him again that is. He's a property developer, by the way, whatever that involves. He seems successful enough. Who knows? Harry gave that impression too, and then nobody wanted to know his furniture. That was a shame,' she added, with a quick glance at Tom. 'You've seen some of his stuff. It *is* beautiful, isn't it? There must be people with money who'd be willing to pay whatever it takes for a really exquisite piece. That was Harry.'

'You still think about him? About Harry?'

'Not if I can help it,' she said smartly, grimacing though as she caught Tom's expression. 'Maybe sometimes. I went with Mary to a stress-busting session. Colour therapy. All that stuff. And when I was drifting about in this garden we had to invent for ourselves, who should be waiting, lurking in the shadows, but him. Harry. Now tell me this, Tom, why? Why did I think of him and not Alex?'

'Any number of reasons,' he said easily. 'The question is, if he asked you tomorrow, would you go back to him?'

She did not answer. They had reached the next set of steps to take them back on to the promenade walk. By mutual consent they headed up them, the sand grating below their feet.

Tom did not prod her for an answer but the question hovered, sitting anxiously between them all the way back to the shop.

★ ★ ★

Clemmie had not made an appointment to see Jonty McKay, so she was aware that she might be on a wild-goose chase but it was a pleasant afternoon, clouded over but still warm and she would at least enjoy the walk over to school.

He was in.

She could see him sitting at his desk through the window as she neared the entrance, saw also that he spotted her, for he gave a sort of half salute. By the time she was in the entrance hall he was out of his office and coming towards her, waving a cigarette.

'Clemmie! An unexpected pleasure.'

'I want a word,' she said. 'Have you a moment?'

'I was just on my way to the library,' he said. 'We can sit in there if you like. Nobody will disturb us. Do you want a cup of tea?'

She nodded. 'Please. That walk seems to get longer every time I do it. Or could it be I'm getting older, Jonty?'

'We all are,' he said, dropping his spent cigarette in a convenient plant pot by one of the windows of the long corridor that would take them to the library. Clemmie loved the library almost as much as she loved the old office. It was such a beautiful south-facing room, a shame almost for the boys to disturb its calm elegance. From its windows they could see fields folding into the distance, a clump of trees, seagulls wheeling and circling overhead. They made their way to a corner by the window, where there were a couple of aged chairs covered in bright-blue fabric and a low table with a small pile of books.

'There you are, Clemmie, take the weight off your feet.'

Once settled Jonty pulled out a mobile phone and spoke to somebody about tea and cakes.

'There we are. All organized,' he told her, slipping the phone back in his pocket. 'You have to keep up with new fangled-technology,' he said, noticing her eyeing the offending instrument with disdain. 'You should get yourself one. People can get in touch any time.'

'No thank you,' she said with a sniff. 'There are times when I wish for complete privacy. Being able to be 'got hold of' at any time appals me.'

'Shall we wait for tea or do you want to fire away?' he said, reaching into his pocket for his cigarettes but restraining himself as he saw her face. 'The co-ed. thing, is it? The board are going to approve it, Clemmie, and I'm sorry if it's going to upset you but there it is. We've got to get at least twenty new boarders signed up next year which will bring us in enough money to keep us floating. I can't keep going to the bank for overdrafts. They won't buy it. They want to see forward projections, that sort of thing, and we have to produce signed up pupils, deposits paid in, to satisfy them.'

'I've told you before, there is no need to go cap in hand to the bank,' Clemmie told him crisply. 'I am happy to dip into my own funds — '

'And don't for a minute think I've not been very grateful for that. But it's not a bottomless pit, is it,' he said, his voice gentle as if he were talking to a child. 'As I've said time and time again, we have to stand on our own feet. We're talking business, Clemmie. And no, I am not going to ask the parents for help. The parents must not have an inkling that we have dodgy finances or they'll whip their boys away in their dozens, grabbing places wherever they can. I can't think of any of them off-hand who would have the guts to stay with a sinking ship. Except Lockwood, the lottery winner, but he's from a different class with different values.'

'Don't bring class into it. I fail to see your point, Jonty. I liked Mr Lockwood,' Clemmie said, recalling the interview with him and his son — *bit of a tosser, my boy, needs to be brought into line*, he had told them before the boy appeared. 'He's relying on us to do something for his boy and I feel very strongly that we must not let him down.'

'I like him too. I wasn't meaning anything.

But parents are selfish creatures, Clemmie. You are one so you should know. If they think we're going under, they won't hang around. They'll have little Johnny booked in somewhere else pronto. It'll be like musical chairs.'

'You're very defeatist, Jonty,' she said. 'And I believe you underestimate the majority of our parents. I know most of them and they will be more loyal than you think, they love the school, they will fight for its survival, and as for our Mr Lockwood, he won't miss one million out of his five, will he?'

'You might be surprised,' Jonty said, pausing as somebody arrived with their tea and a plate of buns. 'Even though I like him, I am not going to bow and scrape before him, not at the risk of his saying no and removing his son. For goodness' sake, he could have sent him anywhere, but he chose here and that boy is going to prove the challenge of the year. I've tried persuasion, but I'm going to have to insist next term on him removing that earring, and on top of that, he doesn't speak our language.'

'He will, given time and I found his accent enchanting. Difficult to understand but not without charm. Thank you.' Clemmie accepted a cup of tea, dropped a slice of lemon into it and declined a cake.

'What can I do for you?' Jonty asked.

'I have come about another rumour that seems to be circulating.'

'What's that?' Jonty raised his eyebrows. 'You can't fart round here without somebody announcing it in the local rag.'

'Really . . . ' Clemmie sniffed her disapproval, although she was inclined to agree with his sentiments. What was she to do with this man? He was in casuals today, a coloured shirt and a ghastly patterned sweater, faded trousers that looked as though they had once belonged to a suit, and scruffy trainers. 'Property developers, Jonty. I have heard a rumour that you are considering hiving off a section of the grounds.'

'Ah, that . . . ' He blew a few crumbs into the air, wiped sticky fingers on his sweater before grinning at her. 'Somebody has approached me, yes. Dangled a juicy carrot my way. And yes, Clemmie, I have to consider it, bring it to the attention of the board of governors. If we did it, it would take all the pressure off at a stroke. It would give us the cushion we need for years to come. And you needn't look like that. It would be a tasteful development they are proposing not a bloody council estate. At the far end of the cricket pitch, very nearly out of sight of the school. A prime site with bay views. The developers are keen I can tell you.'

'I imagine they are,' Clemmie said, feeling a peculiar tightening in her chest. It had been happening on and off for some time now, a squeezing of her heart. Oh dear God, she needed longer yet. She had to keep going for a while longer until this was sorted out. There had been a time when she would have had sufficient clout to sway other members of the school governing body, but not any more. Jonty had edged her out. She saw that now when it was very nearly too late. But if he thought she would give up without a fight, he was very wrong. 'Developers have to get planning permission, don't forget that. And I happen to know — '

'The chief planning bloke,' Jonty chipped in with a sigh. 'It's not come to that yet. The developers are looking at several sites. This was a preliminary recce, if you like, getting the lie of the land, having a provisional word with me, sounding me out. And I didn't say no. It's too important to say no straight off. All right, if I'm honest, I'm not over-keen either but we have to keep the option open and not spit in their faces. He was a nice bloke, the developer. Alex Lawson he's called. Lives out at Fairleven with his parents, although he's thinking of buying his own place. Farming stock.'

'Really?' Clemmie frowned, recalling the

name from somewhere. She would do a bit of ferreting about and scupper this before it landed on the planning desk.

Jonty deftly turned the conversation round to more general matters and Clemmie, tired suddenly, graciously continued to chat to him, although she was beginning to find him a fearful bore these days. He had been here for nearly a quarter of a century and it had taken him a long time to discover 'principles'. He had accepted more than enough help from her in the past and it was frankly insulting that he was now brushing her aside.

'I'm sorry. What did you say?' she asked, as she saw he was awaiting a reply to a question he had fired her way.

'Holiday, Clemmie. I asked if you were planning to go away anywhere?' he said, and she did not miss the swift glance at the library wall clock.

'I rarely go away,' she told him, which he well knew. 'Occasionally Dilys and I might go somewhere. The south coast maybe. But my days of exotic holidays are long gone,' she added, thinking of some of the places she and Anthony had visited.

He had come up with such surprises. *Oh darling, how on earth can we afford to go there?* she would ask when he presented her with a fait accompli, tickets purchased, flights arranged. He always paid for the holidays out of his own funds, being rather good at stretching money, saving for things like a good little boy. The holidays became increasingly extravagant and the last one they took together, on the Orient Express, had cost a fortune. Even then it had never occurred to her to wonder where the money came from, for she had not wanted to spoil his delight.

'I'm off to Wales for a long weekend,' Jonty said, rising as she did. 'Bit of walking. It's a home from home, the guest house I visit. But it's enough to refresh me and then I can't wait for September. I hear your daughter is expecting a baby, by the way. Tom told me. He seems very pleased at the prospect.'

'So is Julia,' Clemmie told him. 'We all are.'

'What about that other daughter of yours? I understand she's been seeing Alex Lawson.'

It took a moment to sink in. Of course. So, the new man was not a brain surgeon. How disappointing and how mischievous of Nina! Nina had this misconception that she was a dreadful snob and teased her about it occasionally.

'Another rumour, Jonty,' she said.

'I'm glad to hear that. No conflict of interest then, on your part,' he said with a grin. 'It would be a turn-up for the book if he was to become your son-in-law, wouldn't it?'

'There's no question of that.' She smiled and shook hands with him. 'Thank you for the tea. I will be in touch.'

'I'm sure you will, my dear Clemmie,' he said drily.

17

Julia sat on a packing crate in the sitting-room of The Old Chapel, surrounded by boxes that still needed to be unpacked. Everything had gone so smoothly, the solicitors had really done them proud and signatures had been exchanged in record time.

Their furniture had arrived, been placed in position and now it was just a question of deciding how best to dress the rooms. It was not like an ordinary house, not at all like the house in Norfolk, its origins as a chapel would always be there, remaining in the very heart of the building. Light flooded in from its big windows, the rooms gave you space to breathe and gone for ever was the cottagey feel of their other home.

Normally it would have been so exciting to be moving in here, but now ... now ... nothing seemed to matter. All that mattered, all that she could think of, waking or dreaming, was the baby that was steadily and greedily growing within her. Even though she knew it was unfair of her, she was so angry with Tom she felt like walking out on him. She would have done so, but she did not know where to go. Frankie would not lose any sleep if she were to go, either. In fact, thinking about it, the two of them, father and daughter, would probably get on a whole lot better on their own. Frankie was very much Tom's daughter and Julia felt sure that, if a choice was presented on a plate, Frankie would opt for him. It was silly that she minded so much because it had been the same for her. She had been drawn always to her father like a magnet and she saw only now how much her mother might have felt excluded from their very special relationship.

Nina had threatened to come round sometime this week to help with the unpacking. They had spoken tentatively on the phone and Julia could not quite remember but rather thought she had ended up apologizing for the vase throwing. Nina in turn had apologized for upsetting her in the first place. Whatever they had said, whoever had said it first, it was a relief. It would be all right. They were sisters and it had to be all right.

Nina was thrilled about the baby.

Tom was thrilled about the baby.

Her mother professed to be thrilled about the baby, once she was over the shock.

Frankie said she was too.

Uncle Tom Cobleigh and all were thrilled about the baby.

Why then, did she feel like this? So angry about it. Goodness knew what it would do this time to her life. Her career had been holding its own down in Norfolk; coming here was a set-back, but one she had been prepared to overcome. But how could she now? She was too old to be coping with it all. To think that by the time this baby was Frankie's age, she would be nearly sixty. It frightened her. The birth. Looking after a newborn. Engaging a nanny. One heard such dreadful tales about nannies and she would really prefer to look after the child herself.

She looked round the room.

Their furniture fitted in beautifully and as she retrieved and put out each small item she unpacked it was feeling more and more like home.

If only . . .

A seventeen-year gap between children was faintly ridiculous. Frankie had taken the news reasonably well although there had been a widening of her eyes, the surprise showing. Damn. Julia felt the ever-ready tears welling up. Impatiently she rubbed at her eyes with her hand, a hand that was grubby from the newsprint in the packing boxes. All the boxes were meticulously labelled and the box she was emptying now contained all the ornaments and pictures that had been in her little study back in Norfolk.

Carefully, she unwrapped them. A wedding photograph taken in the grounds of the school after they had come out of the chapel, both of them smiling nervously to camera. She remembered it so vividly. She remembered Tom turning to look at her as she walked up the aisle towards him. And, at that moment, it had been just the two of them, the happy smiling family friends fading as a blur. She knew then, if she had not known before, how very much he loved her.

There were the small brass animal ornaments that her mother had given her, so they would have to remain: a little brass monkey, bear and elephant. Awful things. She would stick them on a window ledge somewhere. There was a print of Venice, a wide panoramic view, a gift from Nina, a lovely picture but its colours went with nothing else in the old house and it was difficult to know where to put the blessed thing. In addition, there were various things she and Tom had collected themselves over the years. Little mementoes that she was reluctant to pass on to a charity shop.

Then the box of treasures that she kept in her desk drawer.

Silly things. One of her school reports, of all things. *Julia works steadily and is a credit to her form, if a little quiet.* A garter wrapped in tissue paper, the something blue, from her wedding day. One of Tom's rare letters written to her at college, hardly love letters for they had been surprisingly stilted as if he was afraid of somebody intercepting them and censoring them, but letters anyway sent to her when they were apart. She had kept all of them originally but had pared the number down to just a few and then just the one. And look . . . a great heap of cards she had received when Frankie was born. Goodness, she had forgotten that she had hung on to them.

And here was the cutting of the announcement of Frankie's birth, two months late of course because they had not dared to put it in the paper until they knew for sure all was well.

Carrying a heap of stuff in her arms, Julia took it through to the new room that would be her study. She had bagged this room from the first time she saw it, when she'd looked out at the view of the rear walled garden. Unkempt just now but a potential private haven. Busily she put things away; her desk already looked settled in its new position by the window. Not a terribly good position because there was the possibility of being distracted, but she might put up a blind which could be lowered when she was working. Some of her accountancy books were already on the bookshelf — living in hope, rather.

One of the deep drawers she reserved for spare paper, pens, pencils, Sellotape, stapler, drawing-pins: all the usual office items. She picked out a pair of sharp scissors and held them up. On the wall there was a mirror and she caught a glimpse of her reflection; she went closer then to stare at herself.

Goodness! She looked all of her forty-two years: face a little pinched these days, lines round her eyes; a little wear and tear. She had simply scrunched up her hair this morning and tied it back in a ponytail, now she released it and fluffed it out, letting it settle round her shoulders and down her back.

There was a mark on her face from the newsprint and, without make-up, she looked tired and plain. She had missed out so far on the blooming look that some women manage to achieve in middle pregnancy.

She heard the car outside, the door slamming, then the sound of Tom's feet as he came up the path and the front door opening.

His so familiar voice.

'Hello darling, it's me. Where are you?'

She found she was gripping the scissors.

She only had a few minutes before he found her and stopped her.

She raised the scissors.

Looked at her face in the mirror.

Made a stabbing motion.

★ ★ ★

Alex had asked her to come out for the day, a drive over to Cartmel perhaps.

Why not?

As Nina got ready, though, she began to have serious misgivings. What message was she sending out to him? Only one, really, and did she want to send that message out to him? Wouldn't it be better to stamp on it now before it got ahead of itself? He was simply a nice man, but she needed something more than a 'nice man', so agreeing to go out with him again was not quite fair if it gave him hope.

However . . . she had learnt from past experience that sometimes relationships took a while to get off square one, and if you never gave them a chance then it was your tough luck. It felt awful but maybe it was worth persevering with this one.

She was wearing what she considered to be flattering trousers for once, well-cut cream linen that sat nicely over her bum, with a cream satin T-shirt and a cinnamon jacket that struck the right balance between formal and casual. She stuffed her bag with things she might need for the day, then popped into the workroom to have a quick word with Mary.

'Are you quite sure you'll be all right?' she asked, even though they had been over this several times already. Nina had worked most of Sunday at a client's, so she felt she owed herself a weekday off, even though Wednesdays, being market day, were usually one of their busiest and she worried that Mary might get snowed under. 'Just keep things ticking over, Mary. And if there are any design queries, get their number and I'll get back to them. Don't get bogged down if there are other customers waiting.'

'Stop fussing,' Mary told her. 'Off you go.' She eyed her critically, then nodded. 'I like that,' she said. 'Looks good.'

'Should be for the price,' Nina said, looking down at herself. 'I feel a bit like Miss Sobersides in it. It's not my usual glad rags, is it?'

'Exactly.' Mary laughed. 'What *are* you trying to tell him?'

'No idea.' Nina grimaced, knowing she could hide nothing from Mary. Mary was living in high hopes about Alex Lawson, said she could fancy him herself if she wasn't already spoken for.

Knowing she was putting off the evil moment, not sure whether she was looking forward to today or not, Nina picked up her bag, checked her watch.

'Got to go. See you sometime tomorrow. Oh, by the way, I meant to ask you: how is Frankie getting on with her lessons, or is it a big secret?'

'All right, I think. John says she's a natural. She should have no trouble getting through first time. He likes her. He says she's calm. Confident. And always ready to listen. Very co-operative.'

'Really?' Nina raised her eyebrows. 'Try telling that to her mother.'

★ ★ ★

'Why Cartmel?' she asked him, once they were on their way.

'My mother suggested it. I haven't been there for ages. Call it a nostalgia trip if you like.'

'I haven't been there for a while either,' she said. 'My mother comes with her friend Dilys sometimes. She used to come to the races when father was alive. Dad enjoyed a flutter, I think, although he was generally careful with money. He liked to splash out occasionally, surprise her with a holiday or jewellery. She's got some really good jewellery.'

'Whilst we're on the subject of mothers, I must apologize about mine,' he said after a moment. 'I'm thinking about what she said about your father when we first met. It was a bit insensitive of her and I could see it upset you.'

'It was many years ago,' she said. 'You'd think I'd be over it by now, wouldn't you? And I suppose I am. It's just that, now and again, it can hit you like a sledgehammer.'

'I thought so,' he said. 'Car crashes are horrendous. So sudden. And to lose your father in one must have been dreadful for you.'

'Yes.' She smiled, with some difficulty. 'Look, can we change the subject? What have you been doing with yourself since I last saw you?'

'Not much,' he said. 'After we made such a big killing with our last project we've been sitting on our backsides a little, waiting for the right thing to come along. We're looking at some possibilities for a new small development. And I'm also looking at a co-project with a small company in France, acting as their representative here. Second homes. People relocating abroad, that sort of thing. Should be interesting. I'll have to spend some time over there getting the lie of the land.'

'I see.'

'What about you? Have you made it up with your sister?'

'Oh yes. We both apologized. I think. She's moved into The Old Chapel, so I'm going round to help her with the unpacking sometime this week. She shouldn't overdo it, not now she's pregnant and with her previous history. Frankie was premature, you see, and it was touch and go for a while. Julia was fine but the baby was very small and she struggled. Awful time for us all. I don't like to say it because she's very sensitive about it, but at her age Julia must take extra care. We're all scared stiff of her just now. Frightened to death of setting her off. You should see her face, it would be comic if it wasn't so tragic.'

'I see. So, she's not resigned to it?'

'*Resigned* to it?' Nina laughed shortly. 'What a thing to say. Putting it mildly, she's not showing much enthusiasm yet, but she will. It's just hit her hard, coming out of the blue like this. Honestly, can you understand it? If it was me, I'd be dancing a jig on the moon.'

He laughed. 'And you told me you weren't

broody. I seem to recall you saying you were perfectly happy with your lot. Busy career, all that jazz.'

'Oh well. I do love my work and a child would be inconvenient to say the least, but if it happened . . . ' she stopped before she got herself in any deeper, turning the conversation to less awkward matters, relieved when they eventually drove into the little town, driving through and parking beside the race-course and walking back to The Square.

She'd forgotten how delightful it was here. Even though it was the height of the tourist season, with visitors probably packed solid up at Ambleside and Hawkshead, this little gem of a village was quiet, although they had to do a little dance with a group of walkers jostling for space on the narrow pavement.

'It's hardly changed at all,' Alex said, in some surprise.

'What did you expect? A hypermarket?'

'You never know,' he said darkly. 'Would you like to go into the Priory?'

She nodded. 'Please.'

★ ★ ★

It was silent as they approached the Priory, the village sounds fading. An immense Godlike silence. They stood for a moment outside, looking first at the stately building, then beyond to the hills that surrounded them, then closer at the gravestones and the sheep that grazed behind the fence.

Inside, their footsteps echoed on the stone as they trod on the paved floor, over the very graves of yet more ancient souls, Nina tiptoeing respectfully over them, Alex pausing to read some of the inscriptions.

In those days it would seem that many had tried to walk across the bay at low tide and been swept to their deaths.

'Listen to this . . . ' he said. 'An entire family drowned on Lancaster Sands . . . the horse and cart disappeared too.'

Nina did not pause, walking on ahead, immersed in her own thoughts. She stood in front of the great east window, hearing her father's voice suddenly from the very spot where he had stood, a cluster of Florey Park boys before him. In his deeply resonant voice, he had recited that it had been installed in about 1425, inspired, so they said, by the windows of York Minster. *Just look at the stained glass, boys . . . and here, look at this door peppered with bullets by Cromwellian soldiers in 1643.* They perked up at that much more interesting fact. They had come on a school outing, once upon a time, and she had been allowed to tag along after a great deal of pestering and persuading. She remembered feeling a little overawed with all the big boys, holding on to her father's hand. They had picnicked afterwards, looking at the best view of the magnificent building from across the fields, and had arrived home quite late, Mother meeting them rather anxiously back at school, asking if she had behaved herself.

'Behaved herself?' Her father had grinned, ruffled her hair. 'Of course. She's been an angel as usual.'

Alex caught up with her, dragging her back to the present, and they walked round thereafter in silence, each absorbed. They stepped outside eventually, into the same hilly silence, humbled by the experience. An almost reluctant believer, she was aware that God was supposed to be everywhere; it was just that, in some places, he seemed to be undiluted, the presence almost visible. Cartmel Priory was one such place.

Although she would not dream of saying anything about that to Alex, because the last thing she wanted was for him to think she was some sort of religious nut. She had no idea what his views were, his beliefs, and she had no intention of asking. As it was, he seemed suitably overawed by the experience, respectful but no more than that.

They walked slowly back into the middle of the village, pausing a moment to catch their thoughts over a bridge by the gurgling stream that was the River Eea. To her delight Nina discovered a small privately run gallery, which displayed similar items to the ones on show in her shop and they spent some time there, although she was not tempted to buy anything.

'I once walked over to Grange-over-Sands when I was young.' Alex told her. 'On one of our rare family outings, the whole gang of us. You get terrific views of the whole valley . . .'

'I believe my mother did the same, years ago. A bit over ambitious for us today,' Nina said with a smile. 'Perhaps another time.'

'Hope so.'

She recognized the warmth in his voice, but she was beginning to feel uneasy at what was surely to come. What was the matter with her? She had never had such misgivings about a potential relationship before. Normally she was more than happy to let things drift as they would. But this time . . .

After lunch, over which their conversation was a little ragged, they strolled across to the race-course. It was one of the smallest National Hunt courses but there were no races today. No horses. No crowds. No refreshment tents. No fairground. Just cows chewing cud, one letting off a stream of glorious pee, on cue, just as they walked slowly past.

Nina pretended to ignore it but Alex wickedly pointed it out and that made them laugh, breaking what had become a tension between them.

'Nina . . . ?'

She bristled, recognizing the serious sound. This was what had caused the tension, a realization that something had to happen between them, to set their relationship on a different, altogether more serious course. No. Not yet. This was too soon. She should have warned him, told him that, although she and Harry had long since split up, she was still somehow bound to him by a tangle of soft silken thread and love-memories. Maybe she could break free if she wriggled round enough, unloosened enough knots, but the point was, did she want to?

'Let's not talk about the future,' she said firmly. 'I'm a great believer in what will be will be. You can't push it or rush it. It all takes time. And we have time, you and I. Don't we? We're neither of us going anywhere.'

He shrugged but she could see a disappointment in his eyes.

It was very quiet and they were temporarily out of sight of anyone. As he took her hand

and drew her towards him she felt just the slightest relaxation in her body.

It had been a long time since a man had made love to her and as he kissed her she found that her body responded — damn it — as she had known all along it would. He was attractive, available and they were neither of them in the first flush of youth. There comes a time when you have to grab every single chance that comes your way.

'That was nice,' she told him, looking up at him. 'Do it again.'

And he did.

'Must you get back tonight?' he said, smiling at her as he stroked her cheek. 'I know some good hotels round here. I know it's high season but we could see if they have a room. We could book in. Have a leisurely meal. Relax.'

'I haven't brought anything with me,' she said helplessly. 'A nightie, toothbrush and stuff.'

'Oh, come on. I had you down as being impulsive.'

She took her time, making him wait, keeping him guessing, although that was not really her intention. She was not into playing teasing games with him.

She took her time for her own sake. Something Harry once said came back to her.

Live the moment. She was sure he would be doing just that, wherever he was.

'Oh, Alex . . . ' she turned to face him. 'I hope we're not about to make a big mistake.'

18

Frankie was staying at Rosemount for a while. Tom had suggested it, saying that things were in a bit of a pickle at the moment and Julia needed some space.

It was time Julia came to her senses, Clemmie thought, although she did not say as much. Julia was being a pain about all this. Clemmie wanted to tell her to pull herself together but saying that to anybody never worked, so they would have to be patient and let the poor child work it out for herself.

In the meantime, it was nice to have Frankie staying and it would give them every opportunity to 'bond', a new-fangled term for getting to know each other properly.

'Why do you visit Edward Grantham, if you don't like him?' Frankie asked, sitting cross-legged on Clemmie's bed and watching her getting ready. She had done this very thing since she was a little girl, supposedly helping then, but fiddling with things, eventually having to be told not to touch the expensive creams and pretty perfume bottles.

Ignoring the question, Clemmie continued precisely with her make-up routine. Her hair was newly done, looking sleek and wonderful and sometimes, when she was fully made-up, if she sat a little back in her chair and squinted into the mirror, without the benefit of her reading spectacles, it was possible to pretend she was fortyish.

A short sighted and rose-tinted view, of course.

'That hair-do's terrific. You are very trendy,' Frankie assured her now, as if aware of her doubts. 'For your age, Granny.'

'Thank you, dear. I've never understood this permed-hair-and-twinset image some of my generation seem determined to exploit. It's utterly ghastly. I've always liked to keep up with current trends — as far as possible anyway. I have to draw the line at jeans.'

'Oh, I don't know. You're slim enough.'

'I don't feel the grandmother image is the right one for me,' Clemmie went on. 'As you know, I've never knitted in my entire life. Have I been a good grandmother, darling? It matters to me.'

Frankie smiled, her face changing. 'You've been a wonderful grandmother.'

'You're not just saying that?'

'No, I am not,' Frankie said indignantly. 'I wish we'd been able to see more of each other, that's all.'

'Oh, so do I. It's the one thing I regret, not

really watching you grow. And before we know it, you'll be off to college and I shall miss you again.'

'That's a year away,' Frankie said, 'Ages yet.'

Clemmie smiled a little. A year was ages when you were Frankie's age, now it was a mere blip.

'I'm glad you've got black hair,' Frankie went on, seeming determined to cheer her up. 'It suits you.'

'I have no wish to see it going grey,' Clemmie said, pausing a moment. 'If I find myself incapacitated, then will you see to it, darling, that my hairdresser continues to come along and do my hair. Never mind what condition I am in, just don't let it go to the dogs. Even if I'm in a coma, I want my hair and nails done. Promise me?'

'Of course,' Frankie said. For once, she was wearing a dress, a simple blue one, surprisingly pretty, the effect ruined by the clumsy trainers on her feet. 'Why *do* you visit Edward Grantham, Granny?' she persisted. 'I can tell you don't like him. Nina says he's a bit creepy. Is he?'

'Nina has no business saying that. Edward is an old friend,' Clemmie said carefully, spraying wrists with perfume. 'And old friendships are difficult to throw off.'

'I know. I used to be friends with Amy,' Frankie told her. 'Since I came up here we've spoken a few times on the phone, but it's different. I don't see how we're going to be able to stay friends. I don't really want her to visit and I don't think she's bothered either. She's got new friends already. And I haven't got any yet. Not here.'

'You soon will have once you start at school. The school your parents have chosen is very good. Girls only, which is by far the best. I approve wholeheartedly of single-sex schools. You'll work much better with no distractions.'

Frankie nodded. 'It's only for another year anyway. Don't worry. I'm going to work from now on.'

'And you've drawn a line under that other little episode, I hope?'

There was a short silence and Clemmie glanced at her through the mirror, saw the quick flush of colour on her cheeks.

'Well . . . ' Frankie huffed, looked guilty. 'I tried to.'

'Oh dear. Don't tell me you've been in touch with him?'

'I phoned him, Granny. I just had to. It was fantastic to hear his voice. And he still loves me. He told me that.'

'Oh, darling. Weren't you listening at all to

what I said? You have to let this go. What did you hope to achieve by contacting him again?'

'I told you. I want to see him once more. Even if it's only to say goodbye, because we never said goodbye, not properly. He's hoping to come up to Lancaster, to the university, on some pre-term course, so I've decided to go there and see him when he does.'

'I think not.' Clemmie dropped a lipstick into her bag, shut the clasp crossly. She stood up and adjusted the belt of her dress. 'No good at all can come of seeing him again. What would your mother say?'

'She won't say anything. She can't think of anything these days, apart from the baby,' Frankie said. 'There's no getting through to her. And what do you think she's done, Granny? She's cut her hair off. It's horrible.'

'Cut her hair off?' Clemmie paused, her scent bottle in her hand. 'Goodness. Cut it off herself?'

Frankie nodded. 'It looks horrible. It's just chopped off anyhow. You're not to mention it when you see her. Pretend she hasn't. Dad says that's the best way to deal with it. He's very worried that she's losing it.'

'Losing her hair?' Clemmie frowned, wafting her hand this way and that, having dispensed rather too much perfume in her agitation.

'Losing her grip,' Frankie said. 'We don't know what to do with her. She won't talk to anybody about it.'

'Gracious me. She needs to see the doctor. I shall personally arrange something. And I think it's high time I had a word with her. I've been pussyfooting round this problem too long. Now, darling . . . ' she smiled. 'I have to go. Do you want a lift into town?'

'I think I'll pop back home, see how Mother is.'

'We'll drop you off. You must feel free to come and go as you wish. Just let me know when I can expect you for meals so we can lay an extra place.'

'If I suddenly disappear for a few days,' Frankie said, as they went out to the car. 'You'll know where I am, won't you, and you won't say anything?'

'I absolutely forbid you to see that man,' Clemmie said, knowing as she said it that it was like showing a red rag to a bull. Never forbid them to do anything, Anthony always said. Give them your blessing rather and see where that gets us.

True to form, he had indeed given his blessing to Julia and Tom and look where it *had* got them.

The letter was waiting for Frankie when she got home. Her mother was loafing about, lounging on the sofa in the sitting-room, looking miserable as she did these days, shoes kicked off, a little pile of chocolate wrappers beside her.

'Mum . . . You're going to pile the pounds on.'

Her mother shrugged. 'I'm piling them on anyway. It hardly matters. There's got to be some advantage to being pregnant. I can't think of any other.'

Frankie very nearly said *what about the baby* but wisely stayed silent.

Julia slowly unwrapped another chocolate, pointing languidly to the unopened letter lying on the coffee-table.

'If that's from Philip, I suggest you tear it up,' she said. 'It's probably better not to read it at all. And I really can't understand why he writes to you. You would think the last thing he would want is to put anything in writing. I sometimes wonder about the sanity of that man.'

Frankie grasped the letter to her, feeling her heart thud. It was increasingly difficult to make telephone calls to Philip because it seemed that Karen was clinging like a leech just now and it was she who always seemed to answer the phone; probably it was she who had silenced or hidden his mobile. She knew what the letter would be: the confirmation she was waiting for, the rendezvous-point for next week when he was up in Lancaster. She had no idea how she would get there but she *would* get there, even if she had to hitch, although the very idea of that would send her mother into a frenzy of worry and that was why she would not say a thing. She felt she could trust her grandmother not to either. Her grandmother might be appalled but she was not a blabber and she had promised — hadn't she?

She went up to her new room at The Old Chapel. It had been a young boy's room previously and still had the bright blue carpet and the busy Thomas the Tank Engine wallpaper, which was driving her crazy. Auntie Nina was coming to talk about the redecorating with her and, although she could not drum up much enthusiasm, nor could she live much longer with this present set-up. She felt she was camping out; it didn't feel remotely like her bedroom, had as yet nothing of her in it, aside from a few photos in frames and some posters of pop stars.

She held the letter up to the light, as if she might somehow read it without actually opening it, but the cream envelope was too thick and she could see nothing. It had a second class stamp on it, which irritated her rather because it was as if he had not considered it to be of great importance, and surely he would have posted it himself. Before she opened it she needed to consider what she wanted from all this. Her grandmother had unsettled her, because somewhere along the line she knew she was right. She had no idea what grandmother had done in her life but she would guess it to have been a full life and a romantic one, for she had obviously adored Grandfather.

She knew what the sensible thing to do was.

Of course she knew.

She had to let him try to make a new start with his wife and family. How could she think otherwise? What was the choice for him?

Simply this.

Her or Karen.

And she knew he loved her.

It would be the kindest thing to happen to Karen, in the long run, kindest if he left her now, now before the real bitterness started up and it all ended in tears anyway. This way it was just prolonging the agony, useless to try to patch up something that was ripped to shreds. You could say she would be doing Karen a favour.

Divorce and then, eventually, she and Philip would marry.

That was what she wished for, if she allowed her heart to rule her head.

She lay down on her narrow bed, the pastel bedcover completely at odds with the decoration. The window in this room was large. If she raised herself on one elbow she could look out on to the fields, shaking themselves dry today after an early morning shower. The garden was a mess but she had volunteered — madly — to do something with it now that Mum was having to take things easy. There was no guarantee, at Julia's age, that all would be well, especially since her own arrival seventeen years before had not been straightforward.

It was a shock to realize how much she wanted this baby to be born safely. For all their sakes. She remembered nothing at all about being in that incubator, struggling to breathe, but she had seen the photographs they had taken, the tubes attached to her little body, photographs that they knew at the time might be the only things they would have left to remind them of her.

How awful for them. Not just Mum and

Dad but Auntie Nina and Granny too. And now it might all happen again. Perhaps Granny was right: maybe she was the only person who might draw Mum out of this despair. The brief was simple. To make her mum *want* this baby.

Mind you, her shooting off to meet Philip would not go down well if Mum got an inkling of that. If he left Karen he could maybe get a post near to wherever she was going to college and they could then live together while she studied. Yes . . . why had she not considered that before? It was only a year to wait, a year while she got herself together and achieved the grades she needed, the grades she deserved.

She kissed the letter and snuggled it under her pillow.

She would savour it later.

She would read it just before she went to sleep and then perhaps she might dream of him.

He had firm, clear writing and he had addressed it to *Miss Francesca Vasey* which made her smile. He sometimes called her Francesca, at special moments, and she adored the way he said it, the caressing sound to his voice.

Her first letter from him.

Her very first love-letter.

She would fasten a ribbon round it later and put it away, so that when she was Granny's age she could take it out and read it again with an old lady's eyes.

19

'I wish you wouldn't lie to me, Nina,' Clemmie said, glaring at her from across their table in the restaurant at Southwicks. 'I have discovered that this man . . . this man you are seeing is not a surgeon after all.'

Nina pulled a face in apology. 'Sorry. I was just teasing.'

'I know why too. You didn't want me to know who he was and, more to the point, what his intentions were.'

'What are his intentions?' Nina asked innocently. She was beginning to wish she had not agreed to have lunch with Mother. Dilys was incapacitated and Mother had said she did not wish to eat alone, so she really had no choice but to take an extra-long lunch hour, extra-long because the service was abysmal — part of its charm according to Mother — and people had been known to die of thirst as they waited.

'His intentions are to apply for planning permission to build an estate,' Clemmie said, eyes blazing. 'A small housing development of exclusive detached homes in the grounds of Florey Park. Over my dead body, my dear.

And I've told Jonty McKay as much. Jonty is in a very odd mood these days. Full of these crackpot notions of making money.'

'Houses?' Nina put down the menu she had been studying. 'Are you sure?'

'Quite sure.' Her mother's glance was shrewd. 'How involved are you with him?'

Nina picked up the menu again, fanned her face with it. All around them the murmur of gentle conversation, appropriate for the starched-linen look of this restaurant. Nina did not like the new look, which was too half-measures for her. They should have ditched the silver service together with the dark wood. Fresh bay air blew in from the open window and they could see the sands and the sea, the sea far out as yet, but twinkling in the noon sunshine.

'How involved?' Nina echoed, playing for time. She felt like a young girl when her mother was in a mood like this.

Clemmie clicked her tongue. 'Let's not beat about the bush. Are you sleeping with him?' she said, in quite a loud voice, loud enough anyway for a woman nearby to shoot them an amused glance.

'Mother . . . that's none of your business.'

'It most certainly is. Don't you see he's playing a very clever game? Seducing you and putting you in an impossible position. How can I stand up to this and cause a great furore as I intend to do, if, by doing so, it might threaten my daughter's last chance of happiness. I can't be seen to be on the other side of the fence from you and I have no intention of sitting on it.'

Nina stared at her a moment and then laughed.

'Don't be so dramatic. He's not as devious as that. And you needn't worry, Mother. I like him a lot but I'm not madly in love with him, nor he with me, I suspect.'

'Good. Then you won't mind terminating your relationship?'

'What? Why should I do that?'

They paused as the waitress, red-faced and harassed, eventually appeared to take their order, starting off by apologizing for the delay and beginning to launch into the reason why.

In no mood for this, Clemmie interrupted her brusquely and snapped out her choice, Nina quickly giving hers, although she did add a smile too, as the poor girl looked as if she was about to cry.

'He is the enemy,' Clemmie continued, once they were alone again. 'And as such, if you continue to see him, you will be liaising with the enemy, which is totally unaccept-able.'

'Are you mad?' Nina laughed again, but a

little nervously now because mother could get these tremendous bees in her bonnet from time to time. 'I will see whom I like, Mother. I'm not a child any more. I'm nearly forty, for God's sake.'

'You will not see him, Nina,' Clemmie said tightly. 'I don't know what it is with you. You always choose the most awkward sorts of men. Every time. Even before Harry there were some very dubious characters.'

'I haven't known that many men,' she said indignantly. 'As for Harry, he was just unlucky with money. He couldn't really help it if he was totally inept when it came to dealing with figures.'

Her mother flushed, rearranged her cutlery with hands that, most of all, showed her age.

'Be that as it may,' she said. 'People who dabble in property are not to be trusted. This man is totally unsuitable.'

'Let me be the judge of that,' Nina said, feeling her anger welling up. Honestly, her mother treated her sometimes as though she was still a teenager. This was ridiculous because, in all honesty, while she and Alex were getting on reasonably well and while the little 'overnight' in a pretty hotel in the Lakes had been pleasant enough, for he had given her that much-needed sexual excitement once more, it had not raised that important spark

— for either of them. They had not confessed their undying love for each other and nor would they. However, they would continue to see each other, although Nina felt it was just a matter of time before it petered out in an agreeable enough fashion.

That was how she *had* seen it, but now . . .

Now that mother had issued an ultimatum, it was suddenly tremendously important that she should continue to see Alex and if necessary, just to be bloody minded, she might very well champion his cause instead of mother's, although her heart did lie in the preservation of Florey Park's grounds.

Oh bugger.

She was going to see Julia this evening, try to talk some sense into her, get her out of this mood she had sunk into. It was worrying Tom who was muttering about psychiatrists.

The cutting off of her hair had been a call for help surely — something as symbolic as that. Mother's hairdresser had been summoned to try to do something with it and it did look a little better now that the worst of the amateur shearing had been sorted out. Julia looked different though, and at long last was also beginning to look pregnant. This evening, if she could manage it, Nina thought she might bring up the subject of the nursery decoration, see if she could conjure up some interest. She was taking along samples of nursery prints, or they might well settle for a muted scheme in traditional blue or pink. She was also taking some babywear catalogues that Mary had found for her, featuring some gorgeous little outfits. Mary, bless her heart, was offering to knit something traditional.

★ ★ ★

'Jonty McKay has taken leave of his senses,' Clemmie said, in a marginally better mood when they had finished lunch and were heading back to the shop. Nina would run her mother home later, and then she would have to get on with her work. Poor Mary. She seemed to be putting a lot of responsibility on her shoulders these days and it was in the back of her mind that she ought to be thinking of a pay rise. Mary was far too nice to think of asking. She would do some sums, work out the projections on the jobs they had in hand and perhaps, in the meantime, give Mary a little bonus for all her efforts. If Mary decided to toss in her needle and thread, she would be sunk.

'Things have to move forward, Mother,' Nina said, exasperated with her and the way she dismissed everything Jonty McKay suggested. 'We may not always approve of them but ideas have to be looked at and considered and you can't say he's short of ideas, can you?'

'No. He's swamped with them at the moment, all totally insane. Girls in the sixth form from next session. I ask you, is that a recipe for disaster? There will be pregnancies galore.'

'I don't think so. You're not giving the girls much credit, are you? They'll be thinking about their careers and they will know damned well that being pregnant will put a stop to that. They'll be sensible.'

'As Frankie was sensible?'

Nina stared at her. 'Are you saying that she was pregnant?'

'Goodness, no. Where did you get that idea?'

'Well, it did occur to me. I wondered why there was such a rush to get up here. Almost as if they'd *had* to leave Norfolk for some reason. Julia did say she was going to tell me but things are a bit off between us just now. You know, don't you? You know the reason why they had to come up.'

They entered the shop and Mary pounced on her with relief. A problem had cropped up, not something that was insurmountable but it would require instant attention.

Nina looked at her mother. 'I'm sorry,

Mother, I'm going to be tied up for a while. Would you mind . . . ?'

'Not at all. I'll take a taxi,' Clemmie said, inclining her head graciously towards Mary. 'If you would be so kind, dear, as to organize that?'

Mary jumped to attention. Clemmie had that effect.

'I may go round to see Julia,' Clemmie said, as she waited. 'I haven't actually seen her since she was pregnant. I find it faintly annoying that there has been absolute silence from her since she broke the news.'

'She's very upset,' Nina said quietly, not sure whether mother visiting just now was a good idea. 'I'd leave it a while, Mother.'

'No, I shall pay her a visit. Don't worry, I'll be discreet, but she has to realize she can't wallow in misery for ever,' Clemmie said, looking up as the shop bell jangled and a customer wandered in. 'It's terribly self-indulgent of her.'

'Do have a browse,' Nina called to the customer. 'Ask for help if you need it.'

'As I see it,' Clemmie continued, 'Julia insists on carrying the weight of the world on her shoulders. Goodness me, if she'd had to go through what I've had to go through these past few years, I dread to think what she would have done.'

345

'Losing Daddy?' Nina asked, putting her arm round her mother's shoulders and feeling the slight tension there. 'Is that what you mean?'

'Something like that.' Clemmie relaxed under Nina's arm, smiled up at her. 'Thank you, darling. You're a great comfort. And bear in mind what I said about this man of yours. No good will come of it. I will throw myself in front of the bulldozer before I will allow Florey Park's grounds to be ruined.'

'There's the taxi,' Nina said in relief. She needed to talk to Alex about this and somehow get him to see sense. Her mother was far too old to be throwing herself in front of bulldozers.

Bloody hell, if it came to the crunch, *she* would have to do it instead.

★ ★ ★

'You were always on at me to have it cut so now you've got your way, haven't you?' Julia said as soon as Clemmie was through the door.

'You look years younger, darling,' Clemmie told her with a swift glance at it. 'Rather striking in fact. Now, what have you done with this place?' she took off her summer mac and handed it to Julia.

346

Julia sighed as she hung it on a peg in the little downstairs cloakroom. She was not in the mood for a guided tour but she saw that she would have to show her mother round. Clemmie was wearing a long cotton skirt with a rather jaunty striped top and a jingle of silver jewellery.

'Dilys Plowright has gone completely round the bend. She is talking about having breast implants. Her problem is she doesn't know what to do with her money and she likes the idea of spending it on something completely inappropriate,' Clemmie said, following Julia into the vast sitting-room. She stood for a moment in the doorway to admire it. 'Do you think it wise at her age?'

'Absolutely not,' Julia shuddered. 'No reputable surgeon would agree to it. Is she serious?'

'I don't know. I doubt it. She just likes to throw up outrageous ideas from time to time. This is lovely, darling.' Clemmie took stock, picking up the brass ornaments that Julia had dutifully hung on to. 'They look much better in this setting,' she went on, settling herself gingerly on one of the low sofas. 'Now, sit down beside me and tell me all about it, sweetheart.'

'All about what?' Julia said, sitting down as requested although keeping a wary distance.

Her mother in this mood was dangerous. Over-protective, yet able to fly off the handle at any moment. She recognized the signs.

'About this baby of course. This wonderful baby that God has chosen to give you.'

'Oh, Mother . . . ' Julia sighed. 'Don't come religious on me, please. You never go to church.'

'That makes not the slightest difference. I pray in my heart. I do not go to church because I cannot get used to the new minister. It was a sad day when the old vicar retired.'

Julia shuffled in her seat, realizing as she looked down at her trousers that she had grabbed the first thing that came to hand this morning. These were her oldest trousers, the ones she wore for gardening and as yet she had not set foot in this garden. They were elasticated round the waist and reasonably comfortable now that she was spreading, but they looked particularly dreadful.

'It's just going to take some getting used to,' she said carefully. 'This is how I feel, Mother. It's not what I would have wished for myself, not now. I've done it all. Been there, got the T-shirt . . . ' she added, trying her best to lighten up, aware that the jargon meant nothing to Clemmie.

'And now you're doing it all over again,'

Clemmie said. 'Tom is delighted. We all are. Nina's got some ideas for the nursery and you must have help, of course. Is that a problem, darling? Can you afford a nanny?'

Julia shrugged. 'Yes. It's not about money . . . it's . . . ' She struggled to explain her feelings, not even sure herself how she felt and why. 'It's having decisions made *for* me, Mother, and not *by* me. I hate that.'

'Frankie's told me about why you had to come home, why you had to leave Norfolk in a tearing hurry,' Clemmie said. 'Why didn't you tell me? Am I such an ogre? What on earth do you think I would have done?'

'Frankie's told you?' Julia hid her surprise. 'Did you ask her?'

'No, I don't believe so. She just told me. Perhaps she needed to get it off her chest.'

'I'm sorry we tried to be secretive but we felt she had let us down, let you down,' Julia put a hand up to her shorn hair. 'And we had to get her away from him. Don't you see that?'

'Yes I do. But she's still in touch with him. Did you know that? Or was I supposed to keep that secret?'

'There's been a letter,' Julia said wearily. 'From him. I knew it was from him, I recognized the writing and I very nearly threw it away. But in the end I couldn't. She

349

has to see it. Make her own decisions. But I hope she doesn't try to see him again.'

★ ★ ★

In a mad moment, Nina had invited Alex to her place for dinner, knowing only too well that entertaining was not her forte. She had one sure-fire recipe though, and she cheated with the starter and the pudding, both purchased from a great little delicatessan in town; the selection of cheese and biscuits and the after-dinner mints were also bought in, so all in all it might not be too much of a disaster.

She shot up to the flat as soon as she closed the shop. She had tidied up already and the casserole was slowly cooking, so all she had to do was make sure her small dining-table looked presentable and then she could concentrate on herself.

She was very annoyed with Alex for not telling her about this proposed development at Florey Park and she knew it was bound to put a damper on the evening. Mary had been making encouraging noises all afternoon. She had seen Alex and thought him a great catch, even allowing for the ex-wife and the children.

'How would you like to take on another

350

woman's children?' Nina asked her, fed up eventually with all the positive noises and sounding a warning note. 'And one of them is eighteen, very nearly grown up.'

'That's probably better than coping with little ones. They won't bother you much,' Mary said. 'They'll be mainly at a distance and they'll probably be on their best behaviour when you do see them. All you have to do is to keep one step back, not try to take the place of their mother . . . '

'Mary, what on earth do you know about it?' Nina asked.

'I've read about it,' Mary said. 'I read the problem pages. It's never plain sailing being a stepmother . . . '

'Hang on. Aren't you jumping the gun? I hardly know him. We've only been out a few times.'

'And . . . ?' Mary smiled broadly. 'What about the night out?'

'OK.' She felt herself blushing. 'But that was pure lust, Mary. Oh God, I don't know if this is heading anywhere. I hate getting too involved before I've thought things through.'

'Suppose he asks you to marry him, what would you say?'

'I'd say no, of course. I need to know a helluva lot more about him before I embark on that. Anyway, he might not want another

351

baby,' she added, then wishing she hadn't as Mary raised her eyebrows. 'And I wouldn't mind one,' she finished, seeing there was no point in pretending otherwise. 'Whilst I still have a chance.'

'You could do worse,' Mary said. 'He's not bad-looking. He runs his own business. And he's here to stay, isn't he?'

And he is not Harry.

Mary might well have added that, had she known, because that seemed to be the deciding factor. That bloody man had got under her skin and she could not forget him, try as she would. She could always contact him, for old times' sake, but she knew even as the thought crossed her mind that it was a stupid thing to do, two years on. For one thing, he might well have moved on from the last address she had, although she could always contact his mother to find out. And two, he was very likely involved with someone else. Did she want to know that? Or did she prefer to think he was still single and pining for her?

Nina soaked in the bath and decided she was not going to waste a good bottle of wine. They, she and Alex, would enjoy this evening if it killed them and she would try not to mention this thing about Florey Park, not unless he did. Time enough for that later.

She slipped into a dress, a gorgeous soft green and clingy. She had long since given up on loose-fitting stuff. She had a shape so why not show it off. Harry had always loved her shape.

Harry had . . .

Damn the man!

A liar, a cheat, a wastrel . . .

A man, however, who could make her skin heat up with desire from just a single look. And when he touched her, sense and sensibility went out of the window. That was what was missing with Alex. Even if she closed her eyes, it was not the same.

Sighing, she did her make-up, her hair, would have avoided looking at herself in the mirror if she could have because the sadness she had been feeling these last few days was clearly there. It was Julia's fault. That and the irony of it. Julia did not want the baby she was carrying and Nina would give her right arm to be in that position.

It was not fair.

At the same time, she recognized that she must not allow this to rule her life. She had to carry on in the belief that she would not have a child and probably not marry either. Where would that leave her?

Happy if she chose to be.

She could throw herself into the business,

open up another branch somewhere, trickle off between the two, buy herself a proper house, get a couple of dogs, and not be bothered with all the hassle that long-term relationships carried with them, married or not. And also, this time, she could be a real auntie to the new baby, take him under her wing, be a proper auntie to him . . . or her.

There!

She slipped several slim gold bracelets over her wrist, splashed herself with perfume and realized she had another three-quarters of an hour to keep herself in this incredibly sexy beautiful state. What could she do in the meantime, something where she would not get her dress dirty or smudge her newly painted nails?

Sit still, Nina Scarr, and don't move a muscle, her mother's words from long ago came flooding back. If Mother got them both ready Nina could somehow manage to do something disastrous to her outfit or her hair or both, whereas Julia, of course, was always practically perfect.

The phone rang as she was sitting twiddling her thumbs, wondering about the choice of nail colour. She shot towards it, thinking it was Alex making some excuse or other, but no.

It was Julia.

'Nina! I don't know where Frankie's got to,' she said, sounding more worried than usual. 'She's left a note and she's in a state. I think she might have gone walking on the beach. I've looked from the garden but I can't see her anywhere.'

'What's the panic? She's old enough to have a walk on the beach. It's not dark yet for ages. She'll be fine.'

'You don't understand. Tom's not in. He's gone out for a meal with some of his new colleagues. I'm on my own.'

Impatiently, Nina glanced at the clock. Alex would be here any time. What on earth did Julia expect her to do? Drop everything?

'I've got a casserole in the oven,' she said. 'Alex is coming round.'

'So you won't help me then?' The tone was plaintive.

'Help you do what, for God's sake,' Nina said, her impatience winning.

'Look for her.'

'Scouring the sands? You must be joking, Julia. I'm wearing this bloody expensive dress and these crazy shoes. Give me a ring when she turns up.'

'But she's threatening to walk into the sea.'

'She's what?'

'Threatening to walk into the sea. At least I think that's what her note says. It's all a bit ambiguous. I'm trying to keep calm, Nina,' Her voice caught. 'God knows I'm trying but I'm in great danger of screaming at you if you don't get yourself over here now.'

'Oh Jesus!' The doorbell rang and she yelled she was coming. 'We'll be right over.'

She opened the door to a surprised Alex, dragged him in and left him stranded in the living-room whilst she shot off into her bedroom, shouting out the news as she rapidly changed into jeans and trainers, tearing something vital on the dress in her haste.

'Sorry about dinner,' she muttered as she followed him downstairs. 'Just get me there, would you?'

'You bet,' he said, setting off before she had fastened her seatbelt.

Later, she was to remember nothing about the journey along lanes that were not meant for speeding, tearing into The Old Chapel with Alex in hot pursuit. Alex wanted to know if she had called the police but Julia said no, not yet.

He had his mobile and they needed to pinpoint where she was first, so it would not be a complete wild-goose chase.

'You know that beach on the peninsula,' Julia said, once they were in the car and wondering where to go. 'The one we used to go on when she was small. The horseshoe beach with the rocks round about it. She liked that. She might be there.'

'My God, I hope not,' Nina said, quickly instructing Alex, a relative newcomer, how to get there. 'That's Hell's Mouth beach, isn't it?'

Julia nodded, biting her lip.

'I've heard of that. It's supposed to be a death-trap,' Alex muttered in an aside to her, trying not to let Julia hear.

'Don't I know it?' she told him grimly. Everybody knew about it round here. A deceptively beautiful, lonely little beach but with a fast funnelling tide, the sort that sneaks in, leaving unwary people stranded on an ever decreasing spit of sand. Odd current, quicksands, you name it, Hell's Mouth had every bloody thing.

Julia's face very probably mirrored her own, the sheer terror starkly revealed.

Alex roared off.

The early evening summer sky was beautiful, lightly drawn wisps of pink amongst the blue. As they drove along the road that skirted the coast, the water in the bay was shimmering, the lowering sun reflected in it. Gentle ripples moved in a light breeze. It was a scene of great peace and calm, typical of one of Edward Grantham's sand pictures.

Nina comprehended it all in a blur, holding Julia's cold hand.

She dared not say it but the tide was starting to edge in.

20

At last, even though it was far too early to go to bed, Frankie could wait no longer.

She retrieved the letter from under her pillow and slowly opened the envelope, slipping out the sheet of paper. Just a single sheet?

My dearest Francesca, he had written,

It was wonderful to hear your voice again.

I have been sleeping badly; the baby keeps us awake much of the time, and Karen makes sure that she wakes me too when she is feeding Angela. She had a difficult birth but I stayed with her the whole time and . . . how can I say this? . . . the whole experience made me realize just what she means to me.

I cannot believe I behaved as I did. I know ours was a mutual attraction but I ought to have resisted the temptation because, let's face it, it was never going to come to anything. I think I knew right at the beginning that it was just a fling and that, when I came to my senses, I would tell Karen about it and beg her to forgive me.

Which she has.

It can't have been easy for her but she has a generous spirit. Angela looks just like her.

I can't leave them, which is why I've backed out of the seminar at Lancaster.

It's best if we never see each other again. I'm sorry but it is best. You will find someone else and be happy. I know it.

Good luck with your career. I won't forget you.

Love, Philip.

PS. I enclose a photo.

She let out a single sob before tearing it up. She picked up all the pieces, carried them to the bathroom and tried to flush them down the toilet. Bits continued to float in the pan and she tried again and again before they disappeared completely. Her eyes swimmy with tears, she then ran a basin of very hot water and plunged her hands into it, looking down at them, red below the water.

How dare he send a photograph? A happy, smiling, family photograph, with his arm round Karen's shoulders. Karen holding the baby, Karen looking pretty and contented and yes . . . triumphant. The little boy sitting on Philip's knee.

How could he?

A cold rage settled on her. After all her preparations, all the anticipation of what her visit to Lancaster would achieve, after all that . . .

Well, that was it.

Her life was ruined. She knew very well what people might say. A cheerful pat on the back. Plenty of fish in the sea, that sort of thing. Didn't they understand? Philip was her soulmate, the love of her life, and there would never be anybody else to compare. She might as well pack it all in now.

She scribbled a note to her mum, not really noticing what she was saying, leaving it on the bed for her to see when she came up. Then, she went downstairs, carefully avoiding the sitting-room where her mother was. She closed the door quietly behind her.

She needed time on her own. Time to sort herself out without prying, sympathetic eyes on her. She would go to Hell's Mouth beach. It was hard, very nearly impossible to get to, down a very steep path amongst the cliffs but it was so beautiful, if you made the considerable effort. You caught just a glimpse of the sands at first, then it opened out as you got lower and you could see its perfect horseshoe shape.

It was awesome and fascinating to watch from the top when the tide gushed in. It was like a steaming pan of water, bubbling, white-tipped and frothing, always angry water because it was short of space to gentle out. Whenever they used to come here, her mother was always anxious, telling them to check the tide, move back to the shore if it was coming in because, once it started, it whipped in far too quickly.

Dumped.

She had been dumped.

He had made a choice and it was not her.

All the things he had said. All the lovely things he had said to her. And his eyes had not lied. She knew he loved her. So perhaps, after all, he was being incredibly brave and noble, but that was no consolation. It should be Karen feeling like this. Karen had the children as her consolation and it would have been easier for her.

It was further than she thought to the beach and she wished for a second that Amy was here with her. She needed to talk to somebody like Amy, but Amy was not here and there was no going back to her.

The warning sign at the head of the path downwards declared it to be 'dangerous at

362

high tide'. Somebody had scrawled a figure on the board declaring the number of drownings. It made sober reading and Frankie paused at the top of the path, trying to peer down but seeing only the brambles and the vegetation close at hand. Stupidly, there was a handrail for the first few feet which seemed to invite you down, but when that disappeared you had to grab at shrubs and branches. Dislodging small stones and gravel as she moved down, she concentrated on the job in hand, rewarded at last at the halfway point by a view of the bay. The sands below varied from palest beige to a deeper brown, clean from the green-blue waters of the bay, and she saw that she would be the only person to have walked there today. The sea was far out, ebbing, she thought, a silvery ribbon with occasional sandbanks appearing.

At last.

She jumped down on to the beach and looked up now towards the top of the cliff down which she had just climbed. A long way. Rocks all around provided good vantage points and she remembered that they had sat on the rocks sometimes and watched the tide come in, amazed at the speed. One minute it seemed it was just starting to trickle and then — whoosh — it was funnelling in and round, filling up the edges with ever deepening water, leaving the centre undisturbed, sneaking round it, as the centre grew smaller and smaller until it was just a tip of sand surrounded by the fierce sea. One last gulp and it was gone. Many an unsuspecting person had been swallowed whole by that tide, to be regurgitated further up the coast.

'People make the mistake of thinking that there's no real problem,' her dad had told her. 'They think they can just wade through the water if it looks as though they're in any danger but they don't realize how deep it gets and how sloppy the sand becomes.'

She would not make that mistake.

She would not dream of walking on the beach at high tide.

She was safe now.

The tide was going out.

21

Jonty McKay would have a fit if he knew.

Clemmie was totally ignoring his wishes and putting feelers out, having a word in an ear, a particular ear.

The man was coming to tea and she was making a special effort. Mrs Harrison, who could do wonders in the kitchen when she put her mind to it, had made a selection of goodies, which were sitting on doilies on pretty plates on the trolley, protected from flies by a fine cloth. Clemmie peeped under the cloth, checking once more.

There were dainty white and brown sandwiches, smoked salmon, chicken-and-chutney, and cream-cheese with walnut, some of Mrs Harrison's peach scones, her delightful Victoria sandwich-cake, and a plum-and-almond torte.

It was a spread fit for a king or, more important, a lottery-winner.

She had met their lottery-winner, Mr Lockwood, just the once, when he brought his son along for the interview and she prided herself on having helped to put him at ease on that occasion. Jonty McKay was a bit of a snob and had been distinctly sniffy when the first approach was made via Mr Lockwood's newly appointed financial adviser. Clemmie had suggested that Jonty should say they were very nearly at full capacity in the boarding sector but they would be prepared to make an exception and fit him in somehow, also they would waive the usual entrance examination given the extreme circumstances. The boy was virtually unteachable, in grave danger of being excluded from his previous school, and the father had been at his wits' end before he picked the winning numbers and scooped the lot. A roll-about or roll-over or something.

He had made an excellent choice in Florey Park, Clemmie assured him, and his son . . . what on earth was the dratted boy's name? . . . his son would be given the very best education money could buy. A deposit of £500 would secure his place for the coming term. Unexpectedly, Mr Lockwood had promptly lifted a brand-new wallet from the pocket of his brand-new suit and counted out twenty-five crisp twenty-pound notes, asking for a receipt as he passed them over. She and Jonty had exchanged a bemused glance, contrasting it with the efforts they had to go to in some cases to prise out the cash. It was like getting blood out of a stone from some of the parents, particularly the richer and more influential ones, who seemed to be forever burdened by cash-flow problems and waited on final letters before coughing up.

Cash on the nail from Mr Lockwood.

And there was plenty more where that came from.

Clemmie wanted to surprise Jonty. She wanted to present him with a fait accompli, a handsome cheque that would solve their problems in a trice and they could then tell this man of Nina's to forget his plans and, in addition, stop the co-educational idea in its tentative tracks.

Mrs Harrison knocked and came in, hovering by the door.

'Everything all right, Mrs Scarr?' she asked. 'Do you want me to answer the door and show him in when he gets here?'

'Yes, please.' Clemmie wished she did not feel quite so nervous.

'Do you want me to put that cap and apron on?'

'Goodness, no. There is no need for that,' Clemmie said sharply, with the uncomfort-able feeling that Mrs Harrison was being deliberately mischievous. 'I think he will be favourably impressed. Thank you, Jean. You have excelled yourself today with the baking.'

'Hope he appreciates it,' Mrs Harrison said with a sniff. 'He might be more at home with bacon butties and some chips on the side.'

'Now, Mrs Harrison . . . ' Clemmie chided her gently.

'I hope I never win the lottery. You know that saying about a leopard not changing its spots. Well, it's a fact that is. You can't change what you are, Mrs Scarr. You can have all the money in the world, but underneath, you're just the same person you ever were.'

'Quite.' Clemmie glanced out of the window as a car drew up. A pale-blue Rolls. She watched as he climbed out. 'Here he is,' she said. 'Let the bell ring and make him wait just a few minutes before you answer it. And you can bring in the teapot after about quarter of an hour. That will give us time to have a chat first.'

She heard feet at last on the tiled floor of the hall, then Mrs Harrison knocked and showed the man in.

Clemmie rose to meet him with a smile. He was in his late forties, she judged, quite an attractive man with a fresh-air ravaged skin. Fair-haired and blue-eyed. She would bet he had been the bonniest babe.

'Nice to meet you again, Mrs Scarr,' Mr Lockwood said. 'Call me Eric, by the way, I don't stand on ceremony.'

'Oh, I see.' Taken aback, Clemmie was not sure what to say, could not bring herself to ask him to call her by her Christian name.

He smiled pleasantly, taking the point.

'This is not about Darren, is it, Mrs Scarr? Only he seems to be settling in quite well. I know it's early days after one term but he had a good report. Well, sort of good, better than he used to get, anyway. He likes it at Florey Park, Mrs Scarr, likes the individual attention he's getting. I hope you're not going to tell me that he's not fitted in.'

'Darren is a credit to the school,' Clemmie assured him, not having the faintest idea where Darren fitted into the scheme of things in the classroom. 'Do sit down . . . Eric. We'll be taking tea shortly, but in the meantime I hoped we might have a little chat. I always insist on doing this with the new parents. A little private chat without Mr McKay. He's a wonderful man but an academic,' she added with a knowing smile. 'Gifted but not always very practical.'

Mr Lockwood sat down on the elephant-print chair opposite her, glancing round the room and obviously finding it to his satisfaction.

'Quite nicely done,' he told her. 'Good detailing. I like the cornice. My line of business, or rather, it used to be.'

'Interior design?'

'No. Painting and decorating, not poncing

about,' he said with a grin. 'I've just had my new place done up. To be honest, I did think about doing it myself, you know where you are then, and I still have a discount card, so I can get things on the cheap. It's hard to get out of that habit, looking for bargains. Mind you, Mrs Scarr, they only made a moderate job of it. They charged a bomb, twice what I used to charge, and I could have done it better myself. They didn't prepare well enough. It's lucky I went round myself with the fine sandpaper or it would have been a right botch-up.'

'You've moved house then?' She adjusted her long, burgundy, pleated skirt which she wore with a pink tailored top, trying not to look at him. He was wearing a good suit, a light-grey three-piece, a white shirt and a discreetly striped tie and he, or somebody, had polished his shoes. He had gone to some considerable trouble, which she found rather sweet; it made her wonder what he had looked like before, as she tried to imagine him in working overalls.

'You bet I've moved house,' he said. 'But we're staying in the same area because we're used to it. It's a better district where we are now, facing the park. Lovely views. Just round the corner from where we used to live. Me and my wife.'

Clemmie smiled, wondering if she could ask where Mrs Lockwood was.

He told her anyway. 'We divorced a year before I won,' he said. 'To her credit, she hasn't come back asking for money.'

'I see.'

'Just as well,' he said. 'I wouldn't have given her any. It wasn't a happy split. We were at each other's throats. And she's got a new bloke and a new baby, so he can fork out.'

'Have you had lots of begging-letters?'

'Have I had begging-letters?' he chuckled. 'Chucked them all in the bin, Mrs Scarr. And if that sounds hard, I asked myself this: Did I write begging-letters when I was struggling to make ends meet, juggling money so that I wouldn't get the debt-collectors after me, saving a pathetic amount each month and feeling proud? Did I write begging-letters? Did I hell. So, why should they?'

'Five million is a lot of money,' she murmured.

'Five and three-quarters,' he corrected her. 'Nearly six. You're right. It is a lot of money. But I had financial advice. I've got investments now. Safe stuff and some a bit adventurous. I can afford a gamble you see. I'm not bothered about going abroad, don't like the sun much, but I'm thinking of buying a house in Scotland where we can spend the summer. A big house near a loch, somewhere with fishing rights.'

'How lovely for you. Were you advised to give some of your money to charity?'

There was a short silence.

'Charity begins at home.' He took a careful look round. 'I like this house. It's the sort of thing I would have liked but I couldn't face moving from the town where I live. I like it where I am. Bit of a stick-in-the-mud, I suppose. It's a detached house I've got now with a nice garden and conservatory. Double garage. Just the job for me. And I'm mostly on my own these days with Darren being at school during term time. It's not half quiet without him. Like a morgue.'

'It will be easier for him to settle in as a boarder,' she told him gently, feeling his loneliness. A millionaire, six times over, and he was lonely. Poor man.

'He likes boarding,' Mr Lockwood said, recovering himself. 'Like you say, it's better for him to get thrown in at the deep end. I've told him it's his last chance. If he spoils it, then it's his look-out. I'm not going to spoil him, Mrs Scarr. He'll have to work for his living. He'll get no hand-outs from me.'

This was not going to be easy. This man held his money in a tight grip.

'My late husband and I founded Florey

Park,' Clemmie began, determined to set him straight. 'I retain an interest in the school of course and I am more than happy to offer the occasional donation.'

'They were always on at you to give donations at the comprehensive Darren used to go to,' Mr Lockwood said. 'Bloody nuisance. The PTA kept that school going. Books and stuff. Crying shame, isn't it? Thank God it's not like that here. It's nice for him to be at a school that's not up the creek financially. Gives me peace of mind, that does.'

By the time Mrs Harrison had brought the teapot in and he had eaten his way through a good deal of what was on offer he had told her at great length about his ex-business, his ex-wife and the hopes he had for Darren.

And by the time he left she had somehow promised to keep a personal eye on Darren, reporting back immediately if he stepped out of line.

She saw him out, saw the pride in his face as she admired the car.

'My only extravagance. Well, you have to give yourself a bit of a treat, don't you?' He shook hands very firmly. 'It's been nice,' he said. 'Thanks for inviting me. And you know what the best thing was . . . '

'What was that, Mr Lockwood?' She

caught his amused look and quickly added:
' . . . Eric.'

'It's knowing that you invited me because
you wanted me to come for tea, like you do
with all the new parents, not because you
were after my money.'

She caught a twinkle in his eye.

Or was that her guilty conscience?

22

Frankie strolled along the beach near the water's edge. The sand here was darker and ridged and she took off her shoes and wriggled her bare feet in it, feeling the squelchiness of it and the slight grittiness as it oozed between her toes.

The smell was of seaweed, sea and salt. When she was little they had built sandcastles here, or Daddy had and she had helped him, carrying water in her little bucket, slopping most of it over the side before she got back from the rock pool. A thankless task. She would pour the water, what was left of it, into the moat round the castle Dad had built and it would just sink in at once, merely dampening the sand.

'Off you go for some more,' Dad would say cheerfully and off she would indeed go, hoisting up the bucket with her little hands, determination in her every step.

So long ago.

When she closed her eyes and listened to the sea, she tried to imagine she was back in Norfolk, walking along the beach with Amy, but the air was sweeter here, different, and, even with one of her senses shut down, she knew she was here and not there.

What to do now?

First thing, she had to do well in her exams, work really hard next term to make up for last year, and then off to university and . . .

Art and Design.

That's what she wanted to do. Beyond that, she was not sure exactly what she would do. Perhaps teach. She would like that. The family would like that. And then, eventually . . .

It was a shock to realize she was actually making plans in a fashion, plans that did not include Philip. If she had had any thoughts about walking into the sea and ending it, they had never been remotely serious. She couldn't do it for a number of reasons, but mostly because of her mother. Her mother was in a bad enough state as it was and that would have been the final straw.

Somewhere, up above, she could hear voices. Calling her name.

She stopped, looked round and up. Saw them waving and gesticulating.

Shit.

A reception committee.

Couldn't they leave her alone for a minute?

She waved back anyway because they had

seen her and it was too late to pretend otherwise.

She saw her mother setting off down the path, heard Nina yelling at her before she set off too, the man following them both. The path was only wide enough for one person and her mother was first in the procession. What a stupid idea! She might slip.

'I'm coming back,' she shouted, not knowing whether they could hear her. 'Stay there. I'm coming up.'

She turned to retrace her steps and it was then that she realized she had been dwelling on her thoughts for far too long. The tide, rather than going out, was certainly coming in, splashing and plopping at the edges of the rocks, already forming a little channel of water that she would have to stride over once she reached it.

And the sand under her feet was getting more and more sticky and heavy, her feet sinking that bit further with each step.

Panic hit her like a hammer.

'Mum!' she screamed.

23

Julia recognized the danger before the others, intent as she was on checking the tide. It was coming in at a slow trickle as yet but it wouldn't be long before it flooded in like a tap turned on full. Frankie was walking near the water's edge, her figure slight, looking almost like a boy from this distance.

'Frankie . . . ' she yelled, her voice carried away by the wind.

Down below, Frankie did not turn round, had clearly not heard.

'Bugger it, let's get ourselves down,' Nina called. 'Me and Alex. You stay here, Julia. It's too dangerous for you.'

Saying that to the mother of a child who was in danger was plainly ridiculous, and Julia ignored her, already starting down the path. It was dusty and crumbly after the recent dry spell and she dislodged a biggish stone which bounced off the path and tumbled down, gathering a few more as it did so, a mini-avalanche.

'Be careful,' Nina shouted. 'Don't fall, Julia. Let me get past you at least.'

'No time,' Julia said, concentrating fiercely

on putting one foot safely in front of the other. 'Where's the tide now?'

'Marooning her.' Nina's voice came breathily down. 'For Christ's sake, let Alex get past, he can go faster than you.'

Yes, that made sense. Julia paused, pushed back against a shrub, so that Alex could slide past Nina and then her before dashing down, indeed a lot faster than they could.

She was out of breath. And had a stitch.

'I have to . . . ' she stopped, bunched forward as the pain jabbed at her. 'Nina, I'm . . . '

'It's OK,' Nina was at her side, awkwardly drawing her a little further down where there was a blessedly wider bit of path and they could stand in reasonable comfort and take stock.

Frankie was shouting for her now, terrified, and Julia hardly dared look. She'd always been hopeless in an emergency, running out of the house in blind panic once when she had found their old dog having a fit on the dining-room floor. Running away as if that would somehow make things all right.

'Oh, Nina . . . ' she looked at her sister, saw her own horror mirrored in Nina's eyes. 'Oh, God. Call the police.'

'I've already done it,' Nina said. 'They'll be here in a minute and the fire brigade. Don't worry, they can use ladders and things. They'll get her out.'

'Perhaps Alex . . . ' Julia looked down and saw that he was almost at the beach where the channel of incoming tide had widened considerably to the size of a fat stream, leaving Frankie at its edge. 'She's sinking,' she said matter of factly. 'The quicksands.'

They could hear Alex now, authority in his voice, yelling at Frankie to lie down, spread her weight, see him throwing off his shoes, stripping quickly down to his underwear before plunging into the channel.

'Jesus!' Nina breathed raggedly at her side. 'They'll both go. What shall we do?'

Julia did not wait. She continued down the path, slipping now and sliding her way, Nina following, protesting all the while. She could see Alex struggling across the water to where Frankie was now half-lying on the sand, screaming for her — her mum — to help.

As she neared the last few yards, her feet lost their fragile grip and she found herself plunging down, hitting her side on a sticking out rock, winding herself in the process, ending up in a heap on the rock itself, just feet from the water's edge now.

'Frankie . . . ' she screamed. 'Hang on, darling. We're coming.'

'Julia . . . ' Nina arrived at her side. 'Are you all right?'

She brushed the question aside, too intent now on watching as Alex, having plunged through the water somehow started to yank Frankie out of the sand that was trying its damnedest to suck her down. They watched helplessly as he pulled her out and then hoisted her up before sending the both of them back into the sickeningly frothy water.

Frankie screamed.

Nina did too.

Julia was past screaming.

She closed her eyes.

Heard the hammering of her heart and, close at hand, the sound of a siren.

★ ★ ★

Tom's meeting with his new colleagues had ended later than expected.

He tried to ring Julia but there was no reply and her mobile was switched off, as it nearly always was. Not too worried, he stopped off in Greysands to do some shopping before the shops closed. They kept open longer in summer, for the benefit of the tourists. He knew the town reasonably well, as a twice-a-year visitor, but he managed to find a little side street he had not come across before. A bustling little street, quite steep, that reminded him, suddenly in the glorious sunshine, of another street in a northern Italian town. Sunshine did that to people. Brought out the best in them. People smiled at him. Passed the time of day with him.

The baby boutique was halfway up and he passed by it at first before doing an about-turn and marching in before he had time to consider what the hell he was up to.

'Lovely day!' The girl on duty put down her magazine and smiled. 'The forecast says it's going to be like this for the next couple of days and then it might break.'

Tom smiled back. He had had a variation of this conversation all the way from the car park. He hadn't bothered with a ticket — waste of time, Nina told him — because he had not expected to be more than ten minutes or so. He was not a shopper, had little experience, but he knew what he wanted so it should be a doddle.

'Something for a baby,' he said firmly, realizing it was a daft thing to say in a baby shop.

'Boy or girl?' The girl hovered. She had purple fingernails and a nose-stud which drew his gaze.

'Boy,' he said.

'Is he a big baby?' The girl was busily

pulling out a drawer containing white and blue outfits. 'I need to know the size roughly. How much does he weigh? Is he newborn? Or a few months old?'

'Oh. He's not here yet,' Tom said. 'He'll be here around Christmas.'

'I see. Well then . . . how about this?'

He ended up buying three little outfits, all in blue, so tough luck if it was a girl. Why had he done that? Walking back to the car, slowly, his purchases in a smart silver bag, he was reminded of that song from that musical, the one about 'My boy Bill' — great that — and he supposed he felt much the same as that guy had. It didn't bloody matter, one way or the other. Both well, baby and Julia, that was what mattered.

He had a damned lump in his throat the size of a bloody pea and it wasn't like him to get emotional, but somehow, with Julia being so uptight about it all, he had not really had the time to think about what it would mean, not properly. Frankie as a baby had scared him rigid because she had been so very small, but this time it would be different. A healthy full-term baby this time. He didn't want to see that panic again in Julia's eyes. He didn't want to feel so helpless himself either. It had been a tough time; leaning on each other like that had strengthened their marriage for a while and maybe this time it would do that too.

It had better. Things couldn't be much worse than they were just now.

He heard the siren as he reached the car park. Some poor sod in trouble.

And when he reached his car, would you believe it, there was a parking ticket stuck to the windscreen.

24

'Drowned? *Drowned?*'

'Oh, Tom . . . ' Nina was practically incoherent, hysteria firmly trapped in her voice. 'It's been just terrible.'

'Where did you say you were?' he asked, trying to grasp what she was saying. He had arrived home to an empty house, been worried then because of the state Julia was in, had seen the letter from Frankie lying on the table. He recognized the signs of a quick getaway: dinner half-prepared, various items of clothing lying around in the bedroom, not tidied away, so Julia had left the house in one helluva hurry. 'Calm down, Nina. Tell me where you are.'

She gasped out the name of the hospital.

'Julia had a fall, hurt herself, and what with the shock and everything . . . ' Her voice caught and she gave a little sob. 'Oh bloody hell, Tom, get yourself here quick. The doctor says there's a chance she might lose the baby and she'll need you here.'

'I'm on my way,' he said. He put the phone back in its rest and grabbed his keys. Should he ring Clemmie? Or would Nina? Perhaps it might be better if he broke the news to Clemmie? But then again, what did he know of it all? He only had Nina's almost incomprehensible explanation. Frankie had been on the sands at Hell's Mouth and been cut off by the tide. And this Alex guy, this man of Nina's, had tried to rescue her.

How often had he warned her when she was little about the dangers of that beach? It ought to be shut off, but then people would always find a way down and it was seductively inviting.

His heart was cold. Realizing that his hands were trembling, that he was in truth in no fit state to be driving at all, let alone a fair old distance, he set off at speed anyway. It was late and growing dark at last after such a bright beautiful day. On such a day as this . . .

Drowned?

He didn't know the man. Not at all. But he knew he was a youngish guy and that he had had a bit of a thing for Nina. That was good enough for him. What would he be able to say to his parents? How could he ever repay this man who had saved Frankie?

What was it with his lovely daughter? First, she had attracted the wrong man and very nearly wrecked his marriage and now she had caused a man to drown.

How must she be feeling? Poor darling.

And Julia . . . Julia who had witnessed it all, the shock cutting through to her very bones. He had felt that she was hanging on to this baby by a thread, that somehow the baby might guess his mother did not want him, that it would take nothing at all for him to slip away, that Julia would be mightily relieved if that happened.

The bag of baby clothes was still on the passenger seat and he knew now that it had been a mistake to buy them. Tempting bloody fate. She was nearly six months pregnant; if the baby did come now it would count not as a miscarriage but a premature birth, and they knew all there was to know about that.

It would be Frankie all over again. The agonizing. The holding hands over the cot in special care. The helplessness.

Things had improved in seventeen years. The success rate was higher.

Hang on in there, he found himself praying, feeling close to tears. God, just think that today they might have lost Frankie *and* the baby. If that had happened, he would have lost Julia too.

The journey passed in a blur. Thankfully, he got there in one piece, reversing rapidly into a space in the hospital car park, dashing in and locating the ward pretty damned quick. A distraught-looking Nina was there in the corridor, and Frankie was looking dazed.

He wrapped his arms round Frankie, looked over her shoulder at Nina, mouthed a question, dreading the answer.

Nina looked dreadful.

'It's going to be all right,' she said. 'You can go and see her. There was just a bit of bleeding but it's stopped and they think she'll be fine. They're going to keep her in overnight for observation but the baby seems undisturbed by it all. Heartbeat's all right.'

'Thank God,' he said, feeling Frankie trembling under his touch. He sat her down gently on the bench next to Nina. 'Tell me, darling,' he said.

His daughter looked at him, lip trembling, could not say anything.

'We don't know for sure how it happened,' Nina spoke for her, in control now. 'It was just a splash of limbs and shouts that we could hear. And then I saw Frankie half-lying on the rocks, washed up like a bin-bag. I had to climb down and drag her further up so that she wasn't swallowed up again. But Alex . . . ' she looked down, ran fingers through her hair. 'I shouted and shouted, Tom. I couldn't see him. I don't know where he went.'

He nodded, imagining the panic. You don't mess around with tides like that.

'I couldn't see him. I don't know where he went. I couldn't see him,' she repeated, tears in her eyes. 'The police haven't found him yet but they think he must have drowned.'

Tom took hold of Nina's hand, squeezed it.

'I'm so sorry,' he said, knowing it to be inadequate and foolish. 'What can I say?'

Nina shook her head, managed a little smile.

'Go and see Julia, Tom,' she said.

'Stay with me, Auntie Nina,' Frankie said, clutching her arm. 'Don't leave me.'

Tom left them sitting on the bench, Nina with her arm round Frankie, both of them staring unseeingly into the distance.

★ ★ ★

'I thought we were going to lose her,' Julia told him as he sat by her bed.

She was pale, of course, and very sad, but there was something else about her that he could not yet pinpoint. Something different and it wasn't just the hair, which he still couldn't get used to.

'I know, sweetheart,' he said. 'But we didn't. She's fine. None the worse.'

'Poor Alex. He was a good man. What man would do that without stopping to think? Launch himself into that water, knowing the danger, to save a girl he did not know. That's something I have to tell his mother. I must speak to his mother soon.'

'Why was Frankie there? She knows about the sodding tides.'

'She made a mistake. She thought it was going out. She wasn't thinking straight. She'd had a letter from that man telling her it was over. Finally, she believed that. She wasn't going to . . . she didn't mean to harm herself.'

'No, of course not.'

Her hand felt cool and light. Flimsy.

'I'm fine,' she said, smiling for the first time since he had entered the little private room off the corridor. They probably did not want her to be in one of the maternity wards with babies and new mums in case it was too much for her. 'We're both fine,' she added, looking down and stroking her stomach with a strange look, a tender look. 'What's wrong with me?' she went on. 'Does it have to take something like this for me to realize what is important and what's not? I've been so selfish. Why didn't you tell me how selfish I was being?'

'I tried to,' he said quietly, knowing this was not the time for recriminations.

'Something positive has to come out of this,' she said. 'Do you see? For Frankie and for us. We owe that to Alex. And we have to

390

help Nina come to terms with losing him.'

'Was it serious between them?'

She shook her head. 'I have no idea. I don't think so but it's not the sort of thing you can ask now, is it? She'll tell me soon enough. Does mother know? Has anybody thought to ring her? It will be all over the papers tomorrow. I haven't spoken to anybody but there's somebody from the press already been in touch, wanting a statement.'

'Leave all that with me. You're not well enough to talk to them yet,' Tom said, unable to stop a yawn. 'Do you know what time it is?'

She shook her head. 'Are you staying?'

'Of course. We're all staying. And then we can take you home tomorrow.'

'Oh Tom . . . what a thing to happen,' she said softly. 'What an awful thing. You don't think there's a chance he might be alive, do you? He could have swum for it, got further up the coast, he could be lying somewhere . . .'

He shook his head before he kissed her.

'Try to get some sleep, darling,' he said.

She felt light and fragile under his touch and she smelt of saltwater.

★ ★ ★

391

Another funeral.

Although Alex's mother had wanted her to be included with the principal mourners, as if she and Alex were engaged or something, Nina had insisted on being just another guest.

And that was how it should be.

His mother and father were the chief mourners, with his teenage boys, awkward in suits, and his ex-wife, uncomfortable and tearful, a little back from them, as befitted *her* position. There was no sign of the other man but, again, that seemed sensible.

Nina had no idea how she felt.

People kept asking her that.

Tom. Julia. Her mother. Mary.

She had no idea how she felt, other than terribly proud of him, of course. They were just starting out and she was not to know how it would have panned out. They had had one less than memorable night together but who knew, next time might have been better. They might have split up or they might have tried to make a go of it. Looking at the boys, his boys, she saw that one of them looked very like him, unnervingly like him, the other not so much. The ex-wife was dark and curvy under her dark-brown suit. A bit like her. So, maybe that's what he had been subconsciously searching for, a substitute for the woman who had left him.

392

Marian Lawson had insisted that they must all come along, including Frankie. She was not blaming Frankie, not blaming anyone.

'It's all about being in the right place at the right time,' she told Nina. 'Or the wrong place, whichever way you look at it.'

After the service at the crematorium they were all invited back to the Lawsons for the wake.

As usual, at these events, it all developed into rather a good party. Somebody had to be the first to laugh, stifling it as people glanced his way. But it broke the ice. And they began at last to talk about Alex. Nina found herself standing beside his ex-wife, was suddenly unsure whether she ought to be offering condolences, then found herself doing it anyway. Good heavens, the woman might have left him but she didn't want him dead.

'You must be Nina. I'm Sheila, Alex's ex-wife. Marian's been talking about you. Apparently, you and Alex . . . ' She had narrow blue eyes and for some reason Nina took an instant dislike to her, hating doing that on an occasion like this. Give the woman a break, for God's sake.

'We were just friends.' Nina told her hastily. 'It wasn't serious. Not for me anyway and I don't think for him. I don't know what would have happened.'

'I assume he talked about me. What did he tell you?'

Nina laughed nervously. 'I really don't think . . .'

'No, I want to know. I expect he told you that I left him. He liked to say that. It gave him a vulnerable edge.'

Nina nodded, uncomfortable with this but not seeing a way out just now as they were hemmed into a corner and nobody was going to disturb their cosy chat.

'I think you should know that he led me a merry dance,' Sheila said, lips pursed. 'And I'm only here now because of the boys. He couldn't keep his hands off other women. And I grew sick to death of it. And that's why I left him. There is no other man.'

'Should you be telling me this?' Nina asked, after a moment's painful silence. 'Remember, he saved my niece's life.'

'I'm sorry. I know he was wonderful to do what he did and it is just the sort of thing he would do, but Marian . . . ' she glanced towards her ex-mother-in-law. 'She makes him out to be perfect and he wasn't. That really gets up my nose, dead or not. I just wanted you to know that. Alex was full of flaws. It wouldn't have lasted with you. If that's any consolation.'

'Don't tell my sister any of this,' Nina said,

watching Julia across the room, talking animatedly with Marian. 'She's expecting a baby. It's all been a bit fraught. She needs to remember Alex as being perfect. To her, he is. It doesn't matter what else he did. He saved Frankie. And that's how I want to remember him too. If you'll excuse me . . . '

She knew that Sheila had only been trying to help, to ease the pain for her, had no idea whether she was speaking the truth but she wished she had not said what she had.

★ ★ ★

'Alex's company has pulled out of the Florey Park negotiations,' Nina said, sitting on the elephant-print chair. 'You'll be delighted to hear that, of course.'

'Yes I am,' Clemmie said, eyeing her carefully. 'Although I'm sorry it had to happen like this. I hope it isn't because he was drowned. I wouldn't have wished that.'

'No.' Nina shook her head. 'It's not because of that. His working partner favoured another location anyway and I think they had already made up their minds.'

Clemmie tried a tentative smile. It was difficult to know quite how to help Nina just now. The incident had had a tremendous impact on all their lives, on Frankie, Julia and

395

Tom — for the better in their case — and for Nina.

'I don't know how I feel,' Nina said, after a moment. 'If I'm supposed to be feeling devastated then it's not happening. I'm sorry for his family. His mother, particularly. But for myself, I feel I should be more affected. I feel . . . ' she paused. 'Mother, are you listening to me?'

'Of course, darling.' Clemmie sat up straighter. 'Finish what you're saying. I'm trying to think how to help.'

'And I'm just trying to think how I would have felt if Frankie had drowned.' Nina shuddered. 'I can't bear that thought. Or Julia or you. Or Harry . . . ' she added softly.

'Oh, I see. I can't say I'm surprised. Are you in touch still? Have you means of getting in touch with him?'

'Through his mother,' Nina said. 'We've kept vaguely in touch. I used to get on well with her and she still sends me a birthday card, would you believe? I could drop her a note, ask how she is, that sort of thing. Perhaps I could mention Harry.'

'You need to see him one more time,' Clemmie said. 'That will either have the effect of laying the ghost completely, or make you realize that for all his faults, he is the man for you.'

'Yes, but suppose I find out he's got married or he's in another relationship. Do I want to know that? How would I cope with that?'

'Very well, I think. You can't move on, Nina, until you've proved to yourself that it's over. Or otherwise.'

'What would you say if I went back to him? If he wanted me, that is?'

Clemmie laughed. 'I would say you were quite insane but a woman in love is insane in some ways anyway. I certainly was. And you forgive the faults. And, for heaven's sake, stop feeling guilty about Alex Lawson. Nobody made him do that. You couldn't have stopped him at that moment. Fate, darling. And take heart because men have always yearned for a hero's death. Like your father.'

'He was killed in a car crash. How is that heroic?'

Clemmie did not answer.

She had said quite enough.

25

'It's another girl then? You're sure about that?' Nina asked, standing in the middle of the room that would be the nursery.

'As sure as we can be,' Julia told her with a smile. 'From the scan it doesn't look like a boy anyway. I don't know if Tom was disappointed but he says not. And I'm not. I'm looking forward to having a baby girl.'

Julia sat down on the only chair in the room and let Nina do the thinking. She was quite happy to do that, to let somebody else take over the responsibility. She felt at last that she was coming out of the deep, scrabbling to the surface, and letting out a huge breath of relief. There was no point, as Tom said, of harbouring guilt and of course they all felt guilt. She took most comfort from Marian Lawson, who had dealt with it exactly as she hoped she would have dealt with it, given different circumstances. With dignity and pride. She had hugged Julia and then Frankie and whispered to each of them that it was all right.

When she got back from hospital she and Frankie had talked at last. Cuddled together.

She felt Frankie's pain at the way Philip had ended it but, because she was stronger herself, she suddenly found the right things to say, confiding in her daughter about how frightened she had been at finding herself pregnant. That fear had set everything off but it was gone now. Gone because she somehow knew that the baby, given the chance maybe to slip away, had chosen not to. She was staying put. This baby was a fighter as Frankie had been a fighter.

★ ★ ★

'Pink, I think.' Nina said, drawing her back to the present.

'Isn't that a bit naff.'

'No. I like pink. You can change it anyway in a few months if you like but for the start I think pale pink and lots of white. I know the very fabric for the curtains and there's a pretty wallpaper that will look great.'

'All right. Pink it is,' Julia said, determined not to argue. Mother had told her that Nina was going to get back in touch with Harry but so far she had not mentioned that fact to Julia and Julia was not going to press it. She hoped it was not a gut reaction because she had lost Alex, trying to return to the safety of another relationship, for that would be the wrong reason to want to try again.

'Cup of tea?' she asked as Nina fiddled about with her swatches book and her wallpaper samples.

'Oh yes. I'll do it.'

'No. I will. I'm fine, you know. You needn't treat me like an invalid. I've been thoroughly checked out and things couldn't be better and I feel a lot better too. I've got heaps more energy suddenly.'

When she returned with the tray, Nina had discarded her books and was sitting on the wide window-ledge, staring out towards the beach.

'It's going to be tough living round here,' she said quietly, as Julia poured the tea. 'I shan't be able to go for a walk on the beach any more without thinking of Alex and what he did. Nor will you or any of us. It will be just like Daddy all over again. Passing that spot in the road by the bend and always glancing down. It might be better if I move, Julia.'

Julia passed her a cup of tea. 'And that will make everything all right, will it?'

'Probably not. Why did you have to move? You said you would tell me.'

'I'm surprised Mother hasn't told you already. Perhaps she's more discreet than we give her credit for. The fact is . . . ' she took a breath. 'Frankie got involved with one of her teachers at school. He was married with a family. She thought he loved her but in the end he decided to stay with his wife and children.'

There was a silence.

'I thought it was something like that,' Nina said at last. 'Poor Frankie. But she's tougher than that, Julia. She's not going to top herself because some swine of a man ditches her. God, we've all of us had to cope with something like that . . . except you possibly,' she added with a smile.

'Are you going to contact Harry again?' Julia asked, feeling the moment was right to say it. 'Mother told me . . . ' she added with a smile. 'Sorry.'

Nina nodded. 'I've put things in motion. It was his mother's birthday so I've sent her a card and popped a note in it. If there's no reply at all then I suppose I can assume he doesn't want to see me again. I'm not getting my hopes up. And if we were to patch things up, he would have to do a lot of changing. Let me handle the finances for one. I wouldn't let him near a child's money-box in future.'

'I hope it works out,' Julia said, shifting in her seat as the baby kicked. 'If that's what you want, of course.'

★　★　★

It was what she wanted and, despite what she had said to Julia, Nina worried that she was putting too much importance on it. She was willing Harry to get in touch with her, praying that he had not found a soulmate in the meantime; she would come down to earth with a thud if he had done that. There had been a card at Christmas from his mother but not from him, which was faintly ridiculous. No mention of Harry getting married, but then she wouldn't, would she?

At the shop Mary was tiptoeing round her as if she was made of shells, never mentioning Alex after the initial horror of it all. It had been spread in the papers as drownings always are, extra special because of Frankie, Alex branded a hero, which he was.

At last Nina could stand it no longer.

'You can talk about it, Mary,' she said. 'In fact, it might help if you did. The truth is his dying has put me in a very strange position.'

Mary looked at her uncertainly. 'What do you mean?'

'It's made people assume that, because we were seeing each other, we were just about to get engaged or something. And we were not.'

'But you did like him? He put a smile on your face.'

'Well . . . it's a long time since I had a bit of a fling and it always puts a smile on your face, doesn't it?'

'I wouldn't know,' Mary said with a grimace. 'Believe it or not, I've never had one.'

'No, of course not. But I wish people wouldn't keep looking at me as if I were the grieving widow. I'm not. I'm just really sorry that he's dead. I thought he was nice.'

'So did I,' Mary said. 'A twinkle in his eye. One for the ladies, I should think.'

'Yes, well . . . ' Nina would not be drawn into that. 'I was worried about his children, Mary. I wouldn't have wanted to take that on and I don't suppose he would have wanted another baby and that's one of the important things to me just now. Especially now Julia is pregnant.'

The shop bell jangled and Mary went to answer it, returning after a moment, slightly puzzled.

'A man's asking for you,' she said.

'A man?' Nina felt her heart thud, knowing at once who it was, sensing his presence in the other room. Her hand went up to her hair. 'How do I look, Mary?'

'Fabulous . . . ' a voice said, a man's voice. She looked to the work room door and saw Harry standing just inside it, calm as you like.

'Just happened to be passing . . . ' he said with a grin. 'And if you believe that, you'll believe anything.'

'Mary, would you mind?' Nina held on to the counter-top, did not quite dare to look at him, not fully, the briefest glimpse confirming that he still looked as annoyingly attractive as ever, hair a little shorter, perhaps.

She took him up to the flat.

'Ah, Venice . . . ' he said, nodding towards the glass.

'My mother is on cloud nine. She's determined to get us back together,' he said. 'Don't blame me for this.'

'So it wasn't your idea, then?' she asked, disappointed. 'You're just doing this to please your mother.'

'Bollocks!' he said.

The same old Harry.

'Well . . . ' He stared at her, a slow up-down gaze. 'Well, well . . . how are you doing, Scarr face?'

'All right. The business is doing great,' she said. 'And don't call me Scarr face. You know how I hate it.'

'Sorry. Old habits die hard.'

'Exactly,' she said drily. She wanted him to touch her. She could not stop a glance at his face, his mouth, wanted to feel his breath on her cheek, the soft brushing of his lips on hers.

'God, I want to hold you,' he said.

'Wait!' She held up her hand. 'There's a lot to say, Harry. Why did you let me go? Why didn't you come after me? That's what I expected you to do. I didn't think you would give up so easily.'

'Give up?' He laughed. 'You cut through me, Nina. You wanted me out of your life and what the hell could I do? I had to let you go if that's what you wanted. And I didn't steal your money,' he added bitterly. 'I was just a bit loose with it, that's all.' He glanced round the room. 'Is it me or is there a tension in the air? Angry vibes? If you want me to leave, you only have to say.'

She shook her head, watching as he sat down, moving a heap of cushions, watching him and wanting to go to him and stroke his hair and hold his head against her breast.

'Since you left I've been working like a demon trying to get things together again,' he went on, avoiding looking at her now. 'Business-wise. I've finished a few pieces.'

'A few pieces?'

'It's not a production line,' he reminded her. 'They are hand-crafted with love and sweat and more than a few tears, I can tell you. You can't get my stuff from DFS.

Hand-crafted and that's why they cost an arm and a leg.'

'Have you sold any?'

He nodded. 'One definitely and somebody's looking at a chest. And a Middle East gentlemen who's just bought a pad in London is on the look-out for one-offs. He's asked to see a few things. If I can get him interested we'll take off.'

'So you're still based in London?'

He nodded. 'That's where the contacts are, darling.'

'Don't call me darling, not unless you mean it.'

'I do mean it. I've told you I was a fool to do what I did and if I let you go again when I know from your face that there's still a chance, then I'm an even bigger fool.'

'And . . . ?' she said, not quite knowing how to deal with this. She loved him like this. Anger in his eyes, his body tense. She loved him, damn him, in whatever mood he was in. And if she had ever doubted it, seeing him again had kicked all those doubts into touch. 'And . . . ?' she repeated.

'And what? That's as much of an apology as you'll get, Nina. Take it or leave it.'

'Why should I believe a single word you say after what you did to me? You are one bad bet, Harry,' she told him, the warmth in her

406

heart betraying the cold words. 'Still too cocky by half.'

'Maybe I am,' he said, his voice gentling. 'Or maybe I'm like this because I don't know what the hell I am going to do if you give me my packing orders. I've built up my hopes, sweetheart. Have you forgiven me? Can you forgive me? Can we start again? Oh bloody hell, I've rehearsed all this, what I would say to you but now . . . looking at you, all I want to do is kiss you. How I need to kiss you. How I've missed you. Nights. Days. All the time. I love you. Only you.'

She looked at him.

No doubts in his eyes either.

She held out her arms as he came across to where she was sitting. Let him raise her to her feet.

'I must be stark staring mad,' she said, unable to stop her smile.

'We both are. Crazy,' he said softly, drawing her close.

Why was it, when it came to the crunch, common sense and caution went right out of the window? Why was love so impossible to decipher? Why had she known all along with Alex that it was never going to work?

She and Harry.

A definite item.

'One more chance,' she told him, as they

surfaced. 'And you'd better not let me down this time.'

'I will never let you down again,' he whispered. 'Never.'

26

The local burglars would have slavered to see the sight. Clemmie with all the jewellery out, showing it to Frankie.

'It's to be divided up between the three of you,' she told Frankie, as they examined the collection piece by gorgeous piece. 'You, your mother and Nina. My three girls.'

'What about the baby?' Frankie asked. 'She's a girl too.'

'Of course. I shall have to make a codicil. Although I think we may have to wait until she is born, just to be absolutely sure those doctors have not made a mistake and not noticed his little penis.'

Frankie laughed. 'Granny, you are priceless.'

'Being able to know the sex of your child before it arrives is quite the worst thing to have come out of modern technology. Unnatural,' Clemmie went on. 'I'm so glad I did not know until the very moment of birth.'

'But think of the practical side. It makes it much easier to do up the nursery and buy the layette.' Frankie said cheerfully. 'We're doing it in pink.'

'What a surprise! And how unexciting. I would have expected something different from Nina, but then she's hardly herself these days, poor sweet. She's pining for that Harry of hers. Always has been, in fact, but she's managed to keep him at arm's length until now.'

Clemmie looked at her granddaughter fondly. Francesca had come through all this with some credit, showing the correct remorse, of course, for poor Alex's demise but not allowing it to cloud her future. She would never forget what happened, never forget the man who had given her a second chance, but she would get on at last with her life and Philip was now discarded like the damp squib he had proved to be.

'Are they going to go co-educational at Florey Park?' Frankie asked her. 'What a shame I couldn't go there this next year. I would have liked that.'

'It's in the balance,' Clemmie said. 'I tried to get the lottery-winner . . . oh drat, I think it's supposed to be a secret. Did you know we had a lottery-winner's son at school?'

She nodded. 'It's not much of a secret. Dad told me. I don't know his name or anything like that. Dad says he's going to be a challenge.'

'I should say so. But we'll do it. You'll see.

Anyway, Mr Lottery-Winner refused to give us a donation . . . God in heaven, a million wouldn't have hurt him. A mere pittance.'

'He refused?'

'Well, not quite. I was just in the process of asking him for a donation when he turned the conversation round and it became an impossible situation. I revise my opinion of him. I think he's rather clever. He put me in a position where I couldn't ask without losing face. And Jonty refuses to accept any more help from me so he's backed himself into a corner. You must never do that, Frankie: get yourself into a corner. Always make sure there's an escape route.' She stopped suddenly, remembering the sands and the way Frankie had been trapped there. Foolish thing to have said.

Frankie did not seem to notice. She was fingering a diamond bracelet, holding it up to the light so that the sparkles reflected there, glints of blue and red and yellow.

'Beautiful, isn't it?' Clemmie said softly. 'Your grandfather bought me that for our silver wedding anniversary.'

'Wasn't that wonderful?' Frankie's eyes shone. 'You were so lucky to have him.'

'Yes. I was.' Clemmie recovered all the jewellery, scooped it back into the bags and replaced it in the safe she kept in her

411

bedroom. 'Let's go and have a coffee, darling. You can make it and cut some slices of that ginger cake Mrs Harrison has made. We shall have a little picnic, like we used to do when you were small. We'll eat outside, shall we?'

'OK.' Frankie leapt up and they set off downstairs. The phone rang as they were half-way down. 'I'll get it,' Frankie said. She dashed down the last few steps and rushed into the hall where the phone sat on the semicircular polished table, beside a vase of sweetpeas. 'It's for you, Granny,' she announced, not unexpectedly, holding out the instrument until Clemmie completed her careful descent. 'Your friend Dilys.'

'Clemmie, dear . . . ' Dilys's voice trilled over the line. 'Are you sitting down?'

'No. Should I be?'

'Perhaps. I'm so sorry to break bad news over the phone, dear, but it's Edward. Edward Grantham.'

'Edward? What's happened?'

'Dead, darling.'

'But he was all right when I last saw him,' Clemmie said stupidly. 'He was going to visit Scotland for a few days. Fishing.'

'Quite. That's where he died apparently. In his sleep, it would seem. Peacefully anyway. There's a nephew in New Zealand who's seeing to the arrangements. They'll be

412

auctioning off the furniture. Someone from the auctioneers will be having a look round tomorrow as far as I know.' She paused, sighed. 'Isn't it sad? I don't believe he had any real friends other than me and you, Clemmie. I knew you would want to be told.'

'Thank you.' Clemmie replaced the receiver without any further ado. Dilys would put it down, not to rudeness, but to her being upset. Which she was, in a strange way. The dratted man had made her do all that posing over all these years. It was a wonder she had not contracted pneumonia as a result, and yet she still felt a sadness.

The nephew in New Zealand would be on his way by now, no doubt, and before he arrived and, more important, before the man from the auctioneers arrived, there were things she had to do.

'Are you all right, Granny?' Frankie asked, getting the gist of things as she had listened in to her grandmother's side of the conversation. 'Is it bad news? Do you want a glass of water?'

'No. I want you to drive me into Greysands immediately. I have to go to Edward Grantham's house straight away. The man's gone and died up in Scotland. How inconvenient!'

Frankie looked at her oddly. 'I can't drive you.'

'Why not? You've had lots of lessons, haven't you? Nina says you're waiting for a test date.'

'Yes, but I haven't passed it though,' Frankie said, worry in her eyes. 'It's against the law to drive with just a provisional.'

Clemmie sighed. 'I know it's illegal, darling, and we'll be in the most terrible trouble if we're found out but it's a matter of life and death. To the family. There's something dreadfully important I have to do at Edward's house. Your mother and Nina must never find out.'

'What about Mr Harrison? Doesn't he usually drive you?'

'He's away and I wouldn't ask him anyway. This is very delicate.'

'Can't we call a taxi?'

'Not for what we have to do. Francesca Clementine Scarr Vasey . . . ' Clemmie drew herself up, looked her granddaughter firmly in the eye. 'If we're pulled up by the police, I shall fake a heart attack and you will tell them that you are taking your beloved grandmother to the doctor's. We shall get away with it. Now . . . where are the dratted car keys?'

★ ★ ★

Frankie drew the car to a halt outside Edward Grantham's house. She felt quite sick at what

414

she had just done, although she had accomplished it without a hitch. Her instructor would have been delighted with her.

'Well done!' Clemmie told her with a smile. 'Perfectly driven if a little over-cautious. Now, come with me, darling. We shall have to break in.'

'Granny!' Frankie banged her hands on the steering wheel, looked across at Clemmie who was looking composed. 'What *are* you talking about? Mr Grantham's dead, isn't he? Why are we breaking into his house? And what if somebody sees us.'

'Nobody will,' Clemmie said dismissively. 'Nobody can see round the back of the house and he always leaves his utility-room window ajar. You'll have to climb on to the dustbin to reach it, though, and then on to the washing-machine. Can you do that, darling? I would do it myself but my days of climbing through windows are regrettably over.'

Frankie, though utterly bewildered, had no option but to follow her grandmother round to the back of the house, where there was indeed an enclosed courtyard with no prying eyes peeping through lace curtains. The window was ajar but it did mean doing a balancing act on the bin and somehow manoevring herself through the window to land on the tumble-drier, not the washing-machine, and then to get herself down on to the floor. Once that was accomplished it was a simple job to find the door keys, hanging on a convenient hook, and open the door for Clemmie, who sailed through as if it were the most normal thing in the world.

'This is really awful,' Frankie muttered, following her upstairs. The house was cool and silent and it felt very strange, knowing that its usual occupier was dead. A peep into a bedroom revealed a neatly made single bed and huge ugly pieces of furniture. 'Where are we going? What are you going to do, Granny?'

'Blast.' Clemmie had reached a door on the upper floor and discovered it was locked. 'There'll be a key somewhere. Have a look downstairs, darling. I really don't think we are capable of bursting the door open with our shoulders, do you?'

Hastily, Frankie went back downstairs, frightened of somebody knocking at the door and their having to explain their presence. What on earth had got into her grandmother? Finding a batch of keys, she took the lot upstairs with her and, sure enough, one of them fitted.

'Now, darling . . . ' Clemmie opened the door, stepped into the room. 'Before we go any further, let me explain that Edward was

416

an amateur painter and this is his studio. He had rather a grandiose view of his capabilities, thought he was on a par with Leonardo da Vinci. He liked to paint the female nude.'

'Mr Grantham?' Frankie was astonished. She had seen his sand pictures in Auntie Nina's shop, which she thought were pretty ordinary.

'I was his only model,' Clemmie sniffed. 'There are some paintings of me that I do not wish anybody else to see. Do you understand?'

The room had an unfinished look about it, bare floorboards, not sanded and polished, and blinds at the windows. An easel and a huge assortment of paints and brushes were in a corner and, piled against one wall, were heaps of paintings. Opposite the easel there was a chaise longue draped in velvet and other remnants of material.

'Granny . . . ?' Frankie peered at the half-finished painting on the easel. 'It's you.' She felt herself blushing because her grandmother had no clothes on and was reclining on the chaise longue. It was a very good likeness and it was a beautiful study, Frankie knew that, but it was just so embarrassing and so totally unexpected.

'They're all of me,' Clemmie told her crisply. 'Every last one. I want them destroyed, Frankie, before anyone else sees them. We'll burn them. We shall take them back to Rosemount and have a bonfire before Harrison gets back tomorrow. We'll load them into the car now. We can drape material over them.'

'There are over thirty,' Frankie said, doing a quick count.

'That's right. I have no idea how long proper painters take to paint a picture but I always thought him terribly slow. He managed two a year at best. One sitting a month. Sometimes, it was as if he just did a couple of brushstrokes a session. He used to drive me quite mad. Just as well he was slow, I suppose, or we'd have been dealing with hundreds.'

'What if somebody sees us loading them into the car?' Frankie said, feeling she had to be the practical one since her grandmother seemed to have taken leave of her senses. 'And why do we have to burn them, Granny? They're beautiful.'

'We have to burn them for your grandfather's sake and your mother and Nina. I don't want them to know what I have had to do. What your grandfather had to do too. And you can bring the car up the side alley so that nobody will see. And if they do, I'm a friend of Edward's and they will not query it. I shall say I have his permission to dispose of some items to the hospice charity shop. Nobody will dare query that. Anyway, nobody except Dilys knows he's dead yet.'

'You're asking me to bring the car up the side alley?' Frankie sighed. 'It's not a tight turn, is it?'

'I think it is and you'll have to reverse in a straight line.'

'It's my worst thing — reversing,' Frankie said. 'I go all over the place.'

'Oh come on, darling.' Clemmie clicked her tongue, gave her a look that Frankie remembered from long ago. 'This is an emergency. We can't leave them here for the long-lost nephew to find.'

It would be comical if it weren't so important and serious. Carefully, very nearly with her eyes closed at one point, Frankie reversed the car, bigger than the one she was learning in, down the side alley, managing somehow to get it there without bumping into either of the walls. She then took on the job of carrying the paintings downstairs, at speed, and out to the car, where Clemmie bossily told her where to put them.

At last, it was done.

'Now you just have to get us back to Rosemount in one piece and we can have a bonfire,' Clemmie said, as they set off. 'And then, darling, we'll have a gin and tonic to celebrate.'

'I don't drink gin and tonic.'

'Time you did. I want to tell you all about this and I want you to promise me, on your grandfather's grave, that you will not tell anybody about it. Ever. Just think about the timing of all this. It's worked out perfectly. It was meant to be, Frankie, that you and I should share a secret like this.'

Concentrating fiercely on her driving, Frankie got them home safely. She helped her grandmother to unload the paintings and carry them to the compost area of the garden where Mr Harrison had his bonfires. It was only as they began to burn that she felt her grandmother relax at last.

Frankie was riveted to the spot, watching the flames taking hold, the paintings beginning to curl, heaped on top of each other, falling into each other as the fire raged. They had to stay a while to make sure that the fire did its job. Frankie raked through the last of them as the fire died.

'Let's go indoors,' Clemmie said, her voice strange. 'Such a bore. My eyes are stinging and my throat is catching.'

★ ★ ★

Frankie did not drink or smoke. What was the youth of today coming to? Clemmie poured herself a hefty gin with a splash of tonic and seated herself on Anthony's chair with Frankie more at home on the floor. Clemmie was exhausted yet exhilarated. She had dreamed of this moment but had never imagined that she could have been so decisive and so successful in what she had to do.

'Thank you for that, darling,' she told Frankie. 'You've excelled yourself today. I don't know how I would have handled it on my own. And it was so important that nobody saw those paintings. You do see that, don't you?'

'Not quite.' Frankie sighed. 'I suppose they embarrass you and I would probably feel the same but they were very good paintings. It seems . . . criminal . . . to burn them.'

'When I was your age,' Clemmie began, taking a sip of her drink and placing her tired legs on a footstool. 'I was like you. Beautiful. And Edward was a few years older. I rather liked him. He had money of his own so he wasn't after mine and my mother pushed me into an engagement. That used to happen then. We weren't given quite the free rein you are today.'

'Free rein?'

Clemmie ignored the comment. 'I was so

innocent and it did not dawn on me for a long time that Edward was not particularly interested in sex. Although he was an accountant, he was only really interested in painting. And when he asked me to pose for him, without clothes, I did so.' She took another sip of her drink, smiled across at her granddaughter. 'Then I met your grandfather and fell in love properly and behaved dreadfully after that towards Edward. The sittings stopped instantly. Simply because I could not bear the thought of any man other than dearest Anthony seeing me like that.'

'Granny . . . ' Frankie shifted position, a blush on her cheeks. 'You needn't tell me this if it upsets you.'

'It does upset me but I have to tell you, dear. I have to tell somebody. I've kept it secret for too long and I have to unburden myself. We had a wonderful marriage but I never knew how much it mattered to Anthony that I was the one with the money. And it never occurred to me to wonder where the money came from, out of the salary he paid himself, for all the beautiful jewellery he gave me. I think I half-suspected, but I preferred not to know the truth. The truth was he was embezzling it from school funds. He had been at it for years and nobody had guessed. It was rather cleverly done. And then our old accountants retired and we were passed over to Edward and it was Edward who quickly worked it out. He accused Anthony and Anthony confessed. Simple as that.'

'Embezzling? Grandpa? I can't believe it,' Frankie said.

'If it had come out, it would have been a disaster for us. For the Scarrs. For me and for your mother and Nina, who think the world of him. And it was then that Edward started to blackmail us. He would keep it under his hat, sweep it under the blessed carpet and so on but there were conditions attached.'

'What conditions?' Frankie said.

'I didn't know it but Edward spoke to Anthony and told him that if he were to make himself scarce — those were his words — then he would look after me for evermore and keep the scandal under wraps, also for evermore.'

'Make himself scarce? What did he mean?'

'I'm not sure but Anthony took it to mean that Edward was offering him the heroic way out. Handing him the sword. When he went out in the car that day, the day of the accident, he knew perfectly well that it was the last time he would see me. That's why he said goodbye.'

'You mean, he deliberately drove the car

over the cliff?' Frankie asked in a small voice. 'Oh Granny . . .'

'I know. It was very hard. After all those years together, it was very hard.' Clemmie heard her own voice breaking, took a breath and another sip of drink to steady herself. 'But Edward was not finished. In a fit of rage when I broke off our engagement, he had destroyed or painted over the earlier paintings of me. Since then, with nobody to pose for him, he'd had to make do with his dratted scenes and copying from other paintings.'

'He asked you to pose again?'

Clemmie nodded, closing her eyes a moment and putting a hand up to her forehead. 'He offered me the choice of doing that or going to the local paper. What choice did I have?'

'You could have called his bluff. You both could have. You needn't have done it.' Frankie tried a nervous smile. 'We would have survived. The family.'

'Why do you think they moved you up here? Your mother and father? Because it was best for you, of course, but there's another reason. There's something of me in your mother. The same values. I wanted you to know about this, darling, to help you see things in a new light. Your own little problems might not seem quite so important now. And, at last, I am free too. Now that *he* is gone.'

* * *

'Good news, Clemmie,' Jonty McKay said, fussing her into the chair in his office and indicating a letter lying on his desk. 'Mr Lockwood has given us a donation for school funds.'

Clemmie smiled. 'There you are then. What did I say? A word in an ear, a particular one, was all that was needed. So much for that nonsense about going co-educational.'

'Ah!' Jonty grinned back. 'So you did ask him for a sub. Thought you must have. You are wasting your efforts I'm afraid. We're quite determined to do it. Bring girls in. For a number of reasons. You're on your own with this ridiculous opposition, Clemmie. What do you expect from Lockwood? A million?'

She glanced at the letter. 'How much?' she asked.

'Five hundred pounds. Sizeable, you have to admit, and most welcome but hardly your million.'

She managed a tight smile, remembering to be gracious in defeat. The relief she was feeling now that Edward Grantham was gone was having the required effect of making her more agreeable to this fanciful scheme.

'Perhaps you are right after all,' she told a surprised Jonty. 'Perhaps I was a little high-handed. Girls can be a steadying influence on young boys. My granddaughter is seventeen and a treasure. And I would much prefer to see girls at Florey Park than to see half its grounds covered in houses.'

'Me too,' Jonty said with a sigh. 'Bad idea that. Pity about the bloke who drowned though. Wasn't he a friend of your daughter's?'

'Yes, more of an acquaintance really. She has taken up with her ex-fiancé once again. Blissfully happy. He's a rogue but he makes her happy, so there you are. What can a mother do, Jonty?'

'Are they remaining here? In Greysands?'

'Yes. Nina has laid out a set of conditions,' Clemmie said approvingly. 'Wise girl. She will not be letting him loose with any money that's for sure. And I have to say he is extremely talented. He makes furniture. Antiques for the future. Harry Jennings, a name to remember.'

'Sorry to hear the news about Edward Grantham,' Jonty said, puffing on his cigarette. 'Popping off like he did. I thought we might buy one of his sand paintings for the library. We ought to be seen to be supporting local talent. What do you say?'

'If you wish,' Clemmie said.

'Isn't it his funeral today?' Jonty glanced at the clock. 'Aren't you going? It's not like you to miss a good funeral, Clemmie.'

'I am not going,' she told him. 'Personal reasons. Dilys Plowright is representing me.'

'I see,' he said, although clearly he did not. Happily, he stubbed out his cigarette. 'Things are looking up at last. I think we can always rely on Lockwood for the odd top-up and when we get the new brochure out we'll have the girls flocking in next September. You will be at the open day giving your support as usual, Clemmie?' he asked, a trifle anxiously. 'I hope to God I didn't upset you when I said — '

'Not at all,' she interrupted, saving him the bother. 'You were quite right. I should step back a little now, Jonty. Frankly, I am tired and I have my granddaughter living near and both my daughters, so I have much to occupy myself with. You may call on me whenever you feel the need and of course I wouldn't dream of missing the open day.'

★ ★ ★

She thought she had handled that rather well.

Passing Anthony's picture in the school hall, she paused and glanced up at him.

She hoped, if Edward was up there with him, in heaven or whatever approximated to it, that Anthony would give him what for, reduce the man to a gibbering wreck. It was all he deserved. If he had ever loved her and she even doubted that, then he had a very odd way of showing it.

As for Anthony, he had paid the ultimate sacrifice to save the family name. Had it been worth it? And had he read a meaning into Edward's words that was never really intended? She could not quite believe Edward had meant Anthony to kill himself, his face at Anthony's funeral, his futile attempts to console, were proof of his shock.

Being noble was all very well, but Anthony had deprived her much too soon of a husband, the girls of a father. Would it have been better if the world had known him to be less than perfect? Would it have harmed Julia and Nina to have known that their father was an embezzler, a cheat?

So many questions.

And nobody to answer them.

Not yet anyway.

'You were a proud fool, my darling.' she told him gently, reaching out a hand and resting it on the portrait.

She stepped outside into the sunshine and stood quite still for a moment, eyes closed, savouring the warmth of the sun on her aged face, feeling something tugging at her, almost imploring her to stay and yet something else was drawing her on.

It was not over yet.

Briskly, she walked down the drive.

Not looking back.

Epilogue

The photographer, a wild-haired, keen-eyed, thirty-something woman wearing loose white cotton, fussed them all into what she deemed to be the best grouping. She charged the earth, as Clemmie could verify, and was therefore a perfectionist. It took an age to get them all into the most satisfactory position, which was enough to cause the more excitable members of the family, namely baby Antonia and her adoring Auntie Nina, to fidget. Clemmie, used to posing long and still, retained her seat and expression, as all around lost theirs.

At last, and not before time, they were assembled and the earnest photographer was challenged at last to do the deed.

'Are you all ready?' she said, for what seemed to Clemmie to be the umpteenth time. 'That looks absolutely super. If you could just fold your hands in your lap, Mrs Scarr, and Mrs Vasey, could you turn the baby just a little to face me . . . ?'

'Just take it, *Miss* Whitlock,' Clemmie snapped, losing patience with the dratted woman. 'Or we'll be here all day.'

Fortunately, her impatience did not show in the finished photograph, which, in a silver frame of course, was to take pride of place on her mantelpiece at Rosemount for years to come.

Clementine, the matriarch, looking elegant as always in black velvet, with Julia holding the baby on her right and Nina on her left. Standing behind the front group were Tom and Frankie, both smiling broadly and, looking bemused to be included in the family group, but behaving himself as instructed, Nina's Harry.

'Lovely idea, a family photograph,' Julia said, once the photographer was gone and they could resume their family Christmas. 'Good of her to come today.'

'I bribed her, darling,' Clemmie said. 'Made her an offer she couldn't refuse. May I hold Antonia?'

'Of course.' Julia passed the baby over, smiling as she did at Nina, who was enraptured with the little soul. She couldn't get over how quickly Nina and Harry had drifted back into their old relationship, as if they had never been apart. Alex was rarely mentioned, although she was sure that they had all thought about him when they attended the Christmas service in church.

Frankie and her mother seemed close these

431

days, which was nice. She had caught them the other day, huddled in a corner, giggling about something — something to do with Frankie's driving. She had failed two driving tests now, poor love, having made a complete botch of the reverse on each occasion, but there was always the next time.

'Here, let me take her,' Julia said, whipping Antonia up as she started to fret in her grandmother's arms. She carried the child over to the window, newly curtained in one of Nina's more outrageous fabrics, and stared out at the wintry scene. A frosty day, sparkling like the champagne they had just toasted Antonia with, the trees ghostly in their nakedness, frozen catkins hanging like icicles above a garden statue.

'Anyone for a walk?' Nina called.

'You must be joking,' Harry said. 'It's below freezing out there.'

'Just a thought,' she said, not putting up much resistance.

Tom huddled further into the sofa by the fire and grinned at Julia.

'Come here and sit by me. *The Great Escape* is on in a minute.'

'Not again,' she grumbled, going to join him anyway and gently dumping his new daughter on his lap. 'Your turn,' she said. 'And then we'll put her down for a nap.'

Opposite them, Clemmie was looking very comfortable in her chair, the elephant-print one, and Frankie was lounging, as she often did, at her grandmother's feet.

This was more like it, Julia thought happily, as the chocolates were passed round and the stirring music of the film began. As usual, they would miss half of it, talking amongst themselves, getting up to make a cup of tea, Nina would suggest they play a game and everybody would howl her down, the baby would need changing and feeding, Mother would eventually bring up the subject of Dad, reminiscing about Christmas past.

They would then raise their glasses to him as they always did and that usually brought a sniffle from somebody.

All the usual stuff.

The same with all families, a hotchpotch of shared memories, shared disappointments, shared joys.

For a minute, Julia wished she could take a photograph of this moment.

The photograph they had just had taken was the Scarrs on show.

But this was how they really were.

Warts and all.

We do hope that you have enjoyed reading
this large print book.

Did you know that all of our titles
are available for purchase?

We publish a wide range of high quality
large print books including:
Romances, Mysteries, Classics
General Fiction
Non Fiction and Westerns

Special interest titles available in
large print are:
The Little Oxford Dictionary
Music Book
Song Book
Hymn Book
Service Book

Also available from us courtesy of Oxford
University Press:
Young Readers' Dictionary
(large print edition)
Young Readers' Thesaurus
(large print edition)

For further information or a free
brochure, please contact us at:
Ulverscroft Large Print Books Ltd.,
The Green, Bradgate Road, Anstey,
Leicester, LE7 7FU, England.
Tel: (00 44) 0116 236 4325
Fax: (00 44) 0116 234 0205